Canadian Connections

Cristal Ryder
Katheryn Wallis

HOT FUSION
Cristal Ryder

After fleeing her hometown years ago, Kara Sinclair has returned to breathe life back into the bakery her deceased grandmother left behind. She has a history in this town—one that involves her one true love. A boy she'd thought she'd give her life to before circumstance got in the way. She needs to focus on her task, but one look at Maxwell Stone and all the old feelings return. And it isn't long before she can think of nothing else but reigniting the passion they once shared.

Max never understood what drove Kara away all those years ago, and once she returns to their Canadian hometown, he's hell bent on getting her back into his life…and his bed. But when he uncovers the reason she left him behind, he must decide if he can move on from the past and trust his heart with the only woman he's ever loved.

LETTING JACK WATCH
Katheryn Wallis

Edmonton cop Jack has one rule for dating—don't get emotionally involved. A string of short-term flings leaves him dissatisfied, though, and he starts to envy his partner, Jeremy, who's been dating curvy redhead Caitlin for a year.

Then Jack glimpses something forbidden—and realizes a glimpse is not enough.

For Caitlin and Jeremy, letting Jack watch began as an accident and became a game. But they soon realize the game has high stakes—and threatens to tear them apart forever.

Jeremy doesn't want to lose his best friend, but what will he have to sacrifice to keep Jack around? Caitlin knows what she wants, but getting it might destroy everything. And Jack may have come second, but he won't settle for second best. He started out just watching. Now he wants it all.

An Ellora's Cave Publication

www.ellorascave.com

Canadian Connections

ISBN 9781419967283
ALL RIGHTS RESERVED.
Hot Fusion Copyright © 2011 Cristal Ryder
Letting Jack Watch Copyright © 2012 Katheryn Wallis
Edited by Grace Bradley and Brianna St. James.
Design abd Photography by Syneca.
Models: Elina and Christian.

Trade paperback publication 2012

With the exception of quotes used in reviews, this book may not be reproduced or used in whole or in part by any means existing without written permission from the publisher, Ellora's Cave Publishing, Inc.® 1056 Home Avenue, Akron OH 44310-3502.

Warning: The unauthorized reproduction or distribution of this copyrighted work is illegal. Criminal copyright infringement, including infringement without monetary gain, is investigated by the FBI and is punishable by up to 5 years in federal prison and a fine of $250,000. (http://www.fbi.gov/ipr/)

This book is a work of fiction and any resemblance to persons, living or dead, or places, events or locales is purely coincidental. The characters are productions of the author's imagination and used fictitiously.

The publisher and author(s) acknowledge the trademark status and trademark ownership of all trademarks, service marks and word marks mentioned in this book.

The publisher does not have any control over and does not assume any responsibility for author or third-party Web sites or their content.

CANADIAN CONNECTIONS
❧

HOT FUSION
Cristal Ryder
~9~

LETTING JACK WATCH
Katheryn Wallis
~89~

HOT FUSION
Cristal Ryder
∞

Acknowledgments
ಐ

Niagara-on-the-Lake is one of my favorite places in Ontario. When I saw the Oh, Canada! call, I knew the story had to take place there. A very special thanks to Grace for seeing something in my story and putting me through the wringer. I'm glad I came out the other side all squeaky clean, although not much skinnier. And to my fellow partners in crime, Gina Gordon and Stacey Kennedy, you know why. And especially to Mary. To be able to count on someone, like I do you, is a treasure indeed.

Chapter One

ಲ

She was coming home. Back where she belonged and spent so many years with Gram in the bakery. Kara dreaded seeing what kind of shape the shop and apartment were in now, not having been lived in for so long. Guilt soured in her stomach. No matter how hard she tried to justify staying away, it hadn't been the right decision. She should have come back sooner, and whispered a silent apology to Gram.

On the heels of Gram's memory came one of a dark-haired, dreamy-faced boy from long ago, which made her sit upright in her rental car. Even though it had been years since she'd seen him, he haunted her thoughts. She sighed. It only made sense he would cross her mind now, coming home with reminders everywhere.

Her breasts tingled. Even after all these years, her body reacted viscerally to his memory. His first tentative touch had rocked her world when they were virgin teenagers. She'd lost herself in his chocolaty-brown eyes and under his touch when they gave their virginity to each other. A summer love from so long ago still left a powerful impression all these years later.

"Max." His name rolled around her tongue and she gripped the steering wheel tighter when her belly did a little flip-flop. She wondered if he'd stayed on his family's orchard. Max's dream had been to turn it into a profitable wine-making operation and it had been in the fledgling stages of transitioning into a vineyard when she left. Kara hadn't kept track of Maxwell Grimes Stone II for two reasons. One being her focus on her own culinary career, and the other had been something she still refused to think about and a big reason why she had stayed away so long. She was sure Max had no idea what had really transpired to make her decide to leave. But coming home made her wonder.

She knew she had broken his heart when she ran off to Europe fifteen years ago to learn her craft, leaving a very confused and angry Max behind. Gram told her he pined for her, and encouraged her to contact him, but she couldn't bring herself to. He never tried to get in touch with her either, and that's how it was left. When the news of his marriage reached her she had cried for days, and once the wailing was done Kara firmly put Maxwell Stone on the shelf. She had to in order to keep her focus. Kara managed pretty well most of the time, but Max never failed to show up in her dreams on lonely nights when she missed home. He was safe there in her dreams, a lovely fantasy she welcomed with open arms.

Time slipped by quickly and when Gram died suddenly last year, it all seemed to catch up with Kara. Coming home for Gram's funeral and to sort out her affairs took a big toll on her. It was then she stopped her waffling thoughts about coming home and plotted her return from Europe.

Now here she was, about to drive the familiar roads of Niagara-on-the-Lake to her childhood home. The flight from Heathrow to Toronto had been uneventful, yet she'd been wound up most of the time she was in the air, unable to put a finger on the reason for her unease. Her heart fluttered. *Why? Because I might see him, or because I might not?*

Kara forced her thoughts away from Max as she exited the Queen Elizabeth Way. Time enough to think about him later. She had a goal and her timeline was tight. No distractions allowed. Coming home to reopen the bakery excited her and was foremost in her mind. After closing the shop up last year, she expected to be in for a good cleanup. Even though she'd had it checked on regularly, Kara was sure it needed some tender loving care and she was here to do just that.

As she drove deeper into the region, she couldn't believe how many vineyards had sprung up. She drove past the familiar Hillebrand and Jackson Triggs wineries, as well as a new sprawling one that didn't even resemble a winery—it rose out of the earth like a monolith, all chrome and glass, except for the telltale rows of vines fanning out on each side. She could barely take it all in. Sure, she was on the same old Niagara Stone Road, but oh man, had it changed.

Inniskillen, which basically started the Niagara wine industry back in 1975, was on the western edge of the region, close to the Niagara River. *Where we'd found a private little hideyhole to explore each other. Stop it, Kara! Quit with the thoughts already.*

This wasn't a good sign. Max crossing her mind was never a good thing—it roused images of him and set her long-neglected libido aflutter. She needed a man. Wanted one. But purely for sex. The complications of a relationship she could do without. But sex? Yup, scratch that overdue itch and be on her way. *Maybe a nice Canadian boy will walk into my shop and tempt me.* She laughed out loud and promised herself she wouldn't let her hopes get too high.

With her destination just around the corner, Kara realized she was holding her breath and let it out slowly through pursed lips. Rather than take side roads, she turned onto Queen Street and drove right into Old Town. She sighed again, but this time from the sight before her. She was truly home now. Gracious old trees shaded the road and flowers of every kind bloomed in brilliant color.

Typical for a weekday in early July, the street was jam-packed with people, and of course there was no parking. Tourists flowed along the sidewalks, horses and carriages clip-clopped down the street, sightseers gazed into shop windows or sat at one of the many outdoor cafés, sipping wine from area vineyards and noshing on locally grown foods. Niagara-on-the-Lake was the place to indulge one's culinary senses and what originally inspired Kara to become a chef.

She loved it here. Why oh why had she waited so long before coming back? But of course she knew the answer to that. It was the combination of avoiding Max and getting her own career on track. She realized now though, it had been wrong and she should have settled here long ago like she promised Gram, but instead let herself get wrapped up in the glitzy world of Paris and London. Now with Gram gone, working side by side with her would never be.

She shook her head, not wanting the sad thoughts to take hold, and drove slowly, watching for the storefront. There! On the left, set back from the road. She almost missed the red-and-cream brick of the old building. A quick glimpse imprinted in her mind the patio overgrown with vines and jolts of color from the perennials Gram had planted so many years ago. Being set back from the road was a treasure, and it created a nice little spot for café tables. But it looked tired now. The sign above the rolled-up awning peeled just enough to read the original lettering underneath. *Fingertips.*

Kara's heart constricted in despair and she whispered, "Oh Gram. I'm so sorry."

Kara craned her neck to watch the store disappear in her side-view mirror. She swung her gaze back to the road just in time and stood on the brakes to avoid running up the back end of a stopped car. *Sheesh, pay attention.*

"Move it, buddy." Kara punched the horn. It was totally typical for cars to double-park and bung up traffic while the passengers climbed out. Now that she was here, Kara was in no mood to be tolerant.

Summer in Old Town was nuts, and this was just the beginning. Kara was glad she arrived after the Canada Day weekend. It would have been a zoo. People from around the world flocked to Niagara Falls and Niagara-on-the-Lake, causing chaos all around. But it was a short season and she recognized the pros and cons. Kara took a deep breath and tapped her fingers on the steering wheel, waiting for the car ahead to move. Intolerant drivers from behind began a chorus of honking and finally the car pulled away. Kara followed a little too closely, anxious to get to the shop. Parking was on a laneway behind the buildings and she was happy to see the upcoming stoplight turn green. She flicked on her left indicator signal and took a risky turn before a van, which flashed its high beams at her.

She waved an apology and watched for the laneway that led to the parking area. Excitement mixed with anxiety set her heart pounding harder. She pulled up to the back of the bakery and sat in the car for a minute, gazing at the familiar old building. It hadn't changed all that much from the outside. The bushes and neighboring trees were just bigger, a little wilder, and shielded the second-floor deck better from below.

Kara finally climbed out of the car and stood at the back door, jangling the keys in her hand. What was she waiting for? Why the hesitation? She'd come all this way to start a new life and now here it was, imminent across the threshold. She glanced at the antique black iron urn, which weighed a ton, beside the door. It looked lonely all by itself, flowerless, on the little stone patio. She reached into the soil and pulled out the old, dried-up leaves. Soon it would be full of blooms. The keys weighed heavy in her hand and she picked through them to find the right one. It slipped into the lock and turned without protest. Kara paused a moment, took a deep breath and pushed the door.

She was greeted by a hushed silence. Once inside the kitchen, Kara's eyes adjusted to the dim light and she looked around, taking it all in. Sunlight filtered through the shutters, casting an eerie light, and dust motes shimmered on the rays. White sheets covered everything. Nothing had been touched since her last visit when she closed the place down. Kara stood in the center of the room and slowly turned around, giving herself a panning view of Gram's bakery, which was now hers.

She reached out and her fingertips played with the corner of a drop sheet. Kara took a deep breath and pulled the fabric. Inch by inch the island workstation was revealed, its surface a combination of marble and recently installed stainless. She yanked off the second sheet covering the far end. An ethereal image of her as a child, standing on an old chair pushing a rolling pin over pastry with Gram standing close by, ghosted before her on the dusty air. Then it floated away. Kara couldn't hold back the tears any longer. She cried, clutching the white sheet to her, and great sobbing gulps filled with pain racked her chest.

She cried for the parents she never knew, for Gram's love and patience, for lost love and loneliness. Kara let despair wash over her and feed the tears. Finally she could let it all out, but oh how she longed for someone to hold her in their arms so she could cry on a comforting shoulder. After a few minutes the tears subsided. She wiped her hand across her cheeks and blew her nose into a corner of the sheet. *Get it together, Kara.* She wasn't a crier, but this spell was long overdue and she felt a little better.

Kara tossed the balled-up sheet aside and turned around to flip the lights on. A shadowy figure filled the doorway and her heart tripped over itself.

"Who are you?"

A deep, familiar voice tickled her senses, sending a delicious shiver along the back of her arms. "I heard you were back in town."

Max! Kara stood frozen, totally confused by his presence. Had she conjured him, thinking about him on the drive here? Her breath stopped and no words formed. A crazy thought of how horrible she must look was all that filled her stupefied mind.

He stepped into the beams of dancing light. His smile, wide and welcoming, and his eyes—the color of warm chocolate syrup—weakened Kara's knees.

"Oh Max." Kara stepped forward and threw her arms around him. He captured her and lifted her off the ground easily. A low chuckle rumbled from his broad chest and she clutched him.

Gone was the gangly teenage boy, and in his place was a strong, mature and very solidly muscled man. He swung her around until she giggled, her despair from only a moment ago vanished and a glimmer of happiness sprouted.

"Hey, gorgeous. It's good to see you." He set her down and held her away from him, keeping his hands on her shoulders. She shivered when his gaze swept from her toes to her face. Geez, she still responded to him like a virgin teen and knew her nipples had stiffened under her sleeveless blouse.

He smiled and she felt more relaxed by the genuine delight she saw in his eyes. And then his faced clouded. "I was so sorry to hear about Gram."

"Thanks." The underlying sadness that haunted her the past year surfaced with those few words, and she didn't want to get into it now. It was just so good to see him. Kara felt tongue-tied all of a sudden. He must have sensed it and let her go.

"How did you know I was here?"

"It's a small town, Kara, everyone knows everything."

She nodded, true enough. She'd kept in contact with the lawyers and made arrangements through them to have the building checked on regularly. Probably word got around through those channels.

"This old place sure brings back memories." He strode through the kitchen out to the shop proper and Kara followed him, her gaze drinking him in. Seeing him here now, unexpected and amazing-looking, made her realize how much she had missed him. He had matured nicely and filled the room with his presence, as if he belonged here. His trim hips and broad shoulders were so much more muscular now, and his butt, the same wonderful ass amazing in any pair of jeans, caught her attention. Her gaze lingered, and she appreciated the tempting outline behind the denim. *Whoa, Kara.* She shook herself out of the trance she was slipping into at the delicious sight of him. She was still caught in his spell after all these years.

"I think I can still smell the butter and pastries."

Kara dragged her thoughts back. She sniffed, holding her breath to see if he was right. Yes, she could too.

"The walls must have soaked up all those years of Gram's baking."

He reached for the shutters and unhooked one.

"Please, Max, no. Not yet."

He looked over his shoulder, "Why, what's up?" The easygoing nature he had as a boy was still evident, but he carried a different air about him now. Confidence. No-nonsense and strength. A very sexy combination to be sure.

"I'm not ready for the world to come in yet."

He looked puzzled. "You're here now, and it's not a secret."

Kara sighed and stood in the center of the shop, taking in the long glass counter, still sheathed in drop sheets, which ran the length of the store, and the antique maple display shelves on the opposite wall. A series of white-shrouded humps by the front windows were the cast iron outdoor furniture she dragged in off the patio all by herself the last time she was here.

"It's important to bring everything back like she had it."

Kara stepped toward the counter and pulled the sheets off. She sucked in her breath as the beautiful beveled glass and ornate carved wood was revealed. Kara envisioned the mouthwatering show of pastries, cakes, tarts and pies, buns and breads that used to sit in this old display case, waiting for people to buy them.

"I'll bring it back, Max, and it will be even better."

He nodded, watching her from across the room. Their gazes met. Her heart beat double time when he grinned, revealing that devilish dimple on his cheek.

"I know you will."

"I want to keep the antique feel but modernize. Make it the place to gather. Good food, coffee, teas, and if I can get a liquor license, wine too. Bakery by day and wine bar by night. With internet access. That should bring the crowds back."

"I don't think you have to worry about that. All those extra gadgets would only be for the tourists." His eyes held a deeper meaning that set her belly quivering. "We've been waiting for you to come home."

Kara enjoyed the thrill of delight that washed over her. He said "we" but she heard "I". Unsure how to respond to him, she smiled and let the comment slide by. Kara bit her tongue to hold back the inquiring words she was dying to ask. Why was he here? Had he been waiting for her to come back? It didn't seem stalkerish at all, and a little part of her hoped it was because he missed her.

Wow, what a change from just a few hours ago. All her direction had been to get Fingertips back open and now in a few short minutes, Max had become a delightful and potential diversion.

Kara walked toward him, keeping eye contact. Her stomach fluttered and a curl of heat began low in her belly. She placed the folded-up sheets on a shelf, then slipped between him and the shrouded furniture, totally stirred up by his close proximity. She parted the old wooden slatted blinds a little so she could see out. But she didn't really pay attention to what was on the other side of the window, all her nerves were on high alert for Max. She sensed him behind her and a shiver rippled along her spine to settle in hot tendrils around the base. Kara felt the need to fill the tension with mindless chatter. The first thing that popped into her mind was the condition of the patio.

"Does Niagara College still have their horticulture program?"

"Mmm hmm, they do."

All thoughts of talking to the college to find out if students would like to help bring the patio garden back to life vanished when Max's arm slid around her waist and his fingers splayed over her belly. Kara's eyes fluttered closed and she savored the feel of him, letting the delicious thrill of his nearness fill her. Oh he felt so good and her blood pumped a little quicker through her veins. His breath, so close to her ear, fluttered her hair softly. They had fit perfectly together, so perfectly as teenagers, and it didn't seem time had changed that much. He was much taller now and her head fit under his chin with a little bit more room than it had before. She wondered if her curly hair would still tickle his nose. A sudden sense of belonging overtook her and she leaned back into him, his solid muscles feeling so impenetrable next to her, but she still melded perfectly to him. His energy flowed around her and she absorbed it.

"Why, you thinking of getting a student to tidy it up?"

She nodded and murmured, "The thought just crossed my mind. It would give me more time to focus inside." Attraction for him after all these years was still ripe and she was a little ashamed at her body's response. She was turned-on. He had awoken her sexually so long ago, and their perfection together had set the bar very high for any other man whom Kara allowed into her world. But none had held a candle.

She placed her hands on his forearms and wanted to hug him tighter. Part of the reason she had taken off fifteen years ago was because of her weakness. How could she stay, with Max so close, and not be able to be with him? With his mother watching like a hawk over everything they did and the threat of her making Kara's life miserable, it would have been impossible—eventually breaking them up if she had stayed. She couldn't forget the fact he was married either. But it felt so good to be back in his arms now, however casual it may be. She couldn't give in to her desires. The ones he so easily aroused, probably without realizing it.

She had to remain focused on her goal. And keep simplicity in her life. A darker thought of his mother chilled her. Kara extricated herself from his strong arms, feeling an intense and immediate sense of loss. She slipped between him and the tables and tried to find something to busy her hands with. She wondered if he ever found out what had really happened. What had prompted her to leave in the first place.

"Kara."

"Uh huh?" She fussed with the folded sheet, her back still to him. Here it comes, she thought.

"Kara, turn around."

Slowly she turned to face him. A million thoughts raced through her mind as her gaze took him in. He was her first lover, and her heart swelled with the familiar ache blending in perfect harmony with her arousal for him. Keeping an ocean between them had been the wisest thing all these years. Maybe coming home was wrong after all, but in her heart she knew it wasn't wrong. It was right. Kara wanted to be here and didn't want to remember the hurtful words said to her all those years ago, but they came back like a punch in the gut. After she left, a new life began for her abroad and she had survived, pouring everything into her new career and carefully protecting herself from further heartache. There had been other men, but she never fully opened up to them, since most paled in comparison to Max.

The best thing now was to block him out while she reopened Fingertips, using all the skills and business savvy she'd learned overseas. The last thing she needed was his mother's toxic presence spoiling her return, and who knows when she would show up to cause trouble.

Max stepped toward her and she held her hand up. He halted in his tracks.

"Kara, please, I think we should talk." The pained expression on his face told her he still didn't know what transpired all those years ago.

"Oh Max, I just got home. Can't it wait?" Desperate now to keep her space, she walked to the kitchen and he followed.

He laughed and it almost sounded bitter. "For what? Come on, don't you think we have lots to discuss?"

She turned to him and met his gaze. "Maybe, but not right now."

His eyebrows shot up. She knew exactly what he wanted to talk about. But she wasn't ready. She'd just gotten home, for crying out loud, and already conflict was building. She wanted to find out about Patricia, his wife, but if she brought the subject up it would launch into a whole drama of why she left to begin with. Now wasn't the time. She was exhausted and beginning to feel emotionally wrung out. Being here in the bakery without Gram broke her heart and Max standing before her, well, it was just too much to take in right now.

"It was really nice you stopped by, and I-I think maybe you should leave." She couldn't look at him, positive disappointment would show in his face.

"Is that what you really want?" His voice had hardened and she couldn't help but look at him now.

No! I want you to stay and be with me. The words were so close to bursting forth.

"It's for the best, Max. So many years have gone by." Her lips were stiff and she struggled to force the words from between them. It was hard to send him away and she reminded herself she hadn't come back for Max, she came back to start a new life here.

His features hardened and it pained her. She didn't want to hurt him, again, but she knew she was doing just that. There was so much she had to do, and making it more difficult by trying to fix, build, whatever...an old relationship seemed too much to deal with all at the same time.

"One day, I'd like you to tell me why you left."

And before she could say anything further, he walked past her and out the back door, taking with him the energy that seemed to swell in his presence. Suddenly the old bakery seemed empty and soulless without him. It rocked her to the core.

The brief interlude with him after all these years made her realize what he still meant to her. She was torn now. Should she have stayed in London, or was coming home the right thing to do? If only she had been strong enough to stand up to his mother and tell her to go to hell, things could have been so different for both of them now. Kara drew in a big breath and stood tall. It was time to be honest with herself. She still loved him.

* * * * *

Max shut the truck door and rested his hands on the steering wheel. He sucked in a deep breath. That hadn't been easy, seeing Kara after all these years. But shit, it was good to see her and hold her again.

The brief few moments when she'd been in his arms with her head tucked under his chin had sent him careening back in time. He'd felt like a school kid again, all giddy with new love and fiery hormones. She woke him up. He realized how desensitized he'd become over the years when the rush of raw desire for her ignited in his blood, when his nostrils cleared and colors took on a new intensity. He felt good… No, great. A short burst of laughter erupted from him.

Even if she had just basically thrown him out and pretty much stated she wanted nothing to do with him, she breathed new life into his husk of a body. For the first time in a long time a sense of hope took hold and a seed was planted. He'd be back to win her over. But first he'd let her do her thing and maybe, just maybe, she might miss him a little bit. And when that crack appeared, he'd slip right in.

Chapter Two

ಐ

"Wow." Kara drove up the neat paved driveway lined with row upon row of grape vines. She came to a Y just around a curve in the laneway and stopped. A stunning house with a fantastic wraparound porch sat graciously to the right tucked under old maple and oak trees. To the left were similarly designed buildings, which she assumed were the vineyard office and store. Kara turned left.

She hoped he was here. Butterflies flurried in her belly. She was nervous. Kara pulled in a parking space and sat in the car a minute, gazing at the building before her.

When she opened the door, she inhaled the wonderful scent of flowers and warm earth then ducked into the backseat and reached for the large white bakery box full of treats. It was her excuse to visit Max without calling first, and was meant to be an apology for her rudeness the other day when he stopped by.

She climbed the wide limestone steps, taking in the grandeur of the structure. It was beautiful. A wide, wraparound porch, similar in style to the house, led to an opening at the side like an outdoor lounge, where a grouping of Muskoka chairs and low tables were scattered about.

Kara took a deep breath and pushed the tall, highly glossed wooden doors and entered the spacious shop. Slate floors and muted-tone walls gave the room a gracious atmosphere. Gleaming counters and polished chrome shelves ran along the walls, adorned with numerous wine bottles beautifully lit with pot lights. Strategically placed glass-door refrigerators, which blended perfectly with the décor of the room, also showcased wine. She sucked in a breath, stunned by the view from the floor-to-ceiling windows on the back wall. If she didn't know better, Kara would have thought she was looking at a mature vineyard in France or Italy.

But she wasn't. This was Max's winery and she was very impressed.

"Can I help you?"

Kara turned to the voice behind her. "Hello. Yes please, I, um, is Max available?"

"No, I'm sorry. He's in a meeting at present. Is there something I can do for you?"

"Ah well, can you please see he gets this box?" She held it out to the woman.

"Of course. Whom may I tell him this is from?"

Kara smiled. "He'll know. Thank you."

She wandered back out to the veranda and wanted to take a peek at the outdoor lounge she'd spied earlier. When she rounded the corner, a lovely breeze blew past her. There was nothing like the smell of the land with the hot sun warming it up. She inhaled the sweet air. What a great place to sit and take in the panorama with a glass of wine. It also had great potential as an outdoor café. Shielded from the elements and offering a million-dollar view. She stood at the edge of the decking and saw the grand house partially visible through the trees. It looked spectacular from this angle as well.

"Kara."

She had a feeling he might discover she was here and seek her out. She smiled and turned to him. "Hi." Wind blew curls across her face and she peered at him through the strands.

They both spoke at the same time and laughed. "You first," he said.

"I was told you were in a meeting."

"Yes, I was. I am. But I saw you through the window and excused myself for a moment."

She glanced at the wall he indicated, noting a wide darkened pane of glass. She could barely make out a conference table with a few people seated around it.

He placed his hand on her elbow and led her off the deck behind a rose bush covered in pink fragrant blooms. A thrill rippled down her arm at his touch and she gently pulled from his grip.

"What a gorgeous place, Max. It's wonderful here."

He rocked back on his heels, a look of pleasure crossing his face. He gazed across his land. "I kind of agree."

She took the opportunity to really look at him. He was her long-lost love, her teenage dream. He was the same, but oh so different. Still her Max, but all grown up, and still a sexy beast. She cleared her throat, stemming her wayward thoughts but allowing herself one more appreciative glance. He caught her when his gaze swung back.

They paused and stared at each other. Kara held her breath, only to let it go when her heart skipped a beat. He was married and she needed to behave. Why had she come? Oh yes, the box.

"I was rude the other day and I wanted to apologize." He smiled and her heart flipped over. She looked up at a heavy bloom and reached to pull it to her nose, sniffing the sweet scent. She glanced back at him. "Um…there's a box of goodies for you inside."

"Thanks. You didn't have to do that." He stepped closer, riveting her with his gaze. Kara didn't move and the next thing she knew, she was wrapped in his arms. "I'm glad you stopped by. But I do have to get back to the meeting."

She let him hug her, released the flower and snaked her arms around him, resting her cheek on his chest. She tried to make it a simple, friendly hug, but it was hard not to cling. He felt and smelled so damn good.

"No worries." Her words muffled against the fine cotton of his dress shirt. She released her grip and moved to step away, but he hugged tight for a second longer before letting her go. "Take them into your meeting."

They mounted the steps to the open-air lounge and strode to the parking lot.

"Sorry I'm tied up right now."

He held the car door open for her and she slipped onto the seat. "That's okay. I'm busy too. Just wanted to pop by quickly." Kara started the car. "We'll catch up eventually."

She pulled the door shut, sealing herself inside, safe from the temptation of him. Kara waved and drove off, letting out a breath. She glanced at him in the rearview mirror and wondered if they could just be friends. But if she were his wife, no way would she go for her husband having a friendship like that. Kara sighed, the good feeling she'd momentarily experienced in his arms disappearing.

* * * * *

It hadn't taken the two students long to bring the patio gardens back to their former glory. They'd worked hard and finished it after a week. Since it was well into planting season, the college's greenhouses were full of mature plants that filled in the gardens nicely. If Kara did say so herself, they looked so much better. The students planned to turn her exterior renovation into a semester project, which meant she wasn't required to pay them for anything but the plants and supplies. But she had every intention of compensating them for the work. They had done a marvelous job.

She had been surprised at first when tourists stopped to take photos of the patio. But as the plants filled in and created a riot of color, she understood the draw. It made her smile to see the flow of picture takers and knew Gram would be pleased at the newly rekindled interest in the bakery.

Kara had only a little over a week until the doors to Fingertips would once again be open. Until then, she encouraged people to rest their aching feet on her patio. Seats were at a premium along the main street and goodwill at opening the seating was excellent pre-promo. Soon the shady rest stop was filled most of the day. The comings and goings of tourists seeking shade under the umbrellas and a maple tree growing from the center of the patio pleased her. Even dogs became a fixture with their owners and Kara made sure numerous water pails were filled to the brim.

Today had been exceptionally busy and the morning sped by. She needed a break and strolled down Queen Street to check out some of the other shops that tickled her fancy. Maybe she'd stop at an outdoor wine bar too. It was a glorious day as she sauntered along the sidewalk, gazing in the store windows. Outside a little shop the song of wind chimes drew Kara's attention. She decided she had to have some for the patio and took her time looking at them. In the end she chose a couple pretty, sparkly ones and juggled them in her arms, setting up a ring of sound.

"I think this one is the best," a deep, sexy voice whispered next to her ear and Kara froze. A delightful shiver trilled along the backs of her arms. She knew exactly who the voice belonged to and turned to see Max. Her heart melted and she smiled. It was so good to see him. He was focused on untangling a chime from the others hanging in a tree with a riot of noise.

"The rooster?"

"Ya, he's great." And he finally got it unhooked from the branch. "My treat."

"Okay. A little whimsy never hurt anything." She smiled at Max when he handed her the chime.

After paying inside the store full of all sorts of touristy paraphernalia, they wandered down the street, shoulder to shoulder. At times she had to shuffle tight in front of him when they squeezed through the crowd and his nearness triggered all sorts of emotions in her, which she tried to repress. His scent and the heat from his body played havoc with her senses. She was totally in tune to him and her sexual antenna was all abuzz. A sultry, satiny fluidness slipped through her veins and a sexiness she hadn't felt in oh so long hitched her breath a little more quickly. It felt good to feel again. Walking along the street with him made her realize how much she had missed not seeing Max.

She was glad she'd refreshed herself before heading out on her walk. She hadn't really given a second thought when she dressed and pulled on some clothes from the clean pile of laundry, but was grateful what she had chosen was attractive. The short jean skirt came just above her knees and her turquoise toenails matched perfectly with the sparkly, insanely high sandals she wore. She loved shoes and in fact, when she slipped them on earlier an idea popped into her mind to change the name of the bakery to We Bake in Heels. It was perfect—funky and fresh. She hadn't considered changing the name, but the thought had excited her.

Even the fuchsia tank top she wore had blue prisms scattered across the front, which caught the sun nicely. The rich color heightened her newly acquired tan and streaked-blonde curls, making her feel summery. Kara sighed, happy to be out and about in the bustle of the crowd with this sexy guy at her side.

"Wow." Kara looked up at the magnificent structure of the Prince of Wales Hotel. "It wasn't near this elaborate last time I was here."

"When were you here last?"

"Last year." The expression in Max's gaze looked a tiny bit like hurt feelings to her and she felt the need to explain. "It was hard, Max. Gram died so suddenly and I didn't really want to socialize. There wasn't much time to stay either. You know, work and all."

She couldn't tell him how often she'd picked up the phone just to hear his voice, but never completed the call. Kara didn't want to cause any conflict in his life or open up old wounds. Time had healed her shattered heart, for the most part anyway.

He nodded and took her hand. "Well, you should have called anyway. Let's get a glass of wine."

"Seriously?"

"What?" He looked perplexed.

"Max, don't you have your own wine?"

"Sure. But that doesn't mean I can't buy my own wine or taste another. Come on."

She smiled. "I'd planned to stop for a glass anyway. You've read my thoughts." Good thing he couldn't read them all.

He took the bag from her and they turned around, heading back the way they had come. A short walk later, he steered her onto a patio behind a wonderful wall of flowers. It was delightfully shaded with green and red market umbrellas and a tree in the middle of the patio shaded the patrons under its wide branches. At first glance it didn't look as though there were any seats available, but they spied a small café table tucked behind a fountain and Max ushered her to it with his hand hovering at her waist.

It was as if he touched her. The electricity between them almost crackled and she glanced over her shoulder at him to see if he felt it too. His gaze met hers and he smiled, revealing the dimple on his cheek she adored. Butterflies took flight in her belly and the ache for him between her thighs ripened.

He held the chair for her and she sat, but jumped slightly when he ran his fingers across the bare flesh of her shoulder before he sat down. Goose bumps popped out on her arms and her nipples hardened.

Kara needed to distract herself and glanced around for something other than Max to focus on. She was amazed how this old pizza place had been turned into a hopping wine bar. The second-floor patio was packed, and had the most amazing glass roof structure with wooden beams spanning over the seats. She decided to check out the kitchen later, all in the name of research of course.

"Are you hungry?"

"Mmm, actually, I'm starved."

"Let me order then."

Her gaze roamed over his features while he studied the menu. Her belly did a little flip remembering how intimate they had been as teenagers. Learning about each other and exploring things they thought were so adult of them. She smiled and he looked up at that moment, catching her. A blush crept up, warming her cheeks.

"What?"

"Oh, I was just taking a walk down memory lane."

"What kind of walk were you on?" The insinuation in his voice made her blush more.

"Max!" How could he tell? But then he'd always been able to read her like a book. He returned his attention to the menu and Kara let her mind drift. She gazed around. A young, harried server wove his way through the crowded tables to them. She let Max order. Kara sighed and sat back on the chair, her bag tucked between her feet. For the first time in quite a while, she felt relaxed and enjoyed the natural high. It was a nice feeling.

"How's the reno coming?

"Really good, we're almost done. Everything is turning out exactly like I wanted."

"You didn't need any help?"

"We had it all under control, plus I didn't want to bother you."

"It would have been no bother."

The sincerity in his gaze made her feel guilty for not asking him. A pang of missed opportunity flitted through her mind. Yet being here with him now made up for the days spent without him.

The waiter arrived with their drinks and set the slender glasses before them.

"Ice wine? Now?"

"Sure, why not?" He lifted the glass and swirled it, watching the liquid twirl around and cling to the sides with its richness. He sniffed and closed his eyes. "Nectar of the gods." Then he sipped.

Kara did the same and was surprised by the sweet burst of flavor on her tongue. "Oh my goodness! This is fabulous." The sweet heat of the chilled wine raced down her throat and settled in tingly warmth in her belly, sparking her banked arousal to a higher temperature.

"Good, isn't it?"

"Mmm, better than good. Amazing! It's the best I've tasted." She took another sip. "What winery?"

He sipped again and paused, capturing her gaze with his own. "Mine."

She couldn't have been more surprised. "Yours?" She didn't know what to say.

"Yep, mine."

"Wow, Max, this is really good." She took another sip, appreciating it in a whole new light. "We need to talk some business then."

He sat back and laughed. "I thought you'd never ask."

The afternoon slipped leisurely by and Kara enjoyed a mellow languor she hadn't experienced in such a long time. Sure, it was the wine and the company, but this little bit of patio time in her hometown was the best medicine.

Max ordered a scrumptious antipasto plate and slid his chair around the table beside her so they could share. Their knees touched, sending little shock waves of desire along her nerve endings to settle between her thighs, keeping her arousal at a nice, pleasant hum. She didn't move her leg and neither did he. Their connection continued to grow like a live wire sparking between them. She wondered if he was as turned-on as she. And when he glanced at her over the rim of his glass, she knew. The look in his eyes that drove her to distraction as a ripe teenage girl reflected in his gaze now. A little shiver of delight ran down her spine.

She kept glancing at him over the plate of food, unable to take her eyes off him. They had since moved to a nice Pinot Grigio rather than the ice wine and both glasses now sat empty, begging to be filled. She wondered if it was wise to order more. But she longed to continue sitting here with him, sipping wine, people watching and being enveloped in the intoxicating scent of Max and the flowers. Kara was captivated by him all over again.

He draped his arm across the back of her chair in a casual movement and her heart did a little jump when his thumb stroked her bare shoulder. The air between them fairly crackled and she decided the decision had been taken from her. She'd stay. Here, with him, and let jazzy tunes from the hidden speakers wrap them in anonymity.

"So, you liked the wine, eh?"

"Yes, it was very nice. I should do a sweets night featuring your ice wine."

"I like that idea."

"Good." Kara needed to bring something important up but didn't know how, and was afraid it would shatter the fragile ease that was developing between them. But she had to for her own peace of mine.

"Max. A-are you still marr..." He shook his head and Kara let the word trail away. Relief flooded through her and she didn't want to press it further right now, or know the reasons he was now single. Time for that later. The fact he was no longer married was all she needed to know.

He gazed at her intently and raised his eyebrows. "Do you want to know why?"

This time Kara shook her head and wagged her finger back and forth. "Not really. At least right now. I just needed to know your, um, situation."

He sat back and smiled. "Don't want be the *other woman*, eh?"

Kara laughed and covered her mouth with her hand, a little embarrassed. "No, definitely not on my bucket list!" She also felt a little ashamed being so thrilled by the news he wasn't married. Divorce was never easy.

The rest of the afternoon fell to mindless, comfortable banter and Kara's contentment grew. The stress and hectic days prior began to fade away and she relaxed more as the afternoon wore on.

Kara's mind began to wander. What would come next? How would they part? Should she ask him to come back and open another bottle of wine? Worry furrowed her brow and she jumped when his hand cupped her shoulder. His fingers traced up the column of her throat and pushed into the curls at her nape, massaging gently. The movement chased the worry from her.

"Mmm, that feels nice." Kara smiled and faced him. She shivered in delight and he chuckled at her involuntary reaction.

"Cold?"

She shook her head and without a second thought leaned toward him. He encouraged her with a gentle pull. Their gazes stayed connected and just before their lips met, Kara's eyelids fluttered close.

Her breath caught when he kissed her—chaste and gentle, but with an underlying power she longed to unleash. Kara craved it and kissed him back, opening her mouth to dart her tongue out and taste his. He met her with a sudden ferocity that liquefied her insides. She was helpless to him, her muscles slack and weak. If he didn't have his arm around her, she would have dissolved into a puddle of passion at his feet.

Kara forgot where they were, all sense of place and time vanished. Her hand crept up to the back of his neck and her fingers played with his hair at the nape. Sound faded and Kara was only aware of him, nothing else. She sensed the sexual tension building in him and knew they should slow down before they embarrassed themselves in public. But she couldn't stop and moved closer to him, needing the feel of his body next to hers.

The sharp ring and vibrating buzz of her cell phone on the metal table pierced the moment and she jolted away, almost panting. Kara couldn't catch her breath and fumbled to grab the phone and flip it open. It was the bakery number.

"Hel—" Kara cleared the roughness from her throat and glanced at Max, who was flushed and watching her intently. His dark gaze made promises she wanted him to keep. Kara looked away to try to rebalance herself. "Uhm, hello?"

"Hi, Kara." It was Jilly, one of her co-op students. "Hey, are you all right?"

"Uh, sure. Why?"

"You sound kinda weird."

Weird? No, just incredibly horny. "What do you need?" she asked a little too harshly and immediately regretted it.

"Oh, anyway, the health inspector is here."

"What? Holy shit, I completely forgot." Kara's passion extinguished as if a bucket of cold water had been sloshed on her. "I'll be right there."

Kara quickly gathered her bags and turned to Max. "I gotta go. Totally forgot an appointment." She cupped his cheek in her palm. "Thank you, it was a great afternoon."

She stood and ignored the curious looks from the other patrons and dashed from the patio. As she rounded the wall of flowers, she glanced over her shoulder at Max. He leaned comfortably in his seat, his arm once again draped across the back of the chair she had been sitting in. He winked and smiled at her.

Holy crap.

That one simple and utterly sexy look totally reignited her passion for him. How could she possibly concentrate on a boring old health inspector now?

Chapter Three

༂

Everything was ready. The bakery passed all tests with flying colors and Kara was granted a liquor license. She was pleased with herself and proud of pulling it all together in time for Civic Holiday weekend. There would still be time to catch the remainder of the tourist season to give a solid base to head into the fall.

She stood with her hands on her hips and gazed around. Gordon Ramsay couldn't have done a better job if she did say so herself. The We Bake in Heels makeover had turned out more awesome than she could have imagined. The combination of antiques and her goal of keeping the old charm and incorporating a new contemporary feel had blended perfectly. Gram had been meticulous and kept up to date on most things. Kara didn't mind using some of the older utensils, but brought in a good range of new items to help with the mass production she planned later on.

She wandered over to the maple shelves. The honey-gold, aged wood was warm beneath her palm. The newly installed glass doors fit perfectly with the décor and the cabinets showcased the antique pieces no longer suitable for use. She found some real treasures stored away and placed them in the display along with pictures of Gram from the old days. Kara used the numerous old butter and cheese boxes she'd found stashed in the storage area as shelves and holders for a variety of items that needed a home. The carefully placed lighting highlighted her treasures behind the glass. Treasures worth more than gold to her.

Kara collapsed into a deep leather chair and curled her legs under her. This corner inside the front door to the left created a perfect little cozy alcove for people to rest out of the hubbub to sip their latte and browse the net.

Kara placed her cup on the old, battered oak table she'd hauled down from the living room upstairs. Its scarred and hardened surface gave further antique authenticity to the decor of the shop. She dropped her notebook on the table beside her drink. Kara stretched her arms over her head and sucked in a big breath, trying to get the kinks out of her back. She grabbed her book, and for the thousandth time, ran her finger down the list of foods she planned to put on the menu. It was just right. She decided to keep it simple to start with and then add a new item each week. She hoped her plan to launch a new food treat weekly would create a buzz and keep people coming back regularly.

She would offer sweet treats of course, like tarts and squares, pastries, but there would be savory foods too, suitable for lunch. She didn't want We Bake in Heels to be a sandwich bar, so there wouldn't be any on the menu. She still had to decide what tapas and higher-end finger food she would offer on the wine tasting evenings. Kara sipped the latte, glad she'd bought the fancy machine. It had taken a chunk out of her bank account, but was a necessity if she wanted to compete and bring a little bit of Europe to Old Town.

A sigh of contentment slipped from her lips. She was happy. Kara hadn't realized until now how she had simply floated from one day to the next all these years without any direction. Not until she made the decision to come home did she understand how she'd let herself drift through her life.

Sure she had resided in Paris and London. Living the high life. Of course she had learned a lot, been exposed to some pretty spectacular events and met some amazing people, but being home gave her the grounding she missed. Life, for the first time in a long time, felt good.

She had one little dark cloud in her blue sky though. Max. They hadn't seen each other since last week. She thought about him though, lots. When she had a moment to herself she remembered the snippets of time they had together. Of course their romantic afternoon became a naughty fantasy, making her long for the real thing. And the kiss. Well, she relived that numerous times. He hadn't come by, but had called a couple of times and left messages. They were playing phone tag. She fingered her cell on the table. She'd left the last message and hadn't heard from him yet.

What the heck.

She dialed his number and it went to voice mail, the message stating he was out of the country and would reply to all calls upon his return. Well, at least that explained why she hadn't heard from him. Kara didn't leave another message. She didn't want to appear too desperate.

She would have to let their lovely afternoon and kiss carry her through the days and into the lonely nights until she saw him again. Which hopefully would be very soon.

* * * * *

Max loved it in the sun between the rows of grapes. The ripening fruit hung heavy on the vines and he gazed across the plants fanning for acres on either side of him in the rigid rows. The move made all those years ago to switch from a roadside fruit vendor to planting grape vines had been the best decision his family made. Their vineyard had flourished and many of their wines received awards internationally as well as at home in Canada. He assessed the vines with a critical and educated eye.

Everything was ripening to schedule and gave indication it would be another bumper crop. If the weather cooperated, they would be golden. He plucked a fruit, popped it between his lips and pushed his tongue against the grape. His mouth exploded with flavor. He cupped a bunch of fruit and lifted carefully, assessing the weight.

He hadn't had a chance to call Kara since getting back from his business trip yesterday. Their afternoon at the wine bar stayed with him like a sweet memory and the kiss hadn't satiated his need for her, only made it riper. He knew she was as busy as he was. It wouldn't be fair to swoop down on her and whisk her off to bed without a little bit of courting first. He itched to touch her, taste her. He longed to explore her body and make sweet love to her. But his timing was off. He had all kinds of pre-planned conference calls and meetings both here, in Toronto and abroad.

He wished he could blow off some of the meetings, but they were too important to the business. He needed to attend. Max decided he would call her tonight before taking off again. He hoped they'd be able to connect this time rather than miss each other like they had been.

He wandered the vineyard and his thoughts continued to revolve around Kara. God, she looked good. And after seeing her for the first time in so many years, he realized how much he missed her. But why she had left still needed to be answered. They had grown up together, went to the same school and birthday parties. Then at fifteen they discovered each other in a different way, becoming inseparable. He smiled, remembering the fun times in the bakery eating fresh pastries and picnicking down by the river. They sat for hours talking about their future, what they wanted to do when they grew up and even about getting married. It seemed so easy and clear back then, not at all complicated. Until she disappeared. Just like that. Poof, gone.

His lips tightened into a thin line, the pain not easy to forget. He thought his heart had been ripped out and like the old saying goes, you don't know what you've got 'til it's gone. His family didn't seem to care much about it or what he went through. But looking back, they hadn't really embraced Kara, especially his mother, making things very awkward for them as a couple. His father had been too wrapped up in the business to notice much of what went on. His intensity only led to an early heart attack, leaving Max to abandon his ideas of university, traveling to Italy and France for further oenology and viticulture education.

He recognized now how easily influenced they had been by the adults around them. Max kicked a rock, then leaned down to pick it up. He'd been a wreck when Kara hadn't answered his calls. And Gram had only said Kara had left and she was sorry.

His mother said it was for the best anyway and refused to talk to him about Kara after that. Gram had been different though—he could tell she truly was sorry. She'd been gentle with him every time he stopped by the bakery to find out news of Kara. He always left disappointed she hadn't sent a message for him.

He'd almost gone to France after Kara, but when his father died he couldn't. He needed to run the place and his mother made no bones about how foolish it would be to chase after someone who had no interest in him and began to push another girl on him. Patricia Howe. Her family had the neighboring farm, but he kept a wide berth from her and his mother's meddling. He'd stayed and his uncle had come to live with them and help out.

Max got reckless for a while, feeling the need to rebel against the expectations placed upon him and his loss of freedom. But his cavalier behavior caught up with him and he came home to roost when Caroline, another girl he grew up with, tricked him into marrying him, claiming she was pregnant. His mother wasn't thrilled, preferring Patricia, but encouraged the match since Caroline also came from a wealthy family and the Stones could benefit from the connection. Max learned a few very valuable lessons at a young age when they separated shortly after the discovery she faked the pregnancy. After the legal battles were over and their business remained intact, Max turned all his attention to the vineyard.

He kicked another rock along the row, remembering those troubled years, and felt the familiar ache in his heart.

And Kara, well, she had just faded into the past like a distant memory. His anger for her eventually dissipated with time and over the years turned into sweet memories. He knew she completed a Cordon Bleu cooking school in Paris and moved to London, but had no idea when or if she would be back.

He picked up the stone he'd been kicking and dropped it into a rock pile at the end of the row. Max pulled the baseball cap lower over his eyes to shield the sun and mounted the stairs to the sprawling wraparound veranda of the house he'd built. It sat on a rise overlooking the vineyards, shaded by wonderful mature trees. He gazed across his lands and pride filled him. He'd come a long way since then and had an exciting future ahead of him. Only he didn't want to spend it alone. There was a hole in him that no amount of business success could fill.

Kara was still in his blood. No amount of trying to forget the silky feel of her skin, or her enthusiastic response to him when they kissed, or anything about her for that matter, would help ease his want for her. His cock grew heavy remembering their passionate nights down by the river's edge, where they had first made love and become more adventurous together. Her appetite for sex matched his, something he hadn't found since and he certainly had tried. Max groaned and the tightening in his groin didn't help matters. It wasn't just sexual. Oh ya, he desired her, but there was more. She held a special place in his heart.

Now that she had returned, his sweet ghostly memory was no longer indistinct. She was real, alive and here. So the memories of Kara and his teenage love for her began to ripen like the grapes on his vines after the rain. He wanted her back.

* * * * *

A soft summer breeze blew in the open second-floor windows. The sweet scent of roses climbing the front wall of the bakery blended deliciously with scents of the delicacies cooking in the ovens below. We Bake In Heels would be open to the public for the first time since Gram had died, and under a new name. A nervous stomach kept Kara from eating anything, even though she was starved. It didn't matter how delectable everything smelled, she couldn't put anything past her lips just yet. Not even a coffee.

She checked her watch. Ten more minutes. "Oh God. Why am I so nervous?" Because she didn't want to fail, that's why. Could she live up to Gram's reputation?

She heard laughter and shuffling around downstairs. The culinary baking students she'd hired from the college were busy and they seemed to enjoy the steady panic that filled the kitchen for the past week. Part of their program was to acquire co-op training hours, and she needed help. Thank the Lord for Niagara College so close by.

Kara took a deep breath and made her way down the back stairs. Jilly and Shane looked up from organizing cases of baked goods and smiled at her.

"So. Are you ready?"

They both nodded, excitement written all over their faces. "It's going to be great," Shane assured Kara. He was a giant, well over six feet, blond and blue eyed with a passion for cooking that rivaled hers. She was glad to have found him.

Jilly, a friend and fellow student of Shane's, had her dreads pulled neatly back beneath a red-and-white kerchief. She was a unique individual, and never had Kara seen such a variety of tattoos and piercings. Jilly was dedicated and very creative.

"Well, almost time, and looks like you both have it all under control."

Kara hesitated at the counter and took a deep breath before she walked to the front of the shop. She glanced above the counter at the old antique clock she had found in the storage room. Four minutes. Her gaze took in all the wonderful plants and flower arrangements sent from her neighboring businesses, welcoming and wishing her the best. She was so pleased to receive the warm greetings and had sent them thank-you plates loaded with samples of what she would be offering in the bakery.

"Okay, time to open the door." Kara gave a quick glance around—perfect, everything was organized and clean, with extra inventory waiting to be brought to front of house when needed.

The shop itself thrilled her. It was perfect, and she had absolutely no complaints about the restoration. She had delighted at all the little trinkets she found tucked away, which were now on display. She even found a real treasure, a small signed original of a Trisha Romance painting, which Kara had hung in a prominent place on the wall. How on earth Gram managed to score an original painting by Trisha Romance was beyond her. But it definitely was an honor to have it in the shop, especially since her gallery was just around the corner.

The day was going to be hot and Kara decided to run the air conditioner on low so it would help keep heat out of the store while open windows allowed the smell of baked goods to fill the street. Kara refused to think about the hydro cost and justified the expense was worth it to create a presence.

She pulled open the heavy wooden door and propped an old crock full of summer blooms in front of it, then turned Gram's old hand-painted sign around.

Open.

Kara stepped outside to unwind the awning and was shocked to see people already sitting at the iron patio tables waiting for the shop to open.

"Good morning! Please, come inside."

A chorus of "good mornings" greeted her and Kara stood aside while they filed through the door. She glanced up at the old sign. The peeling paint had been carefully stripped away to reveal the original letters underneath. She decided to keep the original sign in honor of Gram. The new large one shaped like a stiletto shoe was fastened to the building beside the door and another one swayed on an iron post closer to the sidewalk.

Kara sighed with relief and the flutter of happiness in her belly banished all anxiety that played there earlier this morning. People had come. It was going to be a great day.

And it was. The day streaked by with barely a chance for them to catch their breaths until a lull came around two thirty. Kara touched Shane on the arm. "Why don't you and Jilly take a break while you can?"

He glanced to the door. "Are you sure?"

"Yes, go. If anyone comes in I can handle it. Grab something to eat and drink and go rest your feet out on the patio."

She watched them snag a few pastries and a drink then collapse in a shady spot out front. Excitement still bubbled in her and Kara coasted on a natural high. She felt great!

The turnout had been huge and they'd restocked the cases several times. After a quick inventory check she knew there would be just enough to carry them until closing and if they were lucky, a few leftover treats. She grabbed a damp cloth and wiped down the counters and café tables at the internet bar. No one had brought a laptop yet, but she wasn't concerned. People expressed surprise to know it was offered, assuring her next time they would bring their computers. Once she tidied everything up, Kara pulled a bottle of sparkling water from the cooler behind the counter. She poured a glass and dropped in a sliver of lime. She finished the bubbling water in a long swallow and poured another one. Sipping while she turned around, Kara nearly choked.

Max.

"Hi!" God he looked good, and she quickly swept a drip of water from her lips.

"Hey, Kara. I couldn't let your opening day go by without a visit." He presented her with a huge basket of different herbs.

Kara laughed. "Oh Max, how thoughtful." She accepted them across the counter and placed the rectangular basket on the window ledge. "I'm glad you came. What would you like?"

"How about you pick me a sampling of your favorites?"

She pushed flyaway curls off her brow and hoped her mascara wasn't smudged too badly. She folded a takeout box together.

"All right then."

She picked a number of items she knew he liked and added some of her favorites — butter tarts, spanakopita, cheese puffs, cream puffs, mini croissants and a few other delectable treats. Then chose a big, flaky chocolate croissant, knowing it was his favorite, and handed the package over the counter to him.

"You remembered." The husky tone in his voice sent thrills of delight along her flesh.

"How could I forget? The croissant will be the best you've ever tasted. Remember, I've had formal training in the art of French delights, er, pastry."

He laughed out loud and the deep timbre warmed her heart.

"How much?" Max reached his free hand into his pocket.

"Don't be ridiculous! I'm not going to charge you." Kara waved her hand, dismissing the idea.

"I insist to pay."

"And I won't take any money from you. My treat." Then she gave him a devilish smile. "Remember the rooster?"

For a moment he looked perplexed and then laughed again. "Okay, but you're spoiling me."

"I know." She smiled, enjoying their flirting.

"Has it been busy?"

"Very, this is the first break all day. So I shooed them outside to take a rest." She nodded to Shane and Jilly sitting in the shade.

"I'm glad." His face was earnest. "It's good to see the doors open at Fingertips again, Kara. But what's with the new sign out front?"

She shivered, loving how her name rolled off his tongue and his gentle tone. "The idea struck me awhile ago. I love to bake and shoes are my weakness, so I combined the two. Do you like it?"

He nodded. "I do. It's original."

"I wish I had done it long ago. When Gram was still alive." Sadness filled her heart. "If only I'd come home sooner."

"Why didn't you?"

Kara didn't expect his forthright question. "Well, um, Max…" She paused, trying to think of what to say. "Now really isn't the time."

"When will it be the right time, Kara?"

"I don't know, but please, can we drop it for now?"

She wanted to avoid the pained look she saw in his eyes, but didn't look away and forced herself to keep his gaze. She would tell him eventually. But not now.

"Max—"

She was interrupted by laughter when Shane and Jilly burst through the door.

"Get ready, Kara, there's a crowd coming!" Shane's voice boomed out. He saw Max and hesitated. "Oh sorry, man, didn't mean to interrupt."

"No worries." He reached his hand out. "Max. I'm an old friend of Kara's."

"Shane." He shook Max's hand.

Max turned to Kara and met her gaze, but a crowd burst through the door and swarmed into the bakery before either could say anything further. Their private moment was gone.

She smiled and shrugged her shoulders at him as he was shuffled to the back of the crowd. He touched his fingertips to his brow and returned her smile, then walked out her front door. Even though the shop was brimming with people, it felt very empty with him gone and she gazed past the throng to try to catch a glimpse of him through the window.

* * * * *

Kara collapsed onto the lounge chair at the end of the day. Her feet ached, she was exhausted and starving, but felt fantastic. Today exceeded her expectations tenfold and there were barely any leftovers, which meant an early rise tomorrow to get baking. She groaned thinking about crawling out of bed at four a.m. Thank God she had the students to help.

Dusk fell quickly and the fresh smell of Lake Ontario drifted on the sultry summer breeze. It lifted and shook the leaves overhanging the second-floor deck at the back of the bakery. The rooster chime Max had given her tinkled in the branches and birds tweeted their good night to the world.

Kara was glad she'd created an oasis for her to escape to. She snagged a few plants from the front patio and had the students lend their creative hands to creating a comfy ambience. She helped thread twinkle lights along the railing and through the potted flowers and arranged cozy patio furniture and outdoor cushions. She knew she would need a place for retreat and the end result was a carefully created, private haven. Even a little fountain gurgled in the corner.

Man, what I wouldn't give for a glass of wine.

It was the only thing that hadn't made its way onto her very comprehensive shopping list. Shocking, considering she lived in wine country. Kara longed for a crisp glass of Chardonnay. She sighed and stretched her toes out, relieving the aches. A foot massage would be divine and would go so well with a glass of wine. She had neither.

The jangle of the old cowbell that hung at the back door startled her. She wasn't expecting anyone and the interruption made her ready to bark at the intruder. She swung her legs off the lounge, tiptoed to the railing and peeked down through the canopy of leaves.

OMG!

Max. She snapped up straight and her hand flew to her mouth. She stepped forward again just in time to watch him give the rope a good yank. Did she want him to go away? She was tired and badly needed some rest and a shower, but she didn't have the heart to send him along. Kara waited a minute or two to see what he would do. Through the green veil she saw him take a couple steps back and look up at her.

"Kara. Answer the door."

Chapter Four

She couldn't hide from him. "What are you doing here, Max?" Kara cringed, realizing she sounded a little bitchy and didn't mean to be.

"I'm here to celebrate."

She stepped forward and leaned over the railing, looking down again, curiosity getting the better of her. "What are you celebrating?"

"Not me, you!"

Me? "What are you talking about?"

"Kara, are you playing dumb? Open the door and let me in."

She realized Max at her door topped the day off with perfection. Even in her exhausted state she was glad he came.

"Hang on a sec, I'll be right down." Kara dashed into the washroom. She looked a wreck after the long day and needed a major repair job, but she didn't have time. So she wiped a cold facecloth over her flushed skin, under the light tank top she'd changed into, freshening up the girls, then dabbed a dash of perfume behind her ears and between her breasts. She smoothed her hands over the shorts. All this in under a minute. She skipped down the stairs, feeling light-footed and happy he showed up at her door.

Once he was inside the kitchen, Max's presence filled the room and damn if her heart didn't do a little flutter. He closed the door behind him and locked it, then turned around and waggled his eyebrows at her. She laughed and rejoiced in the butterflies that took flight in her belly. The old familiar languor flowed through her veins and she would have walked right into his arms had he not handed her a couple bottles of wine and stepped away to rummage in the drawers.

"What are you looking for?"

"An opener."

"Third drawer." It felt so right to see him in her kitchen and she feasted her gaze on him, watching every move he made. With his close proximity, her thoughts ran to the risqué. She was so totally absorbed with her eye candy that he scared the crap out of her when he shouted out his find.

"Aha!" He smiled and raised his hand, holding the corkscrew as if it were a trophy, and took a bottle from her.

Kara returned the smile and let her gaze travel over him, loving the way the muscles in his forearms rippled with his effortless movements as he twisted the screw into the cork and flicked it out with a pop. It didn't matter if she was expecting the sound, it never failed to startle her. Fireworks did the same thing, so she avoided them.

"Scared ya, huh?" He laughed.

"Did not."

"Oh ya, I remember. No matter how hard you try to be ready for it, you never are." He held the bottle up. "Glasses?"

What house in a wine region would be complete without a full set of wineglasses? Kara's place was no different. A wonderful selection of old goblets sat behind the glass doors of cupboards in the kitchen, waiting to be filled with the delicious nectar. Kara removed two and held them to the light, inspecting for spots. Satisfied, she set them before Max on the marble counter. He handled the bottle carefully, cradling it in his palm and tipping enough for a perfect pour into the goblet. He ended with an expert twist to catch the drip. When he set the bottle on the counter, the label faced away so she couldn't see which vineyard it came from. But she fully expected it would be his wine.

Max held a glass to her and shivers rippled up her hand when their fingers touched. The sensation rolled like waves across her body and she shivered in delight. He hesitated a brief moment and looked deep into her eyes. She couldn't look away and her belly tumbled over with pleasure. He let his finger linger next to hers longer than necessary before raising the glass to toast.

Oh God, what was happening?

Kara barely heard his words. He succeeded in distracting her completely and she was caught in his spell. Heat raced along her veins and settled in aching need between her thighs. Her nipples hardened and rose against the light tank top. She felt the urge to cover them but didn't. Feeling slightly wanton, she stood proud and watched to see if he would notice.

"To your grand opening and…" His gaze flickered down and stayed. She smiled. He'd noticed. His voice faded away and all she heard was the rushing of blood in her ears. His gaze rose back and met hers. She wanted to kiss him. Bad.

She craved the heat of his mouth on hers, his tongue probing and encouraging hers to meet his. Kara automatically raised her glass to clink with his when he held it up. She expertly swirled the golden nectar and held it under her nose to inhale the bouquet. Outstanding.

She sipped and its sweet heat seared down her throat, settling in her belly. Warmth radiated out and mixed perfectly with her arousal, heightening her desire for him. Now she really wanted to do more than just kiss and drifted off into a fantasy world with them together. She could almost feel his touch, her imagination so vivid.

"Kara? Where did you go? Lost you there for a bit." She zoned back in on him, in an even higher state of excitement.

Kara took another sip and stepped toward him. She'd be damned if she was going to wait any longer. Time for her to take charge.

Kara snaked one arm around his neck and pulled his head lower. She watched emotions run across his face and for a moment she thought he would pull away, but he didn't. He set his glass down and grabbed her roughly. He yanked her against his chest and the groan he gave when her breasts pressed up against him ignited her excitement tenfold. She exploded into a livewire of heightened nerve endings, and if he didn't have her in such a tight a grip she wouldn't have been able to stand.

His kiss sent her back in time, as if she was a virgin again, not confident or knowing the power of her sexuality. All her lonely nights of fantasizing being in his arms had become a reality. She fumbled in the kiss. So did he. Their teeth knocked and they grappled as if they needed to get inside each other. But then primal need took over and they found their pace. Max backed her into the marble counter where she reached to set the glass down, dimly aware of the clink when it tipped over, spilling the wine across the surface. But she didn't care. His hands ran down her sides and reached around to grip her ass. He squeezed and she sucked in a breath. Kara clung to his shoulders while he assaulted her with his kisses and touch.

He lifted and set her on the counter, their lips never parting. Max nudged her knees open with his thigh and stood between, so wonderfully close to her. Kara tore at the buttons on his shirt and sent them skittering across the floor. She ached to feel the warmth of his skin next to hers and pushed the fabric off his shoulders. She broke away, breathless from the kiss, and leaned back to gaze at his magnificence.

"Oh I've missed you," she whispered, and ran her hands lightly up his tanned arms and over his shoulders. He didn't move and stood still, watching her touch him. She turned her hands over and the backs of her fingers fluttered over the hard planes of his chest, hesitating against his raised nipples. He shuddered when she grazed against the sensitive tips.

"Come closer," she ordered and he complied. Kara slipped her hands and legs around him and wrapped him in her limbs.

She pressed her heels on his ass to bring his hardness next to her wet warmth. Their touch through the clothing was electric, as if they were plugged into each other. The thin top she wore was a hindrance and before she could reach to pull it over her head, Max did. She held her arms up, which raised her breasts provocatively higher. He dropped the shirt and it landed in the spilled wine, soaking the fabric. Her hands in the air, she stilled and closed her eyes when his fingers caressed down her arms and gently cupped her breasts. Delicious shivers rippled along her flesh.

"You're still so perfect." He leaned down to nuzzle the sensitive tips.

"Mmm." She leaned, giving him better access, and arched her back when his lips nibbled along her collarbone. He trailed a path of heat with his tongue and mapped his way to her aching, tight nipples.

"I know what you want." His voice was muffled against her skin.

"Mmm hmm." She couldn't form words and didn't even bother to try, she was so caught up in his touch. Even years ago he had a way of taking her outside herself with feeling. Kara lost sense of the world around her and homed in on the feelings he roused in her, this moment, and absorbed everything he offered. The glory of his touch mingled with the intense emotion for him and she was close to being overcome.

He pressed her breasts together and pushed her back. Kara supported herself with her elbows on the cold marble surface. The chill of it conflicted with the heated rush of her blood and when his lips finally closed over a nipple, she could barely stand it. Her back arched and she reached for his head, grasping him against her. Max supported her with his arms and lowered her closer to the counter.

"I love your breasts the best." And he suckled, driving her wild with his mouth. She wanted him nearer and wiggled her ass to get closer to him. She hungered to feel his cock and damn, the clothes were in the way!

When she finally felt his hardness tight against her pussy she dampened with anticipation of him sliding inside her. Kara reached between them to undo his pants and her back came flush with the marble. She let out a surprised yelp at the cold, which was like a dash of frigid water.

"I can't. Stop." The patio, they should be up there in the oasis she so carefully created. It was the perfect setting to rekindle their passion. Not here on the cold kitchen counter.

He didn't stop and kept fastened to her breast, his other hand now snaked down between them to cup her damp heat through her shorts.

"Max, stop," Kara moaned and pushed at his shoulders.

"What's wrong?" His voice was husky with desire and the passion reflecting in his gaze reached inside and grabbed her heart. She could tell he was turned-on as much as she, everything about his presence told her that. The look in his eyes, his breathing, the tension in his muscles and most evident, the enticing bulge in his jeans. She'd never seen the grown-up Max turned-on and desiring her, only the teenage Max. And boy oh boy, did she like what she saw. His rawness and pure masculinity made her feel feminine and desired. And she loved every minute of it.

Kara reached for him and took his hand, placing it between her thighs. He pressed his fingers into her through the cotton fabric. She closed her legs on his hand and clenched her thighs, heightening her sensation and trapping him.

He growled and leaned in, his face close to hers. "Are you trying to drive me insane?"

But she put her hand on his chest to halt him. "Not here, big guy. Let's go upstairs." And she swept her tongue along his lower lip before she sat farther back to regard him.

Kara shivered with delight at his predatory grin. She slid off the counter and sidled up to him. His hand slipped from between her thighs, over her belly and up to her breast. He grasped it a little too roughly but she didn't care and let out a laugh. She walked her fingers down his belly and slipped lower to grasp him though the fabric. He sucked in a breath and she gently squeezed his balls, and then ran her palm over the hard length of his cock bound tight in his jeans.

"Come on. Grab the bottle." He did as ordered and she took the glasses. He followed her up the back stairs out to the deck.

He glanced around. "You've turned into an exhibitionist?"

She laughed, sat on the lounge and placed the glasses on the table beside her. Kara reclined and brought one heel to rest on the cushion, while the other leg dangled over the side, her legs delectably spread apart to tempt him.

"Not to worry, it's very private here." Her voice sounded unrecognizably husky, even to her own ears. When his gaze dipped lower, her power soared. It welled up and she welcomed it. Her sexuality had taken a severe backseat all these years and she felt an urge to explore her wilder side, but never quite comfortable enough to let it out. But here with Max, she felt safe to unleash it.

Kara thrilled at the look on his face, the intensity in his stance as he watched her run her hands over her belly and up to her breasts. Kara closed her eyes and imagined they were his and delighted at the aching desire that grew within her.

"This is what I want you to do to me," she murmured, opening her eyes to see the passion in his gaze. Her skin was soft and when her hardened nipples pushed against the palms of her hands she moaned right along with Max. Her eyelids fluttered and through half-closed lids she continued to watch him. The wine bottle hung limply in one hand and his other reached to the front of his pants and she knew he held himself. She smiled, seeing his hand twitch against his cock when she ran her fingers back down over her bellybutton to slip inside her shorts.

"Holy shit," he murmured and stepped toward her, placing the bottle alongside the glasses on the table.

Kara arched her back and slipped her hand lower, feeling her swollen heat. But her hands weren't satisfying enough and she only did this to tease him. It carried her on a wave of self-pleasure that she didn't want to continue without his touch and withdrew her hand. She fumbled with the button and zipper, trying to undo them much too quickly. But before she could slip the shorts off, he was there kneeling on the lounge and pushed her hands aside. He grasped the waistband.

"You're killing me," he growled in a voice hoarse with arousal. "Lift."

Kara did as she was told, raising her butt off the cushion. He pulled the shorts down, revealing her nakedness painstakingly slow. At last she was free of clothes. He sat back on his heels and gazed at her nakedness, passion darkening the chocolate color of his eyes.

"Just as I remember…beautiful." He spread his hands over her belly, fanning them in a feather touch.

"Come here." She lifted her arms to him and he didn't hesitate.

But rather than lie next to her, he kneeled at the foot of the lounge and grasped her ankles. She sucked in a surprised gasp and relaxed her muscles, waiting to see what he planned next.

His large, tanned hands gently massaged her calf muscles and then he worked on her feet for a few minutes before sliding higher. She sighed at the pleasure trilling along her nerves. He worked his way up to her knees and smoothed his palm over her flesh. Then he roved up her thighs, massaging and walking his fingers along the taut muscles. Heaven. She sighed and her muscles quivered as he inched closer to her aching heat. Kara's knees fell open and she lay wanton before him, loving every second of his seduction.

He glanced down at her and licked his lips. Another shiver rippled along her limbs and she felt dampness slip from her. She was ready for him. She had to have him in her now, his thickness widening her and pressing deep, but she forced herself to try to relax, to enjoy his touch and not rush things. *Oh but it's been so long!*

She looked at him crouched between her thighs and sweet heat spread from her sex, radiating from the intensity of his focus. She was exposed, vulnerable, and she welcomed it. His fingers roamed up to her cleft and he brushed his fingers against her swollen lips, tugging gently on her curls.

"Ahh," Kara murmured and her back arched at the intimacy of his touch and her passion ripened beyond anything she had experienced before. Waves of orgasm hovered so close and she held on to them, not letting them take over. Yet.

"Max. Now." Kara tipped her hips in invitation.

"Just hang on, darling. I'm having fun discovering you again." And his hands continued their trek. Her muscles quivered in his wake as he remapped her, over the gentle rise of her belly and under her breasts.

"Now you're killing me," Kara whispered and turned her face toward the throw pillow.

"I aim to please." He chuckled and continued to explore. She nearly jolted upright when the wet heat of his mouth closed over her erect nipple. Kara clutched at his head, not wanting to let him go, and wrapped her legs around him. But he wasn't going anywhere. Sweet song of the evening birds filled her hearing and the sultry night air whispered over them, enveloping her in Max's familiar wild and fresh scent. She ran her hands along the corded muscles of his back and down to his hips. Her fingers stumbled over the waistband of his jeans. She had to get them off.

Max nuzzled over to her other breast and she was nearly incoherent with desire. Kara unwrapped her legs and reached between them. She quickly undid the fly and tried to push his pants down. He leaned over her and she didn't have the freedom to remove them completely and only managed to get them to his hips. His lips trailed a blaze of heat to her collarbone and along her chin. When he reached her mouth and kissed her, a moan slipped from her lips only to be breathed in by him. He cupped her breast and his thumb brushed across the aching peak. She opened her lips and welcomed the heat of his tongue. Every touch, taste, whisper of his lips set her nerve endings alight, radiating pleasure to crackle along her veins and settle in throbbing bliss between her thighs.

"Max, your pants," Kara murmured against his mouth. She raised her feet to hook her toes into the waistband, deliciously bringing her pussy into scorching contact with his cock. He reached down and pushed the jeans off until he was naked too, then placed his hands on either side of her head. He steadied himself with ease and rested between her raised knees. The intimacy kicked her arousal into high gear. Kara welcomed him against her dripping wetness and maneuvered her hips, hoping to encourage him to slip right inside.

He pressed into her and rather than fill her, his cock slid along her swollen lips to nudge against her clitoris. She cried out and he shushed her with a deeper kiss. Kara dug her heels into his ass and pulled him to her, grinding herself against him. Exquisite pleasure tightened low in her belly and she ached for the brilliant orgasm she knew would come. She hadn't been this aroused ever, not even when they were teenagers. Max broke away from the kiss and their gazes met. His beloved face hovered so close to hers and emotion swelled within her breast for him. Yet swirled in with her tender feelings was a fierceness that came roaring out of her.

She wanted him to fuck her now, she couldn't wait any longer. Her fingers reached for him and closed around his hard length. She pushed him back and wriggled out from under him. He fell onto his back and lay beneath her on the lounge. Kara's knees braced him and she straddled his thighs, holding him tight. His mature body thrilled her far beyond the teenage boy from so long ago and she reveled in him.

"You're so gorgeous." She fell over him to run kisses along his chest, lightly covered with dark curls, and ran her hand across his pectoral muscles, which rippled beneath her touch.

"Not so bad yourself." His husky voice was edged with desire.

Max's fingertips pushed into her tangled hair and he leaned up, the muscles in his belly flexed when he buried his face in her tresses. "I can't believe you're here and back in my arms. Where you belong." He kissed her neck, up to her earlobe, and suckled on it. "You smell like butter and almonds."

Kara smiled and placed her hand on his cheek, turning him so he faced her. She gazed into his passion-clouded eyes. She knew her love for him was evident and she didn't care. She belonged here, with him.

Kara closed the distance between them and pressed her lips to his, a kiss that told him more than words could ever say. His arms held her tight and they fused together as one. She let everything go. All the worry and concern that had been eating her up for so long, gone. Just like that. Even the nasty words his mother said all those years ago, gone. It was history and she was here in the present, in his arms.

"Lie back," she murmured against his lips and pushed him down. When he was fully reclined, she sat back and gazed down at his superb chest, across his muscled belly, hips and the sharp ridge framing the strip of hair that ran from his bellybutton to the dark curls between his thighs.

That's where her treasure waited. His wonderful cock stood proud, waiting for her. She was also completely exposed and it was so unbelievably erotic to see their nakedness close together. She took him in her hand, curled her fingers around his erection. The firm silkiness slipped easily in her palm and she stroked up, around the head and back down. He was wonderfully hard, and she didn't think getting even more so was possible, but he did under her touch and his groan of pleasure spurred her on.

Kara couldn't wait any longer. She ached to feel him in her and raised her body, balancing over him. She guided him with her hands to her sex and was about to lower herself when she remembered.

"Do you ha—"

Seeming to read her mind, he interrupted. "Pass my jeans."

Kara reached down, picked them up from the deck and handed them to him. He rummaged in a pocket and triumphantly showed her the packet.

"Let me." She took it and tore the wrapping with her teeth while she continued to stroke him. Kara held the condom over the tip of his throbbing penis and waited. She smiled when he raised his hips toward her. He wanted this just as much as she did. Kara rolled it down over him until he was sheathed.

"Now you're ready," she whispered.

"Am I?" He chuckled and grasped her shoulders. Kara's head fell back and Max ran his hands up to the back of her neck and pulled her to him. She sucked in a breath when her breasts pressed against his muscled chest. Erotic heat radiated outward in a rush and returned like ripples on a pond to settle in agonizing pulsing heat between her thighs. *Oh God.*

He shifted below her and flipped her until she was beneath him. A surprised "Oh!" popped out of her mouth with the sudden switch of their position.

"Now you're where I want you." He ran his hands lightly across her collarbone, sending delicious shivers fanning across her flesh. He mesmerized her and she watched the movement of his hands sweep slowly back and forth, raising her arousal to knife-edge sharpness. His cock nestled on her belly and she wiggled her hips, creating a more intimate contact between them. She couldn't tear her gaze away from his fingers as they played with her nipples and plucked them into harder buds. They ached in time with her clitoris, both begging and longing for attention and release.

"So sweet," Max murmured before he ducked his head and flicked his tongue across a nipple then pulled it between his lips. He gently grazed his teeth across the sensitive flesh and slipped his hands down her belly to find her clit. She arched under him when his fingers found what they sought.

"Ooooooh Max...please." She squirmed under him, unable to take much more of his exquisite torture. He pleasured her so deftly Kara's coherent thought vanished and when he wedged his knee between her thighs, she needed no encouragement and opened to him, aching to feel his hard and delicious length fill her.

"Now, Max, now!"

This time he listened to her and pushed into her waiting heat, slow and steady. She opened for him, unable to contain her outcry, and raised her hips to meet his thrusts.

"Harder." Her voice sounded foreign to her own ears. Her teeth clenched and she encouraged him to lose himself in the wild abandon of the raw sexuality she craved. Kara's fingers gripped his ass and he groaned when her nails dug in. He thrust harder and she met him. Max shifted until he sat on the lounge and positioned her on his lap. Kara tightened her legs around his hips, holding him deep within her. The angle placed her in perfect alignment with him and every part of them united. Her clit rubbed against his coarse curls, intensifying her stimulation. He filled her completely, and each thrust created delicious pressure against her G-spot.

Incredible tension built like an elastic band being pulled beyond its limit. Kara clutched his shoulders and rode him. He held her tight and safe in his arms and she let it all go, taking tiny, quick gasps of breath while her vision faded. Kara clung to Max, the intensity of her orgasm catapulting her into a place with no sense of anything except euphoria. Max silenced her cry of pleasure with his mouth and their lips clung.

Chapter Five

※

Kara's pussy tightened around him. He couldn't hold back any longer. With one last hard thrust he came. It was as if he was turning inside out, never had he been so overwhelmed by ecstasy. He held her tight while they rode out the long-awaited blissful pinnacle of their orgasms.

He didn't let her go and they slowly came back to reality. Max lowered her onto the lounge and slowly their breathing returned to normal. They didn't move and after a few minutes, Max disentangled himself from her and rose.

"Be right back." He dropped a tender kiss on her forehead and Kara smiled at him. His heart swelled and he gazed at her nakedness briefly then turned, leaving her to snuggle on the cushions.

He knew where the bathroom was and made use of it. So it had happened. He'd come over here hoping to share a bottle of wine and instead they made love. She'd been like a starved lioness and he loved it. A happy chuckle came from him and he knew he had a stupid grin on his face, but right now he didn't give a shit. He was here with Kara. Something he never thought would be possible again.

A robe hung on the back of the door. She might need it, so he draped it over his arm. In the hallway he stopped and gazed around. She had made some changes, mostly bringing things up to date and decorating with her personal items. He sighed. It was good to be back here.

He went downstairs. It wasn't hard to find food in a chef's kitchen and he loaded a plate with some good-looking grub and trotted back up the stairs to the deck.

The sight that greeted him took his breath away.

Kara had switched on the twinkle lights. The golden glow from the hurricane glass shades flickered across the deck and created a nice ambience. Branches swayed in the night breeze like a shifting natural ceiling and the fountain gurgled in the corner. But it wasn't any of that setting firing his blood again, it was Kara lying on her side, angled perfectly so the candlelight flattered her naked figure. He swallowed and felt his cock stir.

"Maybe I should hire you to be a waiter." She pointedly looked between his legs. "You dressed like that would definitely bring in the ladies."

He put the plate down on the table and poured fresh wine in their glasses. She accepted the one he offered. Kara sipped and he felt her heavy gaze on him.

"Anytime, sunshine, just say the word." He leaned down for a kiss before placing the robe beside her, then grabbed his jeans. "Hope you don't mind, but I was starving." He reached for a pastry, popped it into his mouth and chased it with a sip of wine. "I thought you might like your robe since your clothes are scattered all over the place. It was on the hook in the bathroom."

"Thanks. I'd forgotten how hungry I was too."

He watched every move she made. Even the simple act of slipping her arms into the sleeves and pulling the edges of the turquoise wrap together was crazy sexy. The edges of the satin clung to her breasts and the enticing gap showcased her cleavage. He caught himself glancing down, and thoroughly enjoyed the view. She didn't seem to mind either, if her nipples pushing against the fabric were anything to go by.

He settled into the low armchair before her and stretched his legs out, propping his bare feet on her lounge. He was relaxed. "So. What now?"

Kara took a sip of the wine. "What do you mean 'what now'? I'm quite happy doing just this." She leaned forward to snag a savory lamb puff.

The edge of her robe gaped and exposed the swell of her breasts. She leaned back and closed her eyes, nibbling on the treat, then took another taste of wine. He was still horny. Their one mind-blowing session wasn't near enough to satisfy all the years of neglect and frustration. But it could all be over in the next few minutes. He knew the risk of asking her, but he had to. He wondered how she would react. He was also a little worried about his reaction when she finally told him the reason.

"Kara, why did you leave?"

She kept her eyes closed and tried to remain calm, but took a deep breath as her heart kicked into high gear. She knew he would want answers and she really did owe him some. But damn if his bitch of a mother shouldn't be the one to explain what she did.

"Have you spoken to Joyce?"

He was silent and she opened her eyes to glance at him. His face was unreadable, the cozy easiness of the night seemed to hover on the breeze, about to float away.

"What's wrong?" She sat up and closed the robe. Suddenly feeling uncomfortable.

"Kara, I've asked you a few times and you've yet to explain it." There was hardness in his voice that made her heart clench with concern. It didn't fit with the mood and afterglow of their lovemaking and cold tendrils of alarm trickled down her spine to clutch in icy fingers at the base. It startled her and suddenly she felt as if something was really wrong.

"Max, it was such a long time ago." She hoped that maybe after their lovemaking he would let it drop.

He shook his head. "Kara, why do you want me to talk to my mother?"

Kara was unsure what to say. If she said too much or too little, it could ruin everything. The last thing she wanted was to end this wonderful night on a bad note. She wished he would just let it go, the past was in the past and she said so.

He ran his fingers through his hair and let out a frustrated sigh. He looked at her, his eyebrows pulled together. "Maybe so, but I don't understand why you refuse to tell me what made you leave so suddenly. Your words, all I want are your words."

"There were a few reasons. You know I wanted to go to Europe to study, as you did."

"Yes, yes, but we talked about our future together too. Getting married, opening a business together."

She could tell he was becoming agitated and panic soured in her belly. She didn't want to tell him his mother had instigated the whole thing. She shivered, remembering the horrible things she said to her. Even offering her money to leave. Which Kara refused to take, of course. It was offensive to be offered money and told she wasn't good enough for Joyce's son. That he deserved someone of his own status. Anger simmered in her chest. How she hated that woman for being the puppeteer that changed two lives forever. Kara never felt comfortable around his mother and she was dying to tell him all the horrible things Joyce said so many years ago. But Kara wasn't going to be the one to deliver the news and expose his mother. She had to do it herself.

Clearly what she had told Kara was a lie. If Max didn't marry Patricia, the daughter of a neighboring farm family, they might lose their farm. It was an arranged marriage, combining the lands for a bigger empire. How could a girl raised by her grandmother who owned a bakery ever be good enough for her son? At the time, when she was a young and impressionable teenager, she believed what adults told her, why would she think her boyfriend's mother would lie?

He stood and drained his glass, set it down on the table and paced to the railing to lean on it, facing her. His arms crossed over his chest, the universal body language meaning unapproachable.

Kara sighed and rose. She walked toward him, still saying nothing but hoping she could somehow try to salvage the night. She didn't want to burst his bubble about his mom, but the woman was a mean bitch.

She placed her hand on his forearm. "Tell me, what caused your divorce?"

He blinked, obviously surprised by her question. "What's that got to do with anything?"

"Humor me, Max. Why did you divorce?"

"We shouldn't have gotten married at all."

"But you did and it was pretty soon after I left, right?"

He didn't answer, so she continued. "Your mom wanted you to marry her. I'd make a bet on that. She came from the right side of the tracks." Kara spoke in a low voice, almost hoping he wouldn't hear her and glanced up at him from under her brows to watch his reaction. "And I came from the wrong side."

His gaze dropped to her and the intensity of it bore into her. He grabbed her shoulders. "Who told you that?"

"I think you know who did, Max." The pain clutching her heart right now was worse than all those years ago when Joyce told her she was trash and not suitable for her son. He would make something of himself without Kara and she would only drag him down.

He gripped both her shoulders and pulled her to face him. His anger came through in the power of his grip. "Tell me what she said to you."

"Oh Max. She should." Kara continued to keep her voice low, but she tripped over the words, upset causing bile to rise in her throat. "First, why did you divorce?"

Pain filled his gaze and she wished she could take it from him. The emotion reflecting on his face exposed his vulnerability and all she wanted was for his pain to go away. She desperately wished she hadn't been one of the people responsible for it. For a brief moment he looked like the teenage boy she fell in love with and she leaned toward him, but then his features hardened.

"I didn't love her." He pushed her away and paced across the deck to the rooster in the tree. He took a swat at it. A riotous clanging filled the tree branches while the rooster danced on its string.

He turned and the words pierced her like an arrow. "I loved you then, not her. It was all wrong. I was tricked and it didn't take long for it to come to a head."

He loved her then, but didn't say anything about now. "Max. I'm sorry—"

"Stop, Kara. I'm pissed you didn't come to me about it. Instead you ran off without any explanation."

"But you don't understand!" She didn't want him to be angry with her, and clearly he was. Damn, and all because of his mother. And maybe a bit of her own pride too. That she could fall for something so stupid.

"What I understand is that the women in my life manipulated situations to benefit their own good. I was young and foolish back then. But not now."

Kara shivered. Never had she seen him so angry and it stunned her. To go from their loving just moments earlier to this raw fury was unnerving.

He took his keys out of his jeans pocket and walked to the doorway.

"Where are you going?" Panic filled her. He couldn't just leave like this now.

He hesitated at the door and gripped the handle. "Kara. Holy shit." He dragged his hands through his hair. "What you're implying changes so much. Trust. We were all about trust back then." A brief flicker of pain in his eyes tore her heart out. "You didn't trust me enough to tell me."

"Don't go." She was close to begging him to stay, but he shook his head and was gone. The back door slammed shut behind him and the throaty roar of his truck shattered the stillness of the night.

Kara leaned over the railing and called after him, but it was too late. Only the spray of gravel hitting the fence from under the churning tires was left behind.

Kara couldn't keep the tears back any longer. She cried for their lost years, the tenderness they shared tonight and what she may have jeopardized for all the tomorrows to come.

She let him go. He was angry and felt betrayed. She couldn't change that, but for both of their sakes he needed to know the truth. She had no idea if he would seek the truth from his mother or if he would come back to her. Kara could only hope he would. She wouldn't be going anywhere and if he wanted her, he knew where to find her.

* * * * *

Max ended the call with his mother. He ripped out the earpiece and tossed it into the cup holder. His heart hung heavy in his chest. Kara alluded to the fact his mother played a significant role and ultimately changed the course of their lives. She was right, but that didn't excuse her from not telling him. He couldn't believe the lie his mother had fabricated and that Kara actually believed it!

He had some thinking to do.

Two women in his life had both let him down. His mother for hiding such a bitter secret all these years and Kara for not trusting him enough to tell him what happened. And a third had tricked him into marriage. Not a great track record for building trust and relationships. It didn't surprise him that he had avoided emotional entanglements all these years. But with Kara back and what he thought he felt for her, he needed to figure it out.

Anger sat in the pit of his stomach and he didn't like it at all. Distraction. That's what he needed right now and knew just where to get it. He put the truck in gear and pointed it toward Niagara Falls. A night at the black jack table would do the trick. It wasn't often he headed there, but before he started his heavy thinking, he needed the thrill of the bet and the sound of the slots to clutter his mind.

What a goat fuck. Everything had gone into the shitter in such a short space of time. But for tonight he'd fill the aching void with a few hours of cards.

It wasn't Vegas by a long shot, but the casinos in Niagara Falls would do. A short while later he handed his keys to the valet. Once inside the casino hall, he cruised past the slots and checked out the waiting list for Texas Hold 'em. Too long as usual, so he turned and looked for an empty seat at the tables. Again, all full and minimum bets were now twenty-five dollars. He spied an empty seat and slid onto the stool. The waitress was there in a flash and he ordered himself a draft, double shot of Jack and dropped three hundred dollars on the table. He piled the chips in front of him and placed his first bet.

Go big or go home. He bet a hundred. His heart jumped in his chest when two aces lay face up, so he split them and hoped for twenty-one. The first card was a nine, the second a face and the dealer busted at fifteen. The crowd around him shouted out and just like that he was up money.

He gave the waitress a ten-dollar chip for a tip and settled in for a good night. A few hours and numerous beers later, a commotion at the next table caught his attention. A domestic situation was developing. The guy was hammered, leaning over his cards trying to support his head and making foolish bets while his lady furiously whispered in his ear. But it wasn't all that much of a whisper since the surrounding tables could hear. She expressed her displeasure and told him she was leaving unless he smartened up. He waved his hand at her and she marched away, only to stop and stare at him from ten feet away with her hand on her hip.

Max chuckled, enjoying the scene playing out before him. When she stomped back and gave her guy a shove on the shoulder Max new there would be trouble.

Security wove their way through the crowd and approached the couple from behind. The pit boss must have called them. The guy was going to get tossed on his ass. But rather than abandon her man, the lady stuck up for him and promised to take him from the casino. After much persuasion, he finally slid off the stool and shuffled behind her. She gripped his arm and hauled him across the casino floor, with security close on their heels to make sure they left.

Max sat back in his chair and watched the couple leave with their escort. He missed placing a bet and when his attention was called back to the table, he realized he didn't want to be here anymore. An overwhelming loneliness consumed him. With a sigh he pushed his chips in to cash out.

Even though the couple had fought and she was mad as a wet cat, she stuck by her man and wouldn't let him get tossed out by security. The exchange between the couple made Max realize how much he wanted a partner, a significant other…a wife in his life. How everything he had built around him, the business, his house, the lands, were just *stuff* without someone to share it with. The heavy thinking he thought he'd have to do wasn't necessary after all. He had clarity and all it took was watching the couple at the other table.

He needed to get home, fast. The urgency he felt to bang on Kara's door and capture her in his arms burned like a fire in his belly. He stood and wobbled, grabbing hold of the chair.

Whoa.

Too many beers. Shit! No way could he drive like this. He might be able to manage if he took the back roads slowly, but when he stumbled against a pillar, he knew better than to risk it.

Max was pissed at himself for not keeping track of how much he drank. Kara would have to wait until morning. He needed a room to crash and walked very carefully to the hotel lobby to get one. Lucky for him there was availability. He rode up the elevator, fell through the door and tripped onto the bed fully clothed.

Chapter Six

ಬ

The alarm jolted Kara out of a sound sleep and she immediately felt sick. She hit the snooze. *Why did I finish that bottle all by myself?* She rolled over and buried her face in the pillow with a very unfeminine groan. If only she'd just corked it. But she hadn't and now she was paying for drowning her sorrow in the wine Max had brought.

The alarm blared again five minutes later, jarring her and sending her heart galloping behind her breasts. Kara rolled to the side of the bed and eased to a sitting position. She needed water. And aspirin.

She shuffled down the hall in the dark and turned on the tap, letting the water run cold, then gulped three big glasses. The clink of the cup against the sink was like a gunshot in the early dawn. Not even the birds were up yet. She loved having the bakery, but these early mornings were a killer. Kara rested her hands on the counter and wondered why she was so tender between her thighs. Recollection warmed her blood. Ahh. Max. They had been amazing together, so much better than all those years ago.

Then everything came roaring back and icy fingers gripped her heart. She reached over to check her phone for messages or texts. Nothing. She'd waited all evening, hoping he would call, and when she couldn't stand it any longer, Kara broke down and dialed his number. It went to voice mail. Why didn't he answer?

He must be furious with her to not answer a call. Was he ignoring her or was there another explanation? A multitude of thoughts raced around her mind, but she couldn't come up with anything that made her feel even the tiniest bit better.

The bottle of wine from his vineyard had beckoned and she'd poured a glass, which led to two and opening the second bottle. She thought it would make her feel a little closer to him by drinking his wine. A dumb thing to do, but it sounded good at the time. Kara had worked herself into a state of anger. She felt used and abused by him. How could he just leave like he did and not call? Or answer his phone? They had made love and his desertion tarnished the exquisite tryst. She had no knight on a white horse to ride in and kick some ass. No, she'd have to do that herself.

"Oh God. I'm gonna be sick," she told the dark room and took a breath, holding it. The feeling passed and she let her anger for Max replace the nausea. She had to get dressed and down to the kitchen. On the way back to her bedroom a sound from downstairs stopped her. Keys jangled in the door.

Max! He'd come back. Kara took the old wooden stairs, carefully gripping the banister for support. She was still wobbly and most likely drunk. A light flicked on below. She fully expected to see Max in her kitchen and her stomach dropped when she saw Jilly and Shane setting three Tim Horton coffees on the counter. It wasn't him and it dawned on her he didn't have a key anyway.

"Morning!" Why did Jilly always shout her greetings? Kara's hangover-sensitive ears rang and she cringed.

"Umm, morning." She was horrified to be in such a sad state in front of her employees and Kara inched back to the stairs. She noticed them exchange looks and smile at each other. She was thankful they didn't say a peep.

"Listen, I'm not feeling so great. Do you mind getting a start on things and I'll be down in an hour or so?"

"No problem, Kara." Shane assured her they would be fine and she could stay in bed as long as she needed.

"Mmm hmm, thanks."

"Here, take your coffee." Shane handed it to her. Kara nodded her thanks and trudged up the steps. Back in her room, she had a big gulp of coffee, took a couple aspirins and crawled back between the sheets. After a long sigh she was fast asleep in seconds.

Two hours later she woke to birds singing and sun creeping in to shine across her face. She wasn't as quick on the uptake as she should have been, but a whole lot better than earlier. She took a brisk shower, wound her wet curls into a loose bun and had herself together in fifteen minutes. She picked up the cold coffee and carried it downstairs. She was pleased by the sight that greeted her. She gazed across the trays lined up and said a silent thank you for these two wonderful students who dropped into her lap. Shane and Jilly had everything organized and ready to go.

"Hiya, feel better?" Shane smiled at her.

"Yes, much. Thank you. You guys are great and I totally appreciate your help." Kara leaned against the counter, waiting for her coffee in the microwave to heat up. "Thanks for taking care of things this morning."

"Yep. It's all under control." Shane smiled and carried a tray to the front. Kara followed him. It was coming on seven and everything would be ready for opening at eight thirty. Kara snagged a croissant. She bit into the flaky pastry. The buttery-almond flavor filled her mouth, reminding her of the words Max whispered into her ear last night while making love. She shivered, the memory still very ripe and tangible. Her belly fluttered and heat rushed Kara's cheeks. She closed her eyes and embraced the sweet response her body had to the memory of them on the lounge. It might be all she had left of him. Her anger for him had drifted away in her sleep and in its place, bitter disappointment about the turn of events. And acceptance.

What they had done together and how they pleasured each other, sharing themselves, touched deep in her soul and she knew it would imprint on her forever. Despair filled her mouth with bitterness and soured the sweet croissant. She gulped a mouthful of the Timmy's coffee to force the lump of pastry down her constricted throat.

Now she questioned if letting him back into her heart and bed had been wise. So many years had gone by and they were different people with very different lives. But maybe they could be interwoven? They would have to discover each other all over again all these years later. It could be thrilling and exciting.

She finished her coffee and tossed the cup in the recycle bin. Right now she couldn't let him distract her from her current plan. They had a big day ahead of themselves and she needed to focus. So Kara forced her thoughts away from Max to the shop. It was the Saturday of the Civic Holiday weekend and they would be swamped.

By noon she was proven correct. They had been so busy there had been no time to think of Max at all, or take a break. Once the lunch crowd dwindled down and people stopped to rest their aching feet on the patio, Kara realized there had been no call from Max. She slipped her hand inside the pocket of her jacket and fingered the phone. She was dying to call him. Should she? Or give him some space, which he obviously seemed to need. She made a deal with herself to call him at the end of the day. Kara would reach out to him, come what may. So she left the phone in her pocket and grabbed a few minutes of peace to do some prep for the wine and cheese appreciation tonight.

A couple minutes later her phone vibrated in her pocket. Max! She grabbed a cloth, wiped off her hands and ran into the back room to answer in privacy.

"Hello?"

"Is this Kara?" The familiar voice turned Kara's belly into a block of ice.

"It is."

"Why did you come back and ruin everything?"

"Excuse me?"

"You were supposed to stay away."

Anger flared in Kara. She knew exactly who this was and this time she wouldn't be so easily scared off. "Joyce, I have no interest in speaking with you. Do not call me again."

"You wait, Kara! I want to speak with you."

Kara hesitated and thought quickly. Should she listen to what she had to say? Why not? Information is power and if she was lucky, Joyce might expose herself and her intentions. "What's your problem, Joyce?"

Kara could almost hear her sputter at the other end before launching into a tirade. "You weren't supposed to come back! That was the deal—"

"There was no deal, Joyce. I was young and stupid and you took advantage of me."

"You weren't good enough for my boy back then and you still aren't now." The venom in Joyce's voice hissed through the phone and Kara could almost feel the toxin strike her though the phone lines.

She'd had enough and realized it wasn't worth the effort. Joyce was a bitter old woman who would never be happy and she no longer had any impact on her life. What was done was done.

"Joyce, be quiet. Stay away from me and don't call again. I have no wish to discuss anything with you at all. Goodbye."

Kara disconnected the call in the middle of Joyce's rant. The woman would never change. She refused to let the call rattle her and, in fact, almost felt a sense of relief. That bitch had a way of making Kara feel like an insecure teenager, but not this time and not anymore. She pursed her lips and stuck her chin out. She'd be damned if she let her play *any* role in her life again.

It was curious she would call her today though. The only logical explanation was Max must have talked to her. A nervous flutter in her heart made Kara catch her breath. She couldn't even predict what he might do now. It all depended on what Joyce told him. Now more than ever she needed to talk to Max. She dialed his number and it went straight to voice mail.

"Damn. Where the hell are you?"

Frustration ate at her since she couldn't reach him but she heard voices in the other room. More patrons. She couldn't worry about it now. There was too much to do before tonight's affair and she needed to be on her game. Kara puffed out a ragged sigh and dropped the phone back in her pocket, pushing thoughts of Joyce and Max out of her mind.

* * * * *

Jesus Christ!

He'd arrived home and moments after parking the car heard a huge crash at the end of his driveway.

He looked at the downed hydro pole that had dragged all the phone and hydro lines with it. The three smashed-up cars littered the end of his laneway, and traffic was backed up to the next concession. His cell phone needed charging but it was impossible with no hydro, the land lines were out and he was trapped on the property.

Frustration welled within him. How in the hell could he get in touch with Kara except by friggin' carrier pigeon? And he didn't have one of those!

He stood with his arms crossed and watched the lack of activity in getting the vehicles out of the way. Flatbed tows sat waiting for the Ontario Provincial Police to finish their investigation and give the all-clear to move the wrecks. At least no one had been seriously hurt, which was surprising considering the extensive damage.

At the rate they were going, it would be tomorrow before he could get off the vineyard or hope for hydro. Max tried to calm himself. There was nothing he could do to speed up the process and hoped word somehow reached Kara about the accident. Then she might understand why he hadn't been able to get in touch with her all day. Now he wished he'd called her before he left the hotel. But he'd been all bent on getting to her shop to speak with her in person. The way he took off on her last night, she deserved an in-person apology.

Shit.

* * * * *

Anticipation twitched along Kara's nerve endings and she couldn't wait until seven o'clock. The majority of the invites she sent had been returned with acceptances so she was expecting about thirty people, hopefully more if those who didn't reply decided to show up. Max had been invited too, and he had RSVP'd yes. Kara wondered if he would come and hoped he would.

Shane and Jilly were ready, along with a few student friends they brought along to help out. They would handle the food and wine so Kara could mingle with the guests. It had been a long, painful day, but her excitement overtook exhaustion and she was raring to go. Tonight was going to be fun, entertaining and hopefully very productive.

The jazz band set up their gear on the patio and a carefully worded sign at the entrance stated it was a private party. Jazzy tunes seeped into the bakery, which they had transformed into an upbeat wine gastro pub. The newest rage combining good eats, drinks and tunes.

Kara schmoozed with grace among the guests, ensuring their every need was attended to. An easy ambience wrapped around Kara and her guests. Titillating aromas tempted the palate and all was washed down with a variety of fine Niagara wines. Seductive and cozy lighting totally transformed the bakery into a hot night spot. Kara was thrilled and decided she would make this a recurring event. What a great way to establish We Bake In Heels as the go-to catering company as well as supplier to the area cafés and restaurants. She moved among her guests, satisfied she had taken a step down the path for her shop to be the purveyor of choice.

As the minutes ticked into hours she grew more disappointed Max hadn't shown or called. She steered clear of the wine tonight and whenever she saw a bottle with his vineyard label, Rockpile, her heart hammered and her upset ripened. She couldn't let her emotions intervene with business at hand and did her best to push Max out of her mind. Once she did, she relaxed again and continued to enjoy the evening.

She carried a tray of goodies to a cluster of people laughing on the patio. "Thanks so much for coming."

"Kara, it's a delight you have come home. Why did it take you so long?"

Kara laughed. "Well, it's hard to explain. But I'm so glad I'm home now." And she drifted off to be a charming and savvy hostess to the next grouping of guests.

Before she knew it, Kara was saying goodbye to her last guest and the night was over in a whirlwind. It proved to be a huge success and she had a list of interested business partners. She waited on the patio while the band packed up their last items and loaded them into the truck at the curb. She waved goodbye and let the quiet night wrap around her.

He hadn't come. She gazed wistfully down the street, looking for any headlights that might indicate he was a late comer. But nothing. So she flicked off the patio twinkle lights and closed the doors.

Inside, Jilly, Shane and their helpers finished the last of the cleanup and had even prepped items for the morning baking.

"You guys were great. Thanks for all your help." Kara gave Shane and Jilly a big hug and walked them to their car out back. Shane tried to hide a yawn, but Kara saw it and chuckled. They looked exhausted.

"Don't come in before ten o'clock tomorrow. Sleep in and get here when you can." She felt sorry for making them work such a long day, but they were young and had a helluva lot more staying power than she.

They climbed into Shane's car and shouted goodbyes, waved and drove off into the night, leaving Kara standing alone on the driveway. She sighed and enjoyed the comfortable sense of well-being that swelled within her. It had been a great night.

Kara leaned back and gazed at the sky. Stars twinkled through the leaves. Max was under the same night sky as her. Was he thinking of her? Kara shook her head. She was way too tired to do any more thinking and couldn't wait to crawl into bed.

Back inside, she let the door swing shut behind her and made a last round before switching off the lights. She paused at the back door to bolt it and jumped. A shadowy figure on the other side of the glass startled her at first, but she immediately knew who it was. Her heart tangoed in her chest and she held her breath.

She wanted to rage at him for ignoring her since last night and didn't wait for him to knock. Kara pulled the door wide and stood with her hands on her hips, ready to do battle. He didn't say anything and she tapped her stiletto-clad foot, waiting to see what he would say.

"You're mad," he stated simply.

"Really? Any reason you can think why I might be?" Kara was trying hard to be angry with him and to make him suffer a little bit, but when she noticed how haggard and worn he looked, whatever tendrils of anger she held for him dissipated on the night breeze.

"What's wrong?" Concern edged her voice and she pulled him inside.

He sighed and ran his hand through his hair. "There was an accident."

"Where? Are you okay?" She looked him over for any sign of injury and ran her hands along his muscular arms, relieved she couldn't see anything evident.

"Yes, I'm fine. Out in front of my place."

"Was anyone hurt?"

"Thankfully not serious, but I couldn't believe the damage."

"Come and sit down." She led him through the kitchen to the comfy leather chairs out front. At the bar, she poured them both a glass of wine, which he accepted with a tired smile.

"I don't think I've ever seen such wreckage before. It's a miracle no one was killed."

"Tell me."

He shook his head and gulped the wine. "It was incredible people walked away without serious injury. But it took them forever to remove the vehicles and the congestion to clear. Hydro had to come and fix a broken pole, so did Bell." His gaze captured hers. "I'm surprised you didn't hear about it."

Kara shook her head. "No, not a word." Relief flooded her. Now she knew why he hadn't called her all day or picked up his phone.

"I'm starved. You've got to have something to eat in this place, don't you?" He smiled at her and stuck out his long legs, resting one booted foot over the other on the scarred coffee table.

"Oh I think I might be able to find something. I'll be right back." She squeezed his shoulder and was pleased when he leaned back in the leather chair. His chest rose and fell with a big sigh and he looked as if all the tension in his body dissipated.

She fixed him a big sandwich, selected a few appetizers left over from earlier and set them on a platter. He could pick and choose what he liked. Kara smiled to herself. It was so good to see him resting in her chair, in her shop, and looking so comfortable. He had come to her after all and reached out for her company when upset. Kara's heart swelled with love for him. Urgent need to take care of and tend to him overwhelmed her.

She didn't bother to turn the lights back on, satisfied with the cozy glow the exterior street lights cast into the room. Romance and intimacy surrounded them. He looked very inviting stretched out on the chair and delicious memories of their tryst last night rushed back, igniting her desire for him.

"Here you go." His eyes were closed when she put the platter on the table in front of him.

"Thanks." Max sat up with a groan. "This is quite a spread."

He reached for the sandwich and she watched every move he made. The strength in his tanned forearms seemed to dwarf the sandwich he held in his hands, reminding her too well how they cradled her last night. Her thoughts quickly ran to the erotic. It had always been hard to stay mad at him and it was so much nicer being turned-on by him.

They still needed to discuss things and why he had left so abruptly last night. She would broach it later, and for now was content to watch him eat. Her gaze roamed over his body. They sat in comfortable silence, noshing on the goodies until he sat back and patted his stomach. "Thanks, that was good."

"You're welcome." It pleased her when people took pleasure from her cooking. Kara ignored the glass of wine she poured for herself and was about to get up for some sparkling water when his hand reached out for her. She halted mid-step when his strong fingers stayed her.

"Kara, I know what happened."

"Pardon?" *What happened when?*

"Mother. I spoke with her last night."

Kara sucked in a breath. Oh! "S-she told you?" Kara hesitated. "Now, after all this time?"

He nodded. "Yes. I know she told you to leave, that you weren't good enough for me." He shook his head with a bewildered look on his face. "And even tried to pay you to leave." He watched her intently.

Ah! Her heart stilled, waiting to see what else he might say. When he didn't she added, "I didn't take any money from her."

"I know! I wasn't saying you did. Just what she told me."

Kara nodded, unable to form words, and tears pricked behind her eyes.

"Kara." His voice was so low she barely heard him. "It kills me that you ran without talking to me. We could have figured it out."

"I couldn't!" The words burst from her and tears slipped down her cheeks.

"Why?"

"Oh Max, come on. We were kids. And you know what she was like. I couldn't believe what she was saying to me." Kara hesitated, trying hard to contain her feelings. "And she is your mother! What could I do? I couldn't put myself between you." Kara took a long breath. "And you knew I wanted to go to Europe to school. I thought it was the right thing to do at the time."

Looking back now, she could have stayed and told him. But she didn't and it set both of them on completely different paths. "Then by the time I considered returning, you were married to Patricia. I couldn't come back then."

"Patricia! She told you that?" He shook his head and took a long drink of wine, then met her gaze. "I married Caroline after she tricked me, saying she was pregnant when she wasn't." He sighed. "Well, after the conversation I had with her last night, I highly doubt she'll be trying any other manipulations."

Kara was blown away by that revelation. Caroline! Geez, his mother was a piece of work. "She phoned today."

"Are you kidding me?" He sat up, his face thunderous. "She just doesn't get it."

"Get what?"

He didn't answer right away, but the intensity in his gaze caused her breath to hitch. *What was he going to say?*

"I love you, Kara."

Silence filled the room. Had she heard him right? A smile broke wide and she threw herself on him, raining kissing over his face. He loved her!

Kara laughed when his arms reached around and held her tight. His lips found hers and the passion in his kiss spoke louder than any words ever could. She wanted to tell him so much, but she was overcome with joy, passion and could only laugh and kiss him back.

Kara shifted so she straddled his lap and cupped his cheeks in her hands, keeping their lips fused together. She recognized the expression on his face when it shifted to smoky heat with his arousal. Their gazes held and it set her heart galloping. He had that special look she had seen so many times when they were teenagers. She gripped him tighter and her lids fluttered closed.

He loves me!

Kara was giddy with happiness and the tenderness in her kiss quickly became more passionate. He responded to her demands and his reaction stole her breath. Max's firm grip against the small of her back pressed her intimately next to his belly. The willowy sundress she wore rode up her thighs, leaving only the barrier of her cotton panties and his shirt between them.

She sucked in a breath at their closeness, but it wasn't close enough and she pulled his top up, desperately needing to feel the heat of his flesh. She thrust her hips forward against the very evident ridge of his erection still trapped within his shorts. Tremors swept through her body.

Max's hands caressed up her back, over the filmy fabric into her hair and she tipped her head back, baring the column of her throat to him. He massaged her scalp, giving rise to exquisite sensations that shivered through her whole body right down to her toes. It didn't matter where he touched her, it was oh so perfect. She moaned in ecstasy, hoping he wouldn't stop.

As if he could read her mind, Max leaned forward and nibbled along the pulsing vein up to her earlobe, murmuring incoherent words to her, sending more shivery delight radiating over her flesh. He brushed his fingers across the side of her neck, moving her hair aside, and stroked the curves of her ear. Kara ground her hips down on him, feeling herself dampen in readiness. He knew every erogenous zone and hadn't forgotten after all these years.

"Oh Max," she sighed, unable to control her tremulous muscles.

"You're trembling," he whispered next to her ear.

Kara nodded, sucking in her lower lip. "Mmm hmm."

"I like that."

She smiled and a husky laugh burst from her lips. Kara dropped her head forward and her curls surrounded them in a golden curtain. Max thrust his hips up and his cock bumped deliciously against her damp heat. She enjoyed the feel of him next to her, but it was time to get rid of the clothes. Kara reached between them, pulled the zipper down and freed him. It didn't take him long to pull her panties aside, tearing the delicate stitches until there was nothing left to keep them apart.

She clenched her thigh muscles and rocked her hips back and forth, sliding deliciously over his cock. Her body jerked slightly every time the tip of him bumped against her clit. It roused her further and at the same time readied him for her. He groaned and gripped her tighter, the length of him growing harder with each thrust she made. This time she was in charge and planned to stay on top. She lifted herself and he held her hips steady.

Kara kissed him and reached between them to grasp his cock in her hand. She positioned him then slowly lowered herself. He filled her and her groan of pleasure expressed everything as he stretched her wide. She accepted him. Her muscles relaxed and clasped him in delicious tightness. He flexed inside her and a deep, guttural groan slipped from his lips. A powerful tremor rippled through his body and she rode him. He held her hips tight, their lips fused together, tongues tangling. They rocked in perfect harmony, born to be together.

Kara gloried at his firm muscles and tickle of hair beneath her fingers. She forgot she still wore the sundress until Max slipped his hands under it and pushed it up. The movement broke their kiss and Kara raised her arms so he could remove it — her bare breasts perfectly in line with this face.

"What a view."

He leaned forward and pulled an erect nipple between his lips. The sensation of his mouth suckling on her, his hard cock buried deep inside and her clit rubbing against him drove her to a higher level of bliss. Kara clutched him tight and he thrust into her. She matched his stride. They were synchronicity, giving and taking against each other. Her breath suspended and she sucked little gasps when the wonderful tightening pulses began in her pussy and her muscles clamped around him. She struggled for breath with each thrust and a low moan began in her throat.

"Come for me, baby," he encouraged her, his voice hoarse with desire. Max tensed and groaned. Instinctively she knew he was close, as was she. She rolled her hips, anxious to bring them both to orgasm, and then it was there. The contractions began in a sweet roll of ecstasy, beginning in her belly and dipping lower to her clit. The pulsing carried her into shrouded darkness and then exploded into a rhythmic, pounding glory. Her cry of delight filled the dimly lit room and he gave one last thrust, which sent Kara onto another wave of spectacular bliss. He shuddered in her arms with his own release and a low groan muffled into her neck. They drew pleasure from each other. Their movements slowed until they rested in each other's arms, spent and satisfied. Finally able to catch their breath, the silence of the room enveloped them in tranquility.

Kara pressed her lips to his neck, just under his ear and gloried in the pulsing power as his blood rushed along his vein. She breathed in his unique scent. How she loved this man and he needed to know.

"Max."

He hugged her tight and kissed her shoulder. "Yes." His voice was still gravelly with satisfaction.

She shivered and smiled, a husky laugh bubbled up and she leaned back to gaze into his passion-filled eyes.

"I love you too."

LETTING JACK WATCH
Katheryn Wallis
෨

Dedication

To my best friend Lisa, for believing in me and loving me unconditionally for twenty years (and counting!), and for inviting me to move in with her and her family, giving me the financial courage to become a novelist at last.

Acknowledgements

I thank my editor, Briana St. James, and everyone at Ellora's Cave for giving me a shot—you guys rock.

Keith Blount and his team at Literature & Latte deserve a huge shout-out for creating the best writing software I've ever used. Scrivener made the process of writing my first novel only as scary as it had to be and not one iota more, and I look forward to using it for many more novels to come.

I am especially grateful to Evangeline Anderson, whose wonderful books introduced me to erotic romance, and whose kind words and encouragement helped me take the plunge into writing this genre myself.

Last but absolutely not least, a million thank yous to Brooke, my friend, critique partner, Plot Muse, Overlord of Inspiration and Voice of Reason, who earned every one of her titles through the course of my work on this book.

Author Note

The Edmonton Police Department as described in this novel is itself a work of fiction, and does not necessarily bear any resemblance to the real Edmonton Police Service. I admire and deeply respect the Edmonton Police Service, but I don't presume to be an expert on their structure, equipment, procedures or operations.

Captain Tractor, on the other hand, is a real band, really from the Edmonton area, and they are at least as awesome as described herein. I encourage any interested readers to check them and their music out.

Chapter One

൭

Jack Bucholski tried to concentrate on what he was saying, but it was hard to stay focused with Caitlin Cook's intense green eyes fixed on him. "Okay, look," he said, tearing his gaze away. He took a quick chug of beer and then set the can down with the others on the kitchen counter. "The beer cans are my stones, the cooler bottles are your stones and the counter is the sheet of ice. Basically, we both try to slide our rocks down the sheet into the house on the other end, and whoever's stone or stones end up closest to the button—the center of the bull's-eye—scores that end."

"Right," Caitlin said, standing on tiptoe to study the arrangement of "rocks" on the counter. The petite redhead took a sip from her corner guard—a half-full bottle of orange-flavored vodka cooler—and then replaced it carefully. "I understand the basic premise of the game, or at least I think I do. What I don't get is the strategy. Or what sweeping does."

"Here, I'll show you," Jeremy Richter, Caitlin's boyfriend and Jack's best friend, leaned over to help.

Jack watched as Jeremy outlined the basics of sweeping, sliding bottles up and down the smooth gray laminate, his girlfriend listening intently. Caitlin had already been a fan of hockey when she moved to Edmonton, Alberta, from Princeton, New Jersey, almost two years ago, but she still found curling—the other winter sport about which many Canadians were extremely passionate—somewhat puzzling.

Travis Eddelton, Jeremy's roommate, wandered into the kitchen as Jeremy finished talking about sweeping and moved on to strategy. "Must be nice," he said when Jeremy paused for breath. "I wish my girlfriend liked curling and hockey. She can't stand either."

"Time for a new girlfriend then," Caitlin joked. "Where is Cindy, anyhow?"

"At a movie, I think," Travis said. He helped himself to one of Jack's "stones", twisted off the cap and took a swig. "She said she didn't feel like coming over tonight, with a bunch of guys getting drunk and talking sports."

"You gotta admit, that is what we're doing." Jack chuckled.

"Right," Travis agreed. "So what about you? Where's...Rachel? Rebecca?"

Jeremy laughed, cutting in before Jack could answer. "I think you mean Leanne. Rachel was last month."

"Leanne?" Travis gave Jack an incredulous look. "You're seeing someone new again? Christ, Jack, how do you do it?"

"I don't know, animal magnetism, I guess," Jack muttered, shifting uncomfortably. He had dated a girl named Rebecca as well, six months ago. Or was it seven? If he couldn't keep them straight himself, he could hardly fault his friends for being unable to do so. "Doesn't matter though—we broke up last week."

"Oh," Travis said. He looked somewhat uncomfortable, and Jack guessed he wasn't sure whether to offer condolences or congratulations. That made perfect sense to Jack—he wasn't sure himself which he needed. "Well, they all hated hockey, right?"

Jack nodded, but Travis, taking another sip of beer, didn't notice.

"That's disturbingly common," Travis lamented. "In fact, Caitlin's just about the only girl in our circle who doesn't."

"Hey! What about me?" Kristy, who was dating Jack's roommate Mike Cho, shouted from the living room. She was a big sports fan.

"That's what I meant by 'just about'," Travis said defensively. "It's just Caitlin and you."

Jack glanced at Caitlin, who was smiling across the counter at him and Travis. She had such a direct gaze. He wondered if she had any idea how her eyes smoldered when she looked at someone. Or was he the only one to be affected this way?

"Well?" Travis nudged Jack's shoulder, and he realized his friends were waiting for him to say something.

"Yeah," Jack said, trying to sound nonchalant. "They all hated hockey. Unfortunately, girls like Caitlin are pretty rare."

"Aww," Caitlin said, her smile becoming even more dazzling. "You're so sweet."

Jack, realizing what he'd just said, darted a quick look at Jeremy. "I mean, girls who like hockey. Like Caitlin," he amended.

"And Kristy!" That was Mike this time.

Luckily, Jack saw, Jeremy didn't look alarmed or angry, merely amused. "Yep," the tall man agreed, bending to give Caitlin a quick but affectionate kiss. "My girl's pretty special."

* * * * *

They didn't talk sports all night, but the subject had come up often enough that Travis' girlfriend Cindy probably would have been bored if she'd been there, Jack reflected as the party wound down several hours later. So would Leanne, and Rachel and all the other girls Jack had dated over the past year, he mused. Well, that was one nice thing about being single again—he had more time to spend with his friends, doing things they enjoyed.

On the other hand, though, Jack couldn't help wondering what it would be like to still be dating the same girl after such a long time. Jeremy and Caitlin had recently celebrated their one-year anniversary, while Jack's longest relationship had lasted just over eight months. It had ended when his girlfriend had dumped him for some financial executive with a two-hundred-dollar haircut, a Cadillac Escalade and a timeshare in Florida.

Jack tried not to think about that day, but the memory always seemed to be there, waiting just under the surface, ready to remind him that people were not what they seemed and he couldn't trust anyone who seemed to care about him.

He had listened in stunned disbelief as Angela, his tall, willowy, raven-haired girlfriend, explained she was leaving him for someone else, unable to reconcile the cold, distant stranger telling him goodbye with the woman he'd loved. The woman he'd thought had loved him back. Apparently, as it turned out, he hadn't even known her.

Since that day, almost a year ago now, Jack had had a string of brief hookups, none lasting longer than two or three weeks. His friends had started teasing him about his conquests-of-the-week, and Jack played along, professing to enjoy his carefree, playboy lifestyle. But in truth, Jack admitted to himself, it was getting old. Having no strings was great, and it made sense—as he told himself repeatedly—since the easiest way to avoid getting burned was to avoid any emotional attachment. But sense or not, it was also getting pretty damn lonely. Lately, he often caught himself watching Jeremy and Caitlin together, and wistfully wondering what it would be like to have a girl like her.

Speaking of his friends, Jack realized, no one else was in the living room. Travis was in the kitchen, crumpling empty pizza boxes by the sound of it. Mike and Kristy had left right after supper, Mike heading home to get ready for his night shift. They'd offered to drive Jack home then, but Jack had declined, not wanting to leave yet. *Probably should've taken a ride while I had the chance,* Jack thought now. He'd had at least two beers too many to drive himself home.

He rose to his feet, grabbing a couple of empty bottles and some dirty dishes to take to the kitchen. "Whoa, make that three too many," Jack mumbled to himself, as he bumped into the couch on his way.

"Jack! I thought you were asleep." Jeremy laughed, appearing from the hallway with a plastic bag half full of bottles and other returnable containers.

"Not yet," Jack said, handing the bottles to Jeremy and the dishes to Travis, who was now loading the dishwasher. "But I *would* like to crash on the couch, if you guys don't mind."

"'Course not," Jeremy said. "I'll get you some blankets."

"Oh hey, Jack." That was Caitlin's voice, and Jack turned—a bit unsteadily—to see Caitlin in the kitchen doorway. She'd changed into one of Jeremy's t-shirts. It came down to her knees, hanging baggy and shapeless, but the sight of her smooth calves and bare feet, and the hint of nipples through the thin fabric suggesting that she wore no bra, made it a sexy outfit nonetheless. "Are you sleeping over?"

"Yep," Jack said. He watched as Jeremy brushed past Caitlin, with a smile and a brief squeeze, on his way to the linen closet.

Caitlin gave Jeremy a saucy wink, then turned back to Jack, smiling. "Any chance you could make pancakes in the morning, then? Your pancakes are awesome."

"Uh, yeah, sure," Jack said, surprised and pleased. Jeremy and Caitlin had crashed at his and Mike's place one night, after a similar party, and he'd made brunch for everyone the next day. That had been about six months ago. Caitlin had complimented his cooking at the time, but he hadn't expected her to remember it all this time later.

"If he's not too hung over to cook," Travis amended, closing the dishwasher and turning it on.

"And if we're not too hung over to eat," Jeremy added, returning with an armful of bedding.

"Well, *you* won't be," Jack teased, following Jeremy into the living room. "You're so huge, you never get that drunk."

His hulking partner laughed easily. "Hey, I resemble that remark."

Jeremy helped Jack make up the couch, and then he and Caitlin said good night, heading around the corner and down the hall to Jeremy's bedroom. Travis went to his own room as well, leaving Jack alone in the dim living room.

Jack looked at the couch, but hesitated. He felt wide awake for the moment, and a bit too warm. The living room was stuffy. He slid open the glass door to the balcony, and then, as the cool night breeze rushed in, he decided to spend some time in the fresh air.

First, though, he visited the washroom, changing into an old pair of sweats Jeremy had offered him for pajamas, and then got himself a glass of water, icy cold from the filtered pitcher in the fridge.

Jack slipped quietly out onto the balcony, sipping his water. It had been a warm day for mid-October in Edmonton, over twenty-five degrees Celsius, but with the setting of the sun the temperature had dropped rapidly into the single digits and the night air was brisk and refreshing. In the orange streetlights the tree branches, some already bare of leaves, looked lacy and delicate.

The apartment complex was mostly dark, only a handful of windows lit. Jack wondered idly who else was awake at this hour—now almost 2 a.m.—and what they were doing. The flickering blue light coming from one window across the courtyard and down two floors suggested that someone was watching TV. Also across the way, three units to Jack's right and one floor up, a woman stood silently smoking on her balcony. She wore a tank top and pajama bottoms, and her hair hung long over her shoulders. It was probably brown, but in the glare from the streetlights it had an auburn tint, reminding him of Caitlin's glossy red waves.

The woman took a final drag and pitched the butt over the railing into the parking lot below, then went back into her apartment. Jack wondered if she knew that she lived across from a couple of cops. She could be ticketed for littering—or even damage to property if her lit cigarette butts damaged any cars below. At least there was no grass in the courtyard lot to catch fire.

The lights in the woman's apartment went out, and Jack, now starting to shiver in the cold air, turned to go back inside himself. But he noticed a slight movement out of the corner of his eye and paused. Not sure what had caught his attention, Jack took a few steps to his right, his bare feet making no sound on the rough concrete. There was a faint shadow on the wall at the far end of the balcony. It was moving slightly, up and down, and it was this almost rhythmic motion that had caught his eye.

He turned to look for the object casting the shadow and stopped, stunned. He was now standing in front of Jeremy's bedroom window, and through a small gap in the curtains he could see Caitlin and Jeremy on the king-size bed. Jeremy, bare-chested, sat propped against the wall at the head of the bed, and Caitlin lay on her stomach between his outflung legs.

Caitlin was sucking Jeremy's cock.

The room was lit only by a small bedside lamp. From where Jack stood, frozen, the lamp was behind Jeremy and Caitlin, turning their profiles to partial silhouettes. But Jack could see enough to tell that Caitlin was naked. The curve of one full, creamy breast was visible beneath her arm, and the smooth pale skin of her back flowed down to her waist and rose again to her plump, shapely backside, the cleft of her buttocks just covered by the crumpled edge of the duvet.

Jack watched, stunned immobile, as Caitlin's head bobbed up and down. The tousled waves of her hair partially blocked his view, but there was no mistaking what she was doing. After a few moments she pulled back to lick Jeremy's cock, from the root to the broad flaring head. Jack noticed that his best friend's cock was very similar to his own in both size and shape. Caitlin took Jeremy in her mouth again, sucking him in until her lips almost reached the base of his cock, and Jeremy tensed, his head thrown back, his hands coming up to tangle in Caitlin's hair.

Jack's thoughts raced, images flicking through his mind in time with the pulse suddenly throbbing in his ears and the heat surging through his whole body. He couldn't help imagining what it would be like to be in that bed, with his own hands in Caitlin's silky mane and her sweet mouth enveloping his own cock—which was now straining at the borrowed sweatpants. He noticed that Jeremy was still wearing his plaid pajama bottoms, but they were pushed down his hips, Caitlin holding the fabric out of the way with one hand, the other cupping Jeremy's balls.

Jack wondered about the sweats he was now wearing—had Caitlin had ever pulled them down but not off so she could suck her boyfriend's cock, like she was doing now? Jack pressed the side of his hand firmly against his throbbing dick, through the thin fleece. He had never needed to come so badly in his life.

A car door slammed in the parking lot below. Startled, Jack stepped back, away from the window, suddenly burning with embarrassment as well as lust. Water sloshed out of the glass he'd forgotten he was holding. God, what was he doing, spying on his partner, his best friend? And how could he have been staring at Caitlin, his best friend's girl, straining to see more of her naked body, fantasizing that it was his own cock she was sucking?

Jack forced himself to turn away from the mesmerizing sight. He slipped quietly back through the balcony door, sliding it most of the way shut behind him, and crossed the darkened room. He set his glass of water on the coffee table and lay down on the couch, trying to ignore his persistent hard-on and the even more persistent images still filling his head.

But his mind was drawn back irresistibly to the scene he had just witnessed. Just before he had turned away, he'd seen Caitlin tilt her head to look up at Jeremy, smiling at him, even as she took his cock farther into her mouth. What would it be like to have her look up at him like that, with her smoldering emerald gaze, even as his hard cock was sliding in and out of her soft pink lips?

Jack rolled to his feet, stifling a groan. There was no way he'd be able to go to sleep until he had come—but he wasn't going to make a mess on his friends' couch, or in his friend's sweats, for that matter. He padded quietly down the hall toward the bathroom, one forearm braced against his crotch to keep his throbbing erection from bobbing up and down as he walked, and to shield it from view if Travis, Jeremy or—god forbid—Caitlin should come out of their respective rooms for whatever reason.

As Jack entered the short hallway beyond the kitchen, with the two bedrooms on his right and the guest bathroom on the left, he thought he could hear a faint, rhythmic thumping noise coming from Jeremy's room. He wasn't sure if he was only imagining the sound—it was hard to make out over the low purring and clicking of the dishwasher, still running in the kitchen behind him. Then, just as he slipped into the bathroom and turned to close the door behind him, he heard Caitlin cry out—a soft but unmistakable moan of passion and pleasure.

Jack's cock pulsed almost painfully at the sound. With a confused jumble of images pouring through his head—a vision of Jeremy pounding Caitlin hard into the mattress turned into an image of Caitlin writhing with pleasure beneath Jack as he drove his own cock into her tight wetness—Jack twisted the doorknob locked, yanked down his borrowed sweatpants and took himself firmly in hand. With three hard strokes he was coming, catching the glistening white fluid in his free hand, trying not to moan aloud with his release.

Afterward, as he washed his hands, Jack tried to avoid the mirror above the sink. But he looked up eventually, flinching as he met his own gaze. What the hell had just happened to him? And how was he going to face Jeremy, and Caitlin, in the morning?

Chapter Two
ℬ

Caitlin watched as Jack poured batter onto the hot griddle, wondering what was bothering him. He seemed uneasy this morning, subdued, and didn't seem to want to meet her eyes. Or Jeremy's either, Caitlin noted, as Jeremy strode into the kitchen and said good morning to everyone.

Caitlin was distracted from her thoughts as Jeremy walked up behind her and spun her bar stool gently around. Even sitting on the stool—which made her about three inches taller than when she was standing—Jeremy still loomed over her. That was one of her favorite things about him; how big and strong he was—and yet how he would never use his size to hurt or intimidate anyone. Well, anyone except the criminals he apprehended in the line of duty, she supposed.

Jeremy kissed her, gently but thoroughly, and she responded, sliding her hands up his chest to twine them around his broad shoulders. He smelled of aftershave, spicy and musky, and his freshly shaved cheek was smooth against hers.

Jeremy clapped Jack on the shoulder, nodded at Travis and set about making tea for Caitlin and coffee for the guys. As Caitlin watched him, gliding about the kitchen more gracefully than you'd expect a man his size could move, she remembered the day they'd met.

* * * * *

Caitlin was an in-house technical writer for an alternative energy company, and she'd decided to take a self-defense class the company was sponsoring. As Caitlin had stood with the other women who'd signed up for the class, she'd surreptitiously eyed the two tall, handsome police officers talking quietly together in the corner of the room, wishing she'd worn something nicer. But the instructions on the sign-up sheet had said to wear comfortable exercise clothes, so Caitlin had worn a tank top over a sports bra, hip-hugging yoga pants and sneakers.

"Damn, I wish I'd fixed my makeup," Marcie, the third-floor receptionist, had whispered, obviously thinking along the same lines as Caitlin. "That guy is hot." She'd pointed her chin at Jack.

"Yeah, no kidding," Caitlin had whispered back. It was strange to think of now—now that she'd been dating Jeremy for over a year—but it was actually Jack she had noticed first, with his dazzling smile, crisp black curls and vivid, impossibly blue eyes.

But as Jeremy took his turn leading the class, demonstrating different moves and explaining when and how to use them, Caitlin found herself drawn to him too, admiring his strong hands, his incredibly broad muscular shoulders and his deep voice, calm but captivating.

Then they'd split into groups to practice the techniques they'd just learned, and Caitlin, eager to demonstrate what a good student she was, had gotten carried away with an escape move and elbowed Jeremy right in the face.

She had been shocked and mortified, but Jeremy had laughed it off, reassuring her that she was obviously a fast learner, and telling the rest of the class that this was proof the techniques they were practicing would really work. Jack had come over to inspect the damage, chuckling when he realized Jeremy was not seriously hurt, and handed him a tissue to wipe his bleeding nose. "Looks like you've got the hang of things," he'd teased Caitlin.

Caitlin had apologized profusely, and when the class was over, asked Jeremy if she could buy him dinner. He'd accepted…but when dinner was over, he'd insisted on paying. Laughing, Caitlin had threatened to elbow him in the face again, and they'd finally settled on going dutch. And Jeremy had asked her to go to a movie with him on his next day off.

Caitlin had been delighted to find that Jeremy shared her love of zombie movies, and Jeremy was thrilled to discover that she enjoyed hockey and, like him, was a fan of British comedy. They also, as Jack had pointed out on more than one occasion, shared a wacky and somewhat offbeat sense of humor.

Caitlin smiled to herself, remembering. Jack would often shake his head in mock derision, pretending to be unamused while she and Jeremy laughed at something strange. But they both knew Jack was fighting not to laugh as well.

Jack didn't laugh much any more, Caitlin realized. He had changed a lot in the past year—since Angela had dumped him. Caitlin had only met Angela once or twice before that, but from what little she knew of her, Caitlin didn't think Angela had been right for Jack anyway. She just didn't seem to have a sense of humor. And more—Angela was ambitious, elegant and cool, while Jack was easygoing, down-to-earth and fiercely loyal.

Maybe that was why Jack just didn't seem to have gotten over that relationship, even a year later. He certainly hadn't found whatever he was looking for in the string of girls he'd dated since then. Maybe, Caitlin reflected, it wasn't the loss of the woman he'd loved that Jack couldn't get past, so much as the fact of her betrayal. It must be hard to trust anyone again, after that.

* * * * *

"Here," Jack said, and Caitlin looked up from her thoughts to find Jack holding out a plate. "This one's yours."

"Aww! Thanks, Jack," Caitlin said, touched and amused. The three pancakes on her plate had been carefully shaped — one was the letter "C", another a star with rounded points and the third was a heart.

"That one's actually from me," Jeremy said, pointing his fork at the heart-shaped pancake. "It was a special request."

"Yeah, Jeremy always wants heart-shaped pancakes." Jack smirked.

"So why are his all round, then?" Caitlin asked, eyeing the enormous pile of pancakes on her boyfriend's plate. She stacked hers up, star-heart-C, and dribbled syrup over the top.

"Well, I don't want anybody to get the wrong idea about Jeremy," Jack said, unplugging the griddle and sitting down to his own breakfast. "It's for his own protection."

"More like for yours," Jeremy countered, grinning. "He *wants* to make me heart-shaped pancakes, but he doesn't want anyone to know he's got the hots for me."

"I think you've got that backward, pal," Jack retorted. He seemed to be fine now, Caitlin thought. Whatever had been bothering him earlier, he appeared to have forgotten about it, or put it out of his mind. "You're the one who got all sad and clingy when you thought I might move to Toronto."

"I just couldn't stand the thought of having to break in a new partner," was Jeremy's excuse. "It took a whole year to get you trained."

"You were thinking of moving to Toronto?" Caitlin asked, ducking as Jack threw a sausage across the table. Jeremy caught it, saluted Jack with it and bit it in half.

"Not really," Jack said distractedly, now giving his partner the finger.

Travis, who had wisely retreated out of firing range to refill his coffee, shook his head. "You sounded pretty serious about the idea at the time, buddy," he said. "Scared the crap out of all of us."

"Yeah, well, Scott wanted me there. I had to at least think about it," Jack said. At Caitlin's puzzled look he explained. "Scott was my last partner, before I got stuck with Jeremy here."

"Hey!" Jeremy protested Jack's choice of words, throwing what was left of the sausage back across the table at Jack.

"And," Jack continued, catching the sausage and biting into it, "Scott and his wife moved to Toronto, to be closer to her family. He keeps trying to get me to move out there, says there's way more action in the Toronto PD."

"Which there probably is," Jeremy agreed fairly. "Along with a lot more politicking and bureaucratic bullshit."

"Yeah, there is that," Jack said. "I suck at that stuff."

"You suck at everything," Jeremy said.

"Yeah, you wish," Jack retorted. Then, for some reason, he glanced at Caitlin. She thought he might be blushing.

The breakfast battle apparently over, Travis sat back down next to Jack and resumed eating. "So, how are Scott and Liz?" he said. "How many kids have they got now — two?"

"Three," Jack said, and shook his head as Travis nodded appreciatively. "That's a hell of a lot of responsibility. You gotta admit, I've got it lucky there."

"Meaning what?" Jeremy asked.

"Meaning I've got no wife, no kids, no strings," Jack said. "I'm a free man. I get to do whatever I want to do, whenever I want to do it. Don't tell me you guys don't envy that at least a little bit."

"Yeah," Travis agreed, sighing. "I have to admit, sometimes I would like to be let off the leash."

"'Off the leash'?" Caitlin echoed, sounding offended. "God, is that honestly how you guys feel about being in a relationship?"

"Hey, not me!" Jeremy quickly protested.

"Good answer," Travis joked. "You've got him well trained." He nodded appreciatively at Caitlin.

"Seriously," Caitlin said. "Travis, if you're not happy with Cindy, you should break up with her. It's not fair to either of you to stay together if that's really how you feel about it. And

Jack," she turned to face him, across the table. "What about you?"

"What about me what?" Jack said. He was cutting his last pancake into smaller and smaller pieces, but not eating any of them.

"Do you really think being in a relationship is that awful?"

"I don't know," Jack mumbled uncomfortably. He tried to meet Caitlin's gaze, but her eyes were doing that smoldering thing again. He'd never met a woman who looked so unwaveringly, unblinkingly, into his eyes, her stare at once direct, forthright and yet utterly mysterious.

"Well, maybe it was awful with Angela," Caitlin said gently. "I didn't know her that well, but I know she treated you pretty badly, at least at the end. She wasn't good for you. And I guess you haven't had much luck since then. But maybe things would be different if you were with the right girl instead of the wrong one."

Jack tried to focus on what Caitlin was saying. Had things ever felt truly good, truly right, with Angela? He'd thought they had, but suddenly he wasn't sure. With Caitlin's luminous green eyes trained on him, he found he couldn't even remember Angela's face.

"Yeah, maybe," he mumbled finally. He did remember, dimly, being happy once, feeling secure and confident and cared for. It was a far cry from the purely physical encounters he'd been seeking lately. For one thing, Jack really missed cuddling, having a warm, feminine body curled up against him at night. But he'd learned the hard way that it was damn near impossible to engage in warm, cuddly acts without starting to have warm, cuddly feelings. Damn near impossible for whatever girl he was with, and for Jack himself as well. So, given a choice between awakening those dangerous, vulnerable feelings and protecting himself, Jack had chosen to go without things like cuddling. But suddenly, today, under Caitlin's intense emerald gaze, that decision didn't seem to make as much sense anymore.

"Hey, cut him some slack," Jeremy said. He threw Jack a concerned glance, then tugged Caitlin toward him, planting a kiss on her forehead. "Jack killed a lot of brain cells last night, all that beer he drank. Lucky he can remember his own name, let alone anything else."

"Aw, he's fine," Travis said. "In fact, I bet we can beat you at Wii Jeopardy. What do you say we play after breakfast? You two," he tilted his chin at Jeremy and Caitlin, across the table, and then nodded at Jack beside him, "against Jack and I."

"Jack and me," Caitlin said.

"What?" Jeremy sounded surprised. "Don't you want to be on my team?" Jack looked startled too.

"Of course I do, silly," Caitlin reassured her boyfriend. "I was just saying, it's 'Jack and me', not 'Jack and I'."

All three men stared at her blankly.

Caitlin laughed at their expressions, washing down a mouthful of pancake with a swig of tea. "You say 'Jack and I' when you're the subjects of the sentence," she explained. "Like, 'Jack and I are eating breakfast'." But when you're the objects of the sentence, you say 'Jack and me'. So, 'Will you play Jeopardy with Jack and me'."

"And me," Jeremy insisted, poking Caitlin's side. He knew from past experience that she was very ticklish there.

Travis rolled his eyes as Caitlin squealed and swatted her boyfriend's hand away. "So what's it like going out with a Grammar Nazi, Jer?" he asked. "She correct your English while you guys are in bed, or what?"

"Um, I plead the fifth," Jeremy said, grinning.

"You can't plead the fifth," Caitlin said, smacking Jeremy again. "You don't *have* a fifth amendment. And anyhow," she smirked, turning to Travis, "when we're in bed, he tends to stick to simple declarative or interrogatory sentences. Not much to correct there."

"Oh yeah?" Travis said, laughing. "No whaddyacallems…uh, imperatives?"

"Not from me." Jeremy winked. "She gives all the orders."

"Hey—shut up!" Caitlin protested.

"See what I mean?" Jeremy laughed. He got up and started clearing the table. Travis got up too. He put his dirty dishes on the counter and then headed for the living room.

Jack wasn't laughing, Caitlin noticed, finishing her tea. He was blushing again, and had his eyes fixed on the plate he was rinsing. Usually he was as uninhibited as the rest of them, but this was the second time today he'd gotten all shy and quiet when the conversation turned to sex or innuendo.

Actually, Caitlin thought, at least once the conversation had turned more specifically to Jeremy and her having sex. And with that, she blushed as well, abruptly realizing what might be on Jack's mind.

She remembered last night in bed with Jeremy, after Travis—and, presumably, Jack—had gone to sleep. Caitlin had heard a noise through the bedroom window—a soft sliding sound. It was the noise the patio door made when it opened. Or when it closed.

Had Jack been out on the balcony last night? And if so, had he heard—or even seen—what she and Jeremy had been doing?

"Hey, are you coming, babe?" Jeremy's voice behind her, and his warm, wide hands on her shoulders, brought Caitlin back from her speculations. "Time to kick some butt. Jack and Travis against you and *me*." He deliberately emphasized the last word, to show he'd absorbed the grammar lesson of a few minutes before.

"You bet," Caitlin said, smiling. That was one of her favorite things about Jeremy—all teasing aside, he truly listened to everything she had to say. She let Jeremy lead her into the living room, where Jack and Travis were already hooking up the game console.

Caitlin tried not to think about the scenario that had occurred to her a few minutes before. Jack might not have seen anything the night before, and if he had, well, it was no big deal. They were all good friends—what harm could it do?

By the time they'd finished the first game—which Caitlin and Jeremy won by over eighty thousand dollars—she had forgotten all about her musings. For now.

Chapter Three
ಐ

Jeremy glanced at Jack, wondering what was on his mind. Jack usually let Jeremy drive the patrol car, preferring to handle the radio and computer. Today, though, Jack had grabbed the keys and slid behind the wheel himself. This was unusual. He also seemed tense, drumming on the steering wheel with nervous energy, a muscle moving in his cheek as he repeatedly clenched his jaw.

Through two speeding tickets on surface streets and a fender bender on the Yellowhead, Jeremy held his tongue, hoping Jack would volunteer whatever was on his mind. After a quick lunch at Tim Hortons—chili combo for Jack, club sandwich and soup combo for Jeremy—and an arrest for illegal weapons possession, through which Jack continued to fidget and also began to dart quick, hesitant glances at his partner, Jeremy finally decided to take matters into his own hands.

Normally, he might have waited until they were off work to find out what was going on. So far, only about half of the Edmonton Police black-and-whites had been outfitted with dash-mounted cameras. These could be rotated to capture either the view in front of the car, or—if the officers had picked up a perp and wanted a record of his or her behavior during transport—the back seat of the car. Either way, however, the cameras were required to stay on throughout each active patrol shift, and thus also recorded all conversations carried out between the officers sitting in the car.

Today, however, since he and Jack were not in one of the camera-equipped vehicles, the conversation he was about to initiate wouldn't be recorded. There was obviously something personal bugging his partner and best friend and, right now at least, it was nobody's business but theirs.

"So," Jeremy began when Jack paused in his nervous tapping on the steering wheel. "What's eating you?"

Jack glanced at him, then quickly looked back at the road. He made a right onto 111th Avenue. They passed 109th Street. "Nothing," he said finally, and unconvincingly.

"Something is," Jeremy persisted. "You've been acting weird since the weekend. Spill."

Jack sighed. "Fine," he said. "I just...I owe you an apology. And Caitlin too, probably, only I'd actually rather you didn't tell her about this."

"About what?" Jeremy was surprised. He couldn't remember any incident requiring an apology. And Caitlin and Jack always got along great.

"When I slept over at your place on Saturday night," Jack explained, "I went out on the balcony before I went to sleep. Just to get some air." He squinted, either reacting to the bright sunlight pouring through his window or anticipating a negative reaction from Jeremy.

"And," he continued reluctantly when his partner didn't say anything, "I, uh, accidentally looked through your bedroom window."

"So?" Jeremy was confused. Who cared if Jack saw his bedroom? He'd been in it dozens of times.

"Well, you guys were...I mean, Caitlin was, uh..."

Watching the blush creep up Jack's neck to his cheeks, slightly darkened with stubble though he'd shaved before their shift as usual, Jeremy suddenly remembered what he and Caitlin had been doing that night, and realized just what Jack must have witnessed. "Oh," he said. "Right."

"Yeah," Jack said.

There was an awkward silence for a moment, as Jack eased up to a red light. They watched a couple on the sidewalk next to them, white male and white female, both in their late teens, arguing. The male stepped threateningly toward the female, shouting, and Jeremy put one hand on his seat belt buckle, ready to step out and grab the guy if things looked to get physical. But at the female's retort, the male turned, shaking his head, and walked away.

"So, that's it?" Jeremy asked. "You just glanced in the window?"

"Yeah," Jack said, but then sighed. "Okay, honestly, I stood there for a couple minutes. I was kind of surprised, you know?"

"Don't tell me you're surprised I have sex with my girlfriend," Jeremy teased, trying to ease his partner's tension a bit. Jack was clearly upset about what he'd done. Jeremy wasn't upset himself, though, to his own surprise. He felt like he ought to be mad at Jack, but for some reason, he just wasn't.

"Of course not." Jack grinned. "You guys obviously have a healthy relationship." He looked over at Jeremy again, apparently reassuring himself that his best friend wasn't furious. "Anyway, as soon as I realized what I was doing, I left," he finished. "So, I'm sorry, pal."

"No problem," Jeremy said. "Thanks for telling me."

"You sure we're cool?" Jack still sounded worried.

"Of course," Jeremy said. He meant it. "This is why you've been acting weird since then?"

"Yeah," Jack admitted. "I wasn't sure what you guys would think of me."

"Well, it's best to have everything out in the open, don't you think?" Now that the worst was apparently out, Jeremy thought Jack could stand a bit of teasing, to lighten things up. "Now *I* know that you're a voyeur pervert, and *you* know how amazing I am in bed."

Jack burst out laughing. "I didn't see *that* part, dude— sorry." He shook his head. "I did see that Caitlin's pretty amazing, though," he added, then bit his lip, as if fearing he'd crossed a line.

"Yeah, she is," Jeremy agreed proudly. Maybe that was what was really bugging Jack—was he comparing what he'd seen Caitlin doing with his own experiences, and finding the latter lacking? If so, he could certainly understand that. Jeremy had been with other girls before Caitlin, but sex with her was definitely the best he'd ever had. "How were things with Leanne? Would she…you know, go down on you?"

"Oh yeah," Jack said. "That wasn't a problem." And it hadn't been, not in the sense that Leanne had been willing—if not necessarily eager—to give him a blowjob. Most of the other girls he'd hooked up with in the last year had been willing to as well, at least on occasion. Getting some action when he wanted it wasn't usually a problem for Jack. But somehow, it never felt the way Jeremy and Caitlin had looked that night.

"So, why'd you dump her then?" Jeremy asked curiously. "I thought she was nice."

"Yeah," Jack said. "She was." Leanne had been nice. She was tall—only an inch or so shorter than Jack's five feet, eleven inches—and slender, with curly hair, warm eyes and a sexy, sultry voice. And, after two weeks of dating, she had offered Jack a key to her apartment. And invited him to Sunday brunch with her parents. That was when Jack had dumped her.

Things had gotten ugly after that, before Jack had cut and run. Leanne had called him several things, none of them pleasant. The four-letter words he didn't mind so much—people swore when they were angry, and she'd had a right to be angry. But some of the other words she'd thrown at him—things like "coward" and "commitment-phobe"—had hit a little closer to home.

"I don't know," Jack said finally, realizing Jeremy was waiting for him to go on. "Things were just moving too fast, I guess. Girls always want to jump right in, you know? Do not pass Go, do not collect two hundred dollars, go straight to living together and lifetime commitment. What's wrong with just having a little fun?"

"Is that really all you want?" Jeremy asked. He was honestly curious. "I mean, I hate the dating scene. Going to bars and coffee shops, trying to find a girl who's more than just a pretty face. Don't you want to get past all that superficial stuff and find someone you can really connect with? Really trust?" He smiled, more to himself than to Jack. "Caitlin's amazing. Yeah, she's gorgeous, and she's incredible in bed, and that matters a lot, but she's also fun. And nice, and smart. And I can talk to her—really talk to her. About anything." Jeremy cleared his throat. "I've finally found the perfect girl, and I'm never going to let her go. I can't imagine going through all that again."

"Yeah, well, I thought I had all that too," Jack said, trying not to sound bitter and jealous. It was hard—harder than usual, somehow, after having seen Caitlin and Jeremy in bed together. "With Angela. But then my 'perfect' girl found her perfect guy. Who wasn't me. And she started fucking him behind my back." He sighed, running a hand through his black curls. "You just never know, Jer. You never know."

Jeremy opened his mouth to protest, but before he could speak the radio crackled to life, summoning them to back up some fellow officers on a traffic stop near Kingsway Garden Mall. Jack shoulder checked, then pulled a U-turn while Jeremy grabbed the mike to acknowledge the call.

"Anyway," Jack said when Jeremy returned the mike to its hook. "Are we good? About last weekend?"

"Yeah, we're good," Jeremy confirmed. Now, he reflected as they sped back east on 111th Avenue, all he needed to do was figure out why Jack's voyeuristic revelation hadn't bothered him.

If you'd asked Jeremy a week ago how he'd feel knowing some other guy had watched him and Caitlin going at it, he wouldn't have bothered answering—he would have found the sick fuck and punched the guy's lights out for perving on his girl.

But this wasn't just some other guy, it was Jack. They'd been best friends since they'd met three years ago. Jeremy's previous partner had retired, and he got saddled with the new guy. That was Jack — he'd been a cop for a while already, but when his former partner, Scott, had moved to Toronto, Jack had transferred to Downtown from the Southeast Division.

Their first shift together fell on a Saturday night, and it was hell. A string of DUIs, domestics and disorderly conducts had culminated in an assault suspect pulling a knife on Jack. Jeremy had taken him down without further incident, but they'd both been shaken. Going through shit like that together tended to forge strong partnerships.

But it was the incident a month later that had really made them best friends, Jeremy recalled. A routine traffic stop had netted them a subject with a warrant out of Saskatchewan. Jack tossed the car while Jeremy patted down the driver, a skinny, twitchy guy with a scar snaking down one cheek. The guy swore he had nothing on him, but when Jeremy checked his left jacket pocket, he pricked his finger on an uncapped, used needle.

He'd spent the next two weeks in a kind of numb agony, waiting for the results of his own blood tests and the forced draw from the suspect — who'd been charged with felony assault on a peace officer — to come in. He couldn't concentrate on anything, kept messing things up, 'til finally the sarge took pity and put him on paid leave. Jeremy couldn't sleep, couldn't eat. All he could do was sit there and try not to wonder what would happen to him if he ended up with hepatitis or, god forbid, HIV.

And through it all, Jack was right there by his side. They hadn't put him on leave, just Jeremy, but Jack had swapped some shifts around and then just showed up at Jeremy's place — the downtown bachelor apartment he'd lived in before moving in with Travis. Jack didn't try to offer Jeremy any meaningless platitudes or assurances, as some of the other guys had, and he didn't make Jeremy talk to him, demanding that he be optimistic. He was just there for him. They watched hockey, curling and all the *Alien* movies, silently, side by side on the ugly, sprung sofa. Jack ordered pizza and Chinese food and bullied Jeremy into eating. The second morning was the first time Jeremy had had Jack's pancakes, he realized now.

When the results finally came back negative, after those two weeks of hell, Jack had given his partner a huge bear hug, said "See you at work" and left. As if he could tell Jeremy was about to lose it—which he was—and that he didn't want to be seen bawling like a baby. Which he didn't.

They'd never really talked about it again, but since that day, Jeremy would have done anything for Jack. Up to and including take a bullet for him. And he knew Jack felt the same way.

So he couldn't be mad at his partner—especially not for something that was just an accident anyhow. Jack's confession did leave Jeremy slightly troubled, however—or rather, his own reaction to it did. He wasn't just not mad; he realized he was actually a bit turned-on by the thought that Jack had watched Caitlin going down on him.

He didn't really think Jack was a pervert, despite his teasing comment a few minutes ago. But maybe Jeremy himself was?

*****

"Hey, partner," a familiar voice said in Jack's ear.

"Unh," he croaked, switching the phone to his other ear and peering at the alarm clock. It was 11 a.m. A perfectly reasonable time for most people to make and receive phone calls, but Jack had worked the night shift and had only been in bed for two hours before being awakened by the shrilling of his cell phone.

"Oh crap, did I wake you up?"

"No," Jack said automatically. An exhausted synapse in his brain finally fired. Scott, that's who it was. "Well, yeah, I was sleeping, actually, but never mind. What's up?"

"Not much," his former partner said cheerfully. "Just wanted to check in, see how you're doing." He paused for a breath. "And to let you know the Toronto PD is hiring."

Jack laughed. "You never quit, do you?" he asked. They talked at least once a month and every time Scott managed to work in his usual pitch. "Did they stick you with some rookie who doesn't know his ass from a hole in the ground, or what?"

"Nah," Scott said comfortably. "I'm still with Sandro. He's coming along great. Tied his own boots this week, even."

"Impressive," Jack agreed, smiling. He'd met Scott's partner, Sandro Botelli, when he visited Scott and Liz five months before, and Sandro—who'd been a cop longer than Scott or Jack—was a good officer and a good man. He knew Scott's teasing was really just for show.

"So," Scott asked, "how are things with you? Who's the lucky girl this month?"

"Nobody," Jack said. "I'm a free man at the moment."

"Good," Scott said firmly.

"'Good?'" Jack echoed, surprised. "Why is that good?" He laughed suddenly. "Married sex is so bad you don't want your friends to get any either?"

"My sex life is fantastic, actually," Scott said with feeling. "I said 'good' for two reasons. One, if you're not seeing anybody, you can pack up and move that much easier. Say to Toronto, for example. And two, I keep hoping if you're ever single long enough, you might finally stop and think about what you're doing. And what you really want in a girl."

What he really wanted. Unexpected, unbidden, a memory of Caitlin rose in Jack's mind. Naked, flushed, flaming hair tousled, her tongue circling turgid flesh. Jack shook his head, trying to dispel the vivid images. Since that night, it seemed what he really wanted was his best friend's girlfriend. And that just wasn't acceptable.

"Not gonna happen," Jack said, more to himself than to Scott.

"Which part?" Scott asked. "You coming out here, or you rethinking your playboy lifestyle?"

"Both," Jack said firmly. "Or neither. Or do I mean 'either'?" He trailed off, confused.

Scott laughed again. "Sounds like you've been spending too much time with Jeremy's girlfriend. Caitlin—she's an editor, right?"

"Writer," Jack corrected. "Yeah, you're probably right." Scott must be right. That was all that was wrong with him, Jack reflected. That and the fact that he hadn't gotten laid since he broke up with Leanne—several weeks ago now—and his body was clearly starving for some action. That was why he kept thinking about Caitlin.

"So," Scott said, changing the subject. "How's Jeremy? And how's work?"

"Good," Jack replied, relaxing back against the headboard. The conversation about his personal life appeared to be over, much to his relief. "We busted Relic for possession again," he continued. That was the traffic stop he and Jeremy had gone to assist on the other day. Right after Jack had confessed to Jeremy that he'd seen Caitlin going down on him. Again he tried to push the insistent images out of his mind.

"Relic?" Scott repeated. "That guy from *The Beachcombers*? I thought he was dead."

"Yeah, the actor is," Jack said. *The Beachcombers* was a popular Canadian television show that had aired for almost twenty years in the 1970s and 80s. The chief villain, played by the late Robert Clothier, was a crusty, unkempt man nicknamed Relic. "We just call this guy Relic 'cause he looks like him—he's got the same straggly, thinning hair and he always wears a touque with the brim rolled up. Also, he's a right grumpy old fuck."

"Awesome," Scott chuckled. "So what happened?"

Jack shrugged, though Scott couldn't see him. "Nothing much. Rad and Cheryl pulled him over for rolling a stop sign, smelled weed in the car and yanked him out for a search." Jack referred to two other members of his squad, John Radakovich and Cheryl Hamlett. "Me and Jeremy pulled up just in time to catch the look on Relic's face as they found his stash—weed and some coke. He'd hidden it in a crack in the rear passenger door, figured we'd never find it there. He was some kinda pissed." It had actually taken both Jack and his six-foot-four-inch partner a real effort to subdue the wiry addict after that.

"Guess he won't be giving you guys Christmas cards this year, then, huh?" Scott said. "That was him, right?"

"Actually, that was this other guy, Davey," Jack said. Last year a heroin addict and male prostitute whom Jack and Jeremy dealt with frequently had given them a homemade Christmas card, written in uneven crayon on torn lined paper, badly misspelled and hand-delivered two weeks after Christmas had come and gone. It was one of Jack's favorite memories of his time on the force and Jeremy's as well, Jack knew. They still had the card—had gotten it laminated, in fact—and took turns pinning it to the tiny cork boards on their locker doors in the change room at the station. It was in Jack's locker right now.

"However," Jack went on, "I think it's safe to say that if we were on Relic's Christmas list before, we're definitely off it now. He was not a happy camper."

"Well, keep an eye out for him," Scott said. "You get between a junkie and his fix and you're asking for all kinds of trouble. Remember the grow house we raided in Mill Woods that one time?"

"God, how could I forget?" Jack laughed. He settled himself more comfortably, propping his elbow on a pillow, as he and Scott reminisced about some of their more colorful exploits.

Jack didn't think he'd ever want to move to Toronto. He liked his current partner and his job and his city too much to ever want to leave. Not to mention his friends. Like Caitlin. But he missed Scott too and it was great to catch up with his former partner.

When they finally hung up half an hour later, however, and Jack slid back down under the covers to catch a few more hours of sleep, he was troubled by how quickly his mind returned to the memories he was trying so hard to repress. As his thoughts filled with a kaleidoscope of images—fiery red hair, full lips, warm green eyes and smooth white skin—a part of Jack began to wonder if he would have to leave town to make these insistent, disturbing new thoughts go away.

Chapter Four

ஐ

Caitlin stepped up to Jeremy, standing between his legs and placing her hands on his hips. Sitting on the chair at the breakfast bar in Jack and Mike's kitchen, Jeremy was only a head taller than Caitlin. "Hey, stranger," Jeremy said, smiling down at his girlfriend. "Where have you been?"

"Talking to Danika," Caitlin said. "Her little sister is thinking about going to college." Jeremy raised an eyebrow and she grinned, realizing exactly what had prompted it. "Fine, university then." She'd been in Edmonton for almost two years now, but was still discovering the many—often subtle—ways in which American and Canadian English differed. For Canadians, the word "college" usually meant a community college offering technical programs. Getting a four-year bachelor's degree from an accredited post-secondary institution was always called "going to university" here.

Caitlin didn't mind the learning experience, or the good-natured ribbing from her friends when their definitions or vocabulary differed. Her friends also liked to tease her with hilarious and very bad impressions of their idea of a New Jersey accent. Truthfully, though, Caitlin had grown up in Princeton, a small Ivy-League university town in central Jersey, where much of the population had moved in from elsewhere, and the stereotypical Joisey accent was rarely heard. Her own parents, an engineer and a librarian respectively, originally hailed from Portland, Oregon, and Prince Rupert, British Columbia. So Caitlin's accent was virtually indistinguishable from a native Western Canadian's.

She did use some locutions unfamiliar to her friends, and they joked about these as well. Canadians, for example, apparently stood "in line", not "on line", and things happened to them "all of a sudden", not "all of the sudden", as they did in Caitlin's lexicon. And they pretended to mock her for being snooty and pretentious whenever she said "I've not done" or "I've not had", instead of their more familiar "I haven't done" and "I haven't had".

Jeremy liked teasing her about all this just as much as the others, and she didn't mind. In fact, as she often told him jestingly, it gave her complete license to correct his bad grammar.

She leaned closer, her tummy nestled firmly between Jeremy's legs, and slid her arms around her boyfriend's back. She pressed her cheek against his chest. "What have you been up to?" she asked.

He shrugged, pulling Caitlin close. "Nothing much, just shooting the shit." He'd been talking to Brandon—Danika's husband—but now they had left, and the others were in Mike's room playing video games, leaving him alone with Caitlin in the darkened kitchen. Jeremy wrapped his arms around his girlfriend, lowering his head 'til his lips brushed her hair. He loved her hair—it was feathery soft and always smelled delicious, like apples. "Brandon said he's thinking about getting a camper lot at Alberta Beach next summer."

"Mmm, fun," Caitlin said. She tilted her head up to kiss Jeremy, then nibbled along his jawline.

"Hmm, what's on *your* mind?" Jeremy teased softly, leaning close. Caitlin shivered, as he'd known she would—she loved it when he whispered in her ear.

"Let's go home," Caitlin whispered back, gently nipping his earlobe. "And go to bed." She pressed herself even more firmly against his crotch, and Jeremy felt his cock stirring to life.

Jeremy was about to say yes, but suddenly remembered that Travis had ridden over with them, and was expecting to ride home with them as well. "We can't," he said regretfully. "We have to wait for Travis, and he's in the middle of a game."

"Oh right," Caitlin said. Jack's roommate Mike and Mike's girlfriend Kristy had challenged Jack and Travis to a game of Wii curling. "Damn, that's too bad." She looked up at Jeremy through her long, copper lashes, and licked her lips. "Because I've been wanting you all day, and I'm not sure how much longer I can wait."

At her suggestive words, Jeremy felt his cock surge from half-mast to fully hard. He loved it when Caitlin got playful.

She winked and started to turn away, clearly intending to tease him a bit and then make him wait until later to continue things...but suddenly, Jeremy realized he didn't want to wait. And two could play this teasing game.

He caught her by the shoulders as she turned, pulling her gently but firmly back against him. "Where do you think you're going?" he said playfully, relishing Caitlin's slight gasp as her ass made contact with his hard cock, straining against the seam of his jeans. She gasped again as he slid his hands down to her chest, pinching her nipples through her thin t-shirt and bra.

Jeremy cupped Caitlin's breasts, loving their soft weight. She had large breasts for her petite frame—they completely filled even his wide, strong hands. Her nipples grew harder, aroused by his caresses, and he ran the palms of his hands over the sharp peaks. He wished they were alone, somewhere he could strip her naked and see her glorious breasts with their rosy tips, pale pink but bright against her even paler skin.

He nuzzled Caitlin's neck as he continued to cup her breasts, working one hand up her shirt and into her bra. "You like that?" he said teasingly into her ear, pinching her nipple again, and Caitlin moaned softly in assent.

Jeremy slid his other hand over the front of her jeans, and she moaned again, leaning into his hand. He felt his cock throb even harder at this sign of his girlfriend's arousal. "I want you too," he whispered. "So bad."

Caitlin gripped Jeremy's knees, clenching the fabric of his jeans, and ground her ass into his crotch. It was his turn to moan at the pleasurable friction.

Jeremy tugged at the waistband of Caitlin's jeans, trying to undo the button. Just as it popped open, a particularly loud burst of laughter erupted from Mike's room, carrying down the hall and through the living room. Caitlin froze, her head coming up as she stared, startled, toward the darkened living room and the sounds coming from the bedroom beyond.

"We should probably stop," she said reluctantly, but she didn't move away from Jeremy, and her hips maintained their slow grind against his crotch.

She was probably right, Jeremy thought, also reluctantly. He was fully aroused now, his cock pulsing almost painfully in his pants, and he didn't want to stop. "We could go in the can," he said.

"No," Caitlin said, a bit shakily. Jeremy grasped the zipper on her pants and pulled it slowly down. "We'd have to pass Mike's room to get to the bathroom—what if they saw us going in together? Or both coming out after?"

"Mmm," Jeremy murmured. He ran a fingertip over Caitlin's lacy underwear, then slipped it underneath the waistband, against the smooth skin of her stomach.

"We can't go in Jack's room either," Caitlin continued breathlessly. "That would be rude. Not to mention it's also on the other side of Mike's room."

The thought was surprisingly tempting, though, Jeremy suddenly realized. He remembered Jack's nervous confession the week before, that he'd inadvertently watched Caitlin going down on Jeremy after the party at Jeremy and Travis' apartment. What Jack hadn't said aloud, but which Jeremy could read in his partner's careful tone and sheepish expression, was that the sight had clearly aroused him greatly. With a sudden naughty thrill, it occurred to Jeremy that, far from being offended, Jack would probably be incredibly

125

turned-on to find out that Jeremy and Caitlin had had sex in his bedroom.

He wasn't sure if, or how, he could explain all that to Caitlin, though. He slid a second finger under the thin fabric of his girlfriend's panties, then the other two as well, and began to inch his hand lower. And lower. "Well, then," he said finally, "I guess we'll just have to stay...right here."

"Oh," Caitlin breathed. Jeremy worked his hand even lower, fighting to make room in the tight confines of Caitlin's pants. His middle finger found the top of her slit and he slid it down, feeling warmth and wetness.

"Oh god," Caitlin moaned as he found her clit and pinched it lightly. He began to twist and rub it between his fingertips, and Caitlin gave herself completely to Jeremy's touch, eyes closed, head thrown back against his shoulder.

Jeremy loved how wet Caitlin got, the sounds she made and the way she ground herself against him, her rhythm increasing with her pleasure. But he was even more turned-on by the knowledge that he was touching her in Jack and Mike's kitchen, with several of his friends just down the hall. Any of them — or all of them — might walk in at any moment and catch them in the act. They had never done anything like this before, and Jeremy was surprised at how much it excited him.

At least, they hadn't done anything like this before on purpose. Again Jeremy recalled the day Jack had inadvertently watched them, trying to picture exactly what his friend must have seen, and what his reaction might have been. Jack's confession hadn't made him angry — in fact, to his surprise, it had actually turned Jeremy on a bit. And now, he found himself even more aroused at the memory. What would Jack be thinking now, if he was watching them again? If he could see Caitlin so lost in her own pleasure, moaning and grinding against Jeremy as he fingered her?

Even as he was thinking this, Jeremy caught a subtle movement out of the corner of his eye, and heard a soft sound that might have been a quickly muffled exclamation of surprise. He turned his head slowly, not wanting to alert Caitlin, while he kept rubbing and squeezing her clit.

He'd almost concluded he was imagining things when something moved again, and with the slight motion Jeremy's eyes were suddenly able to make sense of the pattern of dim light and deep shadows.

Jack was standing in the dark living room.

He had an empty bowl in his hand—it was white and seemed to glow faintly, the brightest thing in the room. He must have been on his way to the kitchen to get more potato chips…when he saw what Jeremy and Caitlin were doing.

Jeremy's stomach lurched—partly in guilty surprise, but also, he realized, in excitement.

"Jeremy, please," Caitlin whispered, and Jeremy realized he'd stopped moving his hand.

Jack had seen them. He was still standing there. Jeremy knew he should stop, that he and Caitlin should wait for privacy to finish what they'd started. But he could tell Caitlin didn't want to wait—she was arching her hips impatiently, trying to increase the pressure of his still-motionless fingers on her clit. She was so wet, so ready.

And Jeremy was ready too—he didn't want to stop.

For some reason, he was now forced to admit to himself, the thought of Jack watching them excited him. But he wasn't sure how Caitlin would feel about the idea. Was it wrong of him to continue, knowing Jack was there, without telling her?

Caitlin mewed with frustrated desire, and that decided him. *It's not like Jack can actually see anything, anyhow*, Jeremy told himself, as he resumed rubbing Caitlin's clit. Not only was it dark in the kitchen, but technically, Caitlin still had all of her clothes on. In fact, come to think of it, Jack had probably seen a lot more of her the other night.

For some reason that thought made Jeremy's cock pulse even harder in his pants. He turned Caitlin slightly to the right, so he could reach between her legs more easily—and, incidentally, so she was facing Jack more fully. Jeremy twisted his hand in the hot—and now extremely wet—confines of Caitlin's underwear, reaching down to press two fingers up inside of her, even as he continued to work her clit with his thumb.

"Oh god, yes," Caitlin moaned, and Jeremy increased his pace. He added a third finger to the two thrusting in and out of Caitlin's tight, slick hole, and rolled her nipple between the fingers of his other hand, which was still up her shirt.

"That's it, baby," Jeremy murmured in Caitlin's ear. He stared across the dark living room. It was impossible to make out the expression on Jack's face in the darkness, but he was standing stock still, the faint gleam of his eyes unwavering, clearly riveted by the illicit sight before him. "I want to feel you come. Want to watch you come for—" Jeremy cleared his throat. He'd almost said "us". "Come for me."

"Oh Jeremy, oh my god," Caitlin whimpered, and then her orgasm took her. She arched her back, biting her lips to stop from crying out. Jeremy felt her pussy clamp down, impossibly tight, on his fingers, throbbing and pulsing with her release.

His own cock was throbbing as well, aching with need. Caitlin ground her hips back once more, and the delightful friction was almost too much for him. Jeremy fought to keep control, not wanting to make a mess in his pants. But then he glanced at Jack once more, and realized that his friend had one hand on his own crotch, no doubt pressed against his own raging hard-on. And that realization—that Jack was hard from watching him and Caitlin, from watching him make Caitlin come—suddenly thrust him over the edge.

Burying his face in Caitlin's hair to muffle his groan of pleasure, clutching her hips as he ground his cock against her plump ass, Jeremy came.

Caitlin sagged back against Jeremy, feeling deliciously drained. She watched out of the corner of her eye as Jack, a dark shape in the darker gloom, backed silently out of the living room, retreating into the even darker hallway from which he'd come.

She'd seen him standing there, had heard his soft gasp of surprise when he saw what they were doing. And she suspected that Jeremy had seen Jack too, from the way he'd reacted.

Caitlin remembered the night, two weeks before, when Jack had slept over at Jeremy's apartment. She'd heard the balcony door slide open or closed, and wondered — when he seemed embarrassed the next morning — if Jack had looked in the window and seen the two of them having sex.

Now she wondered if Jeremy had also known Jack was there, that night, on the balcony. If he was touching her like this here, tonight, in order to deliberately let his best friend watch again. Did it excite Jeremy to have someone see him with Caitlin?

It excited her, Caitlin realized. She had never really thought about voyeurism, or exhibitionism — she wasn't even sure which was the correct term in this case — before. It had just seemed to be a silly game — like the thought of using whips and leather masks and calling your partner "master" during sex. But this wasn't some kind of silly make-believe. The look on Jack's face, as he'd watched her and Jeremy, was real. Real, and incredibly exciting.

"That was amazing," Jeremy's voice rumbled in Caitlin's ear, interrupting her thoughts.

She turned to smile up at her boyfriend, nestling against his broad chest. "It was, wasn't it?" Caitlin agreed contentedly.

A soft click indicated that Jack had gone back into one of the bedrooms and closed the door. Caitlin didn't look around at the faint sound. Neither did her boyfriend.

Then Jeremy eased Caitlin back gently and stood up from the stool, adjusting himself in his jeans. He untucked his shirt and tugged it down to cover his crotch. "I guess I'll go tell Travis we want to get going. I need to go home and change my pants now, thanks to you."

He grinned, and Caitlin grinned back. "Thanks to *you*, you mean," she corrected. "That was all your idea."

"Guilty as charged." As Jeremy strode into the living room, heading for the hallway beyond, Caitlin fell into step with him.

"I'm going to the bathroom," she said in answer to his questioning look. She winked saucily at him. "You're not the only one who needs to clean up."

Caitlin left her boyfriend at the door to Mike's room and carried on into the small washroom. Her panties were thoroughly soaked with her juices and, after using the toilet, she decided to take them off. Caitlin didn't usually go commando, but she didn't want to put her wet underwear back on. To her surprise, the feeling of the slightly rough denim against her soft bits wasn't unpleasant, just unusual. She folded her black lace bikini panties and stuffed them in the front pocket of her jeans.

When she came out, the others had finished their game and were all in the living room, saying good night. As Caitlin approached, Travis gave Mike and Jack high fives, hugged Kristy and then bent to tie his shoelaces.

"Oh there you are," Kristy said over Jack's shoulder, looking up as Caitlin approached. She had a blonde bob and mischievous blue eyes—a softer blue than Jack's intense electric gaze. She gave Jeremy a quick hug too, then Caitlin, and stepped back to let Caitlin past her into the foyer. "Sorry we didn't get a chance to talk much tonight." She laughed. "I swear I'll hang out with the girls next time—watching these guys try to curl is the most boring crap ever."

"Hey!" Mike laughed, tugging Kristy down the hall, back toward his bedroom. She was two inches taller than her stocky Asian boyfriend, but the height difference didn't bother either of them. "That's not very nice."

"No, but I bet it's true." Caitlin grinned. "'Night, you guys."

Travis was chuckling too, as he tied his shoes. "It was only boring for her because we kicked their asses. Right, Jack?"

"Right," Jack said. He glanced at Caitlin, then looked at Jeremy. Caitlin thought he was blushing, and he turned to go into the kitchen, mumbling something about cleaning up. "See you guys," he called over his shoulder.

"Oh crap," Travis exclaimed. "Dude, hang on—I left my jacket in Mike's room. Sorry, guys."

"So," Jeremy drawled, turning toward the kitchen as Travis disappeared down the hall. "You have fun tonight, Jack?"

"Uh, yeah," Jack said. He didn't meet Jeremy's eyes at first, focusing on his hands as he wiped the counter. He folded the dishcloth and set it by the sink. "Did you?" He finally looked up.

"I know I did," Caitlin said suggestively, and both men turned to look at her. She saw looks of equal surprise on their faces, and had a sudden idea. Should she do it? Impulsively she decided, why not? She was sure now that Jeremy had known Jack was there, watching them. If Jeremy didn't mind letting Jack watch him finger Caitlin 'til she orgasmed, then he shouldn't object to what Caitlin had in mind now.

"Here, Jack," she said, stepping into the kitchen. "This is for you."

She pulled her damp, lacy panties out of her pocket and held them up so both Jack and Jeremy could see what they were. "A little souvenir."

As Jack stared, stunned, a door slammed down the hall, and footsteps announced that Travis was rapidly returning.

With a swift glance at Jeremy—who, Caitlin saw, was staring with open-mouthed surprise but no apparent evidence of anger or jealousy—Jack snatched the black panties out of Caitlin's hand and stuffed them quickly in his own pocket.

"Sorry about that," Travis said as he reentered the living room, zipping his leather jacket. When no one else said anything he looked around, taking in Caitlin's impish smile, Jeremy's surprised look and Jack's red face. "What?" he asked, confused.

"Nothing," Jeremy said, shaking his head. He reached a hand out for Caitlin, who came to him immediately, standing on her tiptoes to plant a kiss on his jaw. "'Night, Jack," Jeremy said, looking at his friend over Caitlin's head.

"Yeah, good night," Caitlin added. "Sweet dreams."

Jack actually chuckled at that, shoving his hands deeper into the pockets of his jeans. "Yeah, you too," he said.

Chapter Five
ಐ

Caitlin and Jeremy walked into Boston Pizza, looking around for their friends. She spotted Travis waving from a booth in the back of the restaurant and tugged Jeremy's hand to let him know she'd found them. Travis' girlfriend—hockey-hating Cindy—was next to him, and Jack was sitting across from the tall, blond couple. His back was to the door, but when Travis waved he turned, watching over his shoulder as Caitlin and Jeremy approached.

Jack gave Caitlin an intense look as she slid in to the booth next to him. He was smiling but his eyes burned into her, and his face had reddened as Caitlin and Jeremy approached.

"Hey," Caitlin said, glancing quickly at Jack, then looking across the table to include Travis and Cindy with her greeting. She felt a blush rising to her own cheeks as she thought about the last time she'd seen Jack. That was three days before. When Jeremy had fingered her to an orgasm while Jack watched.

Jack said hi to Caitlin and reached in front of her to clasp Jeremy's hand briefly. Caitlin was acutely aware of his bare forearm, lean muscles rippling as he gripped her boyfriend's hand, only inches from her breasts.

"I didn't get a chance to thank you the other day," Jack said quietly, as he handed Caitlin a menu.

"I, uh, borrowed a movie from Caitlin last week," he added for Travis and Cindy's benefit, seeing Travis' questioning glance from across the table.

"Did you like the show?" She smiled at Jack.

His eyes widened at that, and he glanced quickly at Jeremy before meeting Caitlin's eyes again. "Yes," he said firmly. "Very much."

"Good," Caitlin said.

"Do you want it back?" Jack asked. "The, uh, movie, I mean."

Caitlin knew he was talking about the black lace panties she'd pressed into his hand on the way out the door after that exciting evening.

She glanced at her boyfriend and was reassured by Jeremy's quick smile, and the encouraging hand he placed on her thigh.

"Oh no," she said. "You can keep it. If you want to."

"Well, thanks," Jack said. His eyes were like hot blue fire as they bored into Caitlin's own. He leaned a bit closer, his voice dropping huskily. "But I'd rather watch another one, if that's okay."

He leaned back again, apparently conscious of Cindy and Travis watching them curiously from across the table, who seemed to have detected something unusual in Jack's tone, if not in his words. "Caitlin's got some great shows," he said casually. "Really quality entertainment."

Caitlin tried to steady her breathing, which had become ragged at Jack's blatant request, and at the thought of doing this again. Jeremy's left hand on her thigh, inching under the hem of her dress and stroking suggestively, told her what he thought of the idea.

"I think that could be arranged," she replied as casually as possible. "As long as Jeremy doesn't mind, that is," she added archly. "He likes to watch them too."

"I sure do," Jeremy responded with feeling. He and Jack shared a grin of complete understanding.

The sexual tension diffused a bit as they ordered drinks, and then food, but Caitlin found herself getting excited again as Jeremy continued to knead her thigh under the table, and as

Jack shifted on her other side, eventually settling with his right thigh pressed firmly against her left.

She could see Jack glancing down, every so often, into her lap. They were in the rear corner of Boston Pizza, with Travis and Cindy facing out into the restaurant while Jack, Jeremy and Caitlin faced the back wall. There was another booth across from them, on Caitlin's right, but it was unoccupied. Caitlin wondered what, if anything, Jeremy was planning to do.

When she had decided that morning to wear a dress — in a soft leaf green, with a full skirt and an empire waist — she hadn't been thinking of anything but the weather, which had remained unseasonably warm. Now, however, she was acutely aware that her choice of wardrobe afforded other interesting considerations.

For example, she couldn't help but realize that if Jeremy continued to pull her dress up, exposing her underwear, no one else would be able to see it but Jack — and their waitress, if she came by at an inopportune moment. With the dark, sturdy wooden table in the way, neither Travis nor Cindy could see anything lower than Caitlin's chest. Caitlin had a feeling Jeremy had noticed this too. But would he act on it? Not just in front of Jack this time, and in a dark room, but here, in public, and right across from two of their other friends as well?

At this point, as horny as the double entendres with Jack, and Jeremy's obvious approval, had made her feel, Caitlin was ready to take the risks. She glanced over at her boyfriend, smiling her unspoken consent to his actions. Apparently Jeremy was feeling adventurous as well, for with one last subtle shift of his hand, he drew her skirt up to her waist. Then he tugged it to the side, tucking the loose fabric between her hip and his. Her crotch, covered only in thin, almost-see-through pink panties, was now on display for both Jeremy and Jack, whenever they chose to look down.

They were both doing just that, darting quick glances into her lap and then looking away again. Both men tried valiantly to keep up their end of the conversation with Cindy and Travis, which seemed to be about the construction slowing down traffic on Whitemud Drive—Caitlin wasn't really listening. But they could only manage a few seconds before their eyes were drawn inexorably back to the show.

Caitlin risked a glance down herself. Both men were sporting distinct bulges in the crotch of their pants. Her breath quickened as she noticed that Jack seemed to be very well endowed—at least as big as Jeremy, if not more so.

She slouched down in her seat just a bit, and spread her legs apart a few inches. With one hand, she grasped the waistband of her panties and tugged the thin fabric upward, making it pull tight over the cleft between her legs. Caitlin wanted to give both men the best view possible. A hitch in Jeremy's breath on her right, and a sudden clink from the left as Jack nearly dropped his beer, suggested that she'd succeeded.

The muffled clomping of heels, accompanied by the rattling of plates on a crowded tray, announced the approach of the waitress with their entrees. Jeremy quickly removed his hand from her thigh, and Caitlin tugged her skirt back down to her knees as the server arrived, juggling a tray overflowing with food and a metal stand used to hold medium and large pizza platters.

As they dug into their meals, Caitlin tried to focus on the conversation—Cindy, a teacher, was now recounting the latest exploits of her junior high students—but Caitlin remained acutely aware of the men on either side of her. Jeremy laughed at Cindy's stories, and told them about some of his own school hijinks. But all the while his left hand remained on Caitlin's thigh, caressing and gently squeezing through the thin fabric of her dress. Jack too appeared absorbed in the conversation, but his right thigh stayed firmly pressed against Caitlin's, and occasionally he brushed her shoulder with his own.

The waitress returned several times, bringing drink refills, extra napkins and more condiments. At last, they appeared to have everything they needed. Jeremy glanced casually around, then began to inch Caitlin's skirt hem up her thigh once more. With his other hand he kept eating the Spicy Perogy pizza—a BP special—that he was sharing with Travis. Caitlin selected a second piece of her own pizza—an individual pepperoni with extra sauce—and then leaned back, taking a bite.

Jack laughed at something Cindy was saying, took a sip of beer and then, as Cindy turned toward Travis, glanced casually down into Caitlin's lap. Where Caitlin's wispy pink panties were revealed again, as Jeremy once more tugged her skirt up to her waist. As before, Caitlin slouched down in the seat a bit, spreading her legs until they were firmly pressed against Jack's on her left and Jeremy's on her right.

"What do you think, Caitlin?" Travis asked, looking up from his beef dip.

"About what?" Caitlin said apprehensively. She had no idea what the others had been discussing.

"Food," Travis said. "You miss American restaurants and stuff?"

"Oh right," Caitlin bluffed. She wasn't sure how the conversation had turned from school hijinks to international cuisine—but then she really hadn't been paying attention.

"Well, I miss some things, like P.F. Chang's," she said. "That's an Asian chain restaurant. And you folks have a truly pitiful selection of yogurt. But on the other hand, there are some things here that I love, that I wouldn't be able to get back home."

"Like what?" asked Travis.

"What's wrong with our yogurt?" demanded Cindy.

Caitlin swallowed. Jeremy's hand was back on her bare leg, his fingers sliding slowly toward the inside of her thigh. She tried to focus on her friends' questions.

"There are way more flavors of yogurt in the U.S.," she said, answering Cindy first. "Cool flavors, like key-lime pie, strawberry cheesecake, stuff like that. And it's really smooth.

Here, you mostly just have fruit-flavored yogurt—and they all have nasty, slimy chunks of fruit in them. All the ones I've tried, at least."

"Well, when you put it like that, it does sound gross," Jack said. He smiled at Caitlin, brushing thick black hair back from his forehead. As he lowered his hand to his lap once more, his wrist skimmed lightly over Caitlin's naked thigh. She shivered.

"What do you like better here?" Travis asked again. Caitlin had forgotten his question.

"I know," Jeremy interjected. "Old Dutch barbecue-flavored potato chips. Right?" He nudged Caitlin's shoulder playfully, using the gesture as an opportunity to move closer to her, his hand sliding farther into her lap. His fingertips brushed Caitlin's mound.

"What, they don't have barbecue chips in the States?" Cindy looked surprised.

"Not like these ones," Caitlin said. Her voice sounded ragged and she cleared her throat, then took a sip of her drink. "Old Dutch is the best—I love them."

"Well, that's good," Cindy said. "But personally, I prefer rice cakes. They're much healthier than chips, and they taste pretty good."

"If you like eating styrofoam," Travis amended. Cindy took offense at that, and began lecturing her boyfriend on the virtues of a healthy diet.

Caitlin wasn't listening anymore. Jeremy began to run his fingers slowly up and down the cleft between her legs. A blunt fingernail traced lightly over her clit.

Fighting the urge to moan with pleasure, Caitlin inched forward on the seat again. She raised her left knee a bit, trying to spread her legs farther apart. Her knee ended up resting lightly on Jack's thigh, and she felt him tense as her bare skin pressed his denim-clad leg. As Jeremy stroked more firmly, Caitlin's hips arched involuntarily.

Jeremy's hand froze, and on the other side, Jack tensed even more. Travis, Caitlin saw with alarm, was looking at her curiously. Caitlin realized she had stopped eating, and forced herself to reach for another slice of pizza.

Travis' gaze shifted to something behind Jeremy. "Great," he said. "It never fails—whenever I go to a restaurant, I end up with little kids sitting right next to me."

Caitlin, Jack and Jeremy turned. Sure enough, the hostess was leading a mom, a dad and three little kids—two ambulatory and one in a car seat—to the booth across from theirs.

Jack quickly crossed his legs, and Jeremy withdrew his hand from Caitlin's crotch as she hastily tugged the hem of her dress down once more.

Caitlin sat up straight, trying not to wiggle in her seat, taking a bite of the pizza she found herself holding but no longer wanted. Trying to get herself under control. She supposed it was a good thing they'd been forced to stop what they were doing—she'd been mere minutes away from orgasming in a family restaurant. Right in front of several of her closest friends, for god's sake. Never mind how incredible it felt, how much—to her own surprise—she was enjoying the illicit thrill…this was something they just shouldn't do. At least…not here.

Beside her, Jack was twisted slightly to the left, his right arm clamped stiffly against his side. Caitlin supposed he was trying to hide his erection from the family now seated across from them. On her other side, Jeremy also had his legs crossed, one muscular arm in his lap to conceal his still-bulging crotch. With his other hand, he was toying with his beer glass, making overlapping rings of condensation on the table. He met Caitlin's gaze and smiled ruefully.

They all looked up as Travis' cell phone rang. "Brandon, hey," he said, checking the display before answering. "How's it going?"

Brandon was another friend of theirs. He had gone to high school with Mike. Unlike most of the men in their circle—Mike, Travis, Jeremy and Jack—Brandon wasn't a cop. He and his wife owned a construction company. Caitlin liked Brandon and Danika Kowalchuk. Despite being a couple of tax brackets ahead of the rest of them, they weren't a bit snobby. They also frequently hosted parties in their new five-bedroom, three-story Windermere home.

"I'm in for sure," Travis was saying. "Lemme check—hang on." He grinned at the others watching him. "Too windy to golf, apparently," he said. Brandon and Danika spent a lot of time on their local course, and were eager to get in as many games as possible before winter ended the season. "So they're wondering if we want to come hit the pool."

"That sounds like fun," Cindy said.

"Hell yeah," Jack agreed. He turned to look at Caitlin and Jeremy. "You guys in?"

He held Caitlin's eyes with his own for a long moment, and Caitlin felt a rush of heat return to her loins. Was he picturing her in her bathing suit? The last time they'd swum at the Kowalchuks' Caitlin had worn a moss-green two-piece that Jeremy loved—he said the color perfectly matched her eyes. She remembered twice turning around and seeing Jack watching her from across the pool house. He'd seemed to like it too. Maybe he was hoping to see her in that bikini again. She found herself hoping, in turn, that he was.

"Sure," Jeremy said. He put an arm over Caitlin's shoulders, hugging her against his broad chest. "Sound good, babe?"

"Yeah," Caitlin said. She had a sudden vision of horsing around in the pool with Jeremy and Jack, naked torsos dripping, muscles rippling, as they both laughingly tried to pick her up and toss her in the water. She swallowed. "Sounds great—let's go."

Chapter Six

෯

Brandon stood up and swung his legs over the raised side of the hot tub. "This is getting too hot for me," he said. "I'm gonna cool off in the pool."

"It *is* pretty hot in here," Jack said suggestively, as Brandon dove into the pool. Only the three of them were left in the jacuzzi—Caitlin, Jeremy and Jack. Caitlin's stomach fluttered at the thought of continuing what seemed to be fast becoming an erotic tradition among the three of them.

They'd paid up and left the restaurant after Brandon called, heading home to get their swim gear. Travis went with Jeremy and Caitlin, and Cindy went with Jack. Jack pulled out his cell phone as they left, intending to invite his own roommate, Mike, and Mike's girlfriend Kristy, if they weren't busy.

As it turned out, Brandon had already called Mike, and soon all nine of them were gathered in the large house in Windermere, built three years before in one of the fastest growing communities in the southwest of Edmonton.

The girls changed in one bathroom, the guys in another, while Brandon and Danika, already in their bathing suits, brought out drinks, set out a stack of towels and turned on the stereo. *Flurry* by Social Code, an alternative band from the Edmonton area, was first up.

Caitlin slipped into her green bikini, tucked her rolled clothes into her bag, and headed for the poolside bar, which was just a short counter with a built-in mini refrigerator and sink.

"Hey, Caitlin," Brandon said, holding up a selection of the bottles and cans he was loading into the fridge. "What'll it be?"

"Strongbow, thanks." Caitlin chose a tall can of British cider. As she turned, popping the tab with her thumb, she was conscious of Jeremy and Jack lounging poolside, beers in hand. They both watched as she approached.

"Hey, sexy," Jeremy said, drawing up his long legs so Caitlin could sit on the chaise lounge with him.

"Sexy yourself," Caitlin said. She spoke to Jeremy, but included Jack with her smile. He grinned back. As Caitlin perched on the side of the wooden lounger, Jack leaned over and clinked the neck of his bottle against her supercan.

They drank, lounged, swam and played frisbee in the water—badly; they all missed often, and Caitlin almost gave Travis a black eye with a wild toss she'd meant for Danika. Mike, Kristy and Travis trounced Caitlin, Jeremy and Jack at an aquatic round of volleyball. Through all this, Caitlin continually felt both men's eyes on her, their gaze kindling a slow fire in the pit of her stomach.

Then Jack turned down Mike's challenge to a second round of volleyball, gesturing toward the corner jacuzzi, where Brandon was sitting alone, lazily watching the action in the pool. "Nah, I'm gonna relax for a while—you go ahead."

"You're just afraid you'll get your ass kicked again," Mike taunted. He turned to Caitlin and Jeremy. "What about you guys? You chickenshit too?"

Caitlin glanced up at Jeremy, then watched as Jack slipped into the hot tub. He met her gaze as he sat down next to Brandon, the intense blue of his eyes undiminished by the steam rising around him. Jeremy, holding Caitlin's hand under the water, gave it a squeeze. She thought she knew what he was suggesting.

"I guess we are," Caitlin said to Mike. "'Cause I need a break too."

"Yeah," Jeremy agreed. "Sorry, dude. Hot tub sounds good about now."

They waded to the edge of the pool, leaving Mike to shake his head in mock disgust. As they climbed out and headed for the hot tub, Mike started cajoling Cindy, Danika and Brandon to play instead.

The setup was perfect, Caitlin realized, settling into the hot, bubbling water. Now that Brandon had joined the others, everyone else was now in the swimming pool, which was behind and below Caitlin and Jeremy. From the pool, no one could see anything of them but the backs of their heads. Jack, on the other hand, had a front-row seat for anything that Jeremy and Caitlin might do, and would also be able to alert them if any of the others left the pool and started coming their way.

Jack was grinning at Jeremy, eyes twinkling, clearly daring him to begin. Jeremy turned to Caitlin, sliding his left arm around her shoulders and drawing her close. She responded immediately, leaning into him, and he smiled down at her, his eyes intense, his breathing coming faster as she gave her unspoken consent to continue the game.

Jeremy kissed her then, nuzzling along her jaw and gently biting her earlobe. He knew she loved that. Her nipples grew instantly hard. She wondered if Jack could see that, through the water. Jeremy clearly could. He reached up and pinched her right nipple, making her gasp. "Shh," he warned, but she could tell from the warmth in his voice that he was smiling as he said it.

Jack shifted a bit. Through the rippling water Caitlin saw his right hand move into his lap. She wondered if he was just adjusting things in his swim trunks, or actually stroking himself through the thin fabric. The thought made Caitlin instantly wet.

Jeremy was pulling her closer, resettling her on his lap. He was definitely enjoying this. She could feel his already hard cock pressing against her ass. Now she was sitting higher in the water, not so high that the others behind her in the pool—splashing and shouting—would be able to see anything, but high enough that her breasts were just out of the water. The cool air on her nipples made them stand up even more, and she shivered deliciously.

Jack was watching Caitlin intently, nodding slightly in appreciation. She knew he was smiling, but only because the corners of his eyes were crinkled—she didn't look away from the intensity of his gaze.

Jeremy cupped her breasts with both hands, squeezing firmly. She glanced down and then up again, her gaze alternating between Jack's deep blue eyes and the fluttering white shape that was his right arm, under water. It was moving rhythmically, back and forth, up and down. He was definitely stroking his cock through his shorts.

The thought—that Jack was hard for her, touching himself while watching Jeremy touch her—made Caitlin almost reckless with desire. She arched her back, grinding against Jeremy's cock. He kissed her neck, licking and sucking hard, pinching and rolling her nipples between his fingers. It was all she could do not to moan aloud at the pleasurable sensations, and his rapid breath in her ear told her he felt the same way.

Then Jeremy slid the tips of two fingers underneath the thin fabric of her bikini top. He ran his fingers up to the strap, and tugged it an inch to the side, baring the top of her breast.

Caitlin gasped again, and he froze, clearly wondering if she was about to protest. But it was not fear or a sudden attack of propriety that had made her gasp. It was sheer excitement.

"Yes," she whispered breathlessly. She wanted this, needed it. She'd never imagined doing anything so reckless, so over the edge, but now that it was happening, she wanted it more than anything. "Do it, Jeremy, please."

But Jeremy didn't, not yet. "Jack?" he murmured teasingly. His breath on Caitlin's neck made her shiver. "You want to see?"

"Yeah," Jack breathed. His voice was hoarse and he had to clear his throat. His face was flushed—not just from the heat of the water, Caitlin was sure. His chest heaved as he drew in a deep breath. "I want to see." He looked directly into her eyes. "I've always wanted to see you naked, Caitlin."

His words seemed to ignite a fire between Caitlin's legs. "Oh," she breathed, and then Jeremy tugged at her bathing suit again. The shoulder strap slid down her arm, and his deft fingers pulled the soft fabric down and aside. He squeezed her nipple one more time, sending an electric shock coursing through her, and then lowered his hand.

Caitlin's breast was exposed for Jack to see.

"God," Jack said. He leaned forward for a closer look. Her nipple was rosy pink, pointing slightly out from the full globe of her breast. Caitlin arched her back even more, and turned slightly toward Jack. She wanted to give him—and Jeremy—a good show.

Caitlin was more turned-on than she had ever been in her life. The whole situation was indescribably exciting. To be touched by her boyfriend, with another hot guy—his best friend and partner—watching, excited, almost near enough to be touching her too. And to be doing all this right next to a bunch of other people who had no idea what was going on, and might interrupt them at any moment, discovering their illicit little game.

Jeremy worked at the other side of Caitlin's top, tugging at the thin fabric until her other breast was exposed too. Jack scooted even farther forward, perching on the edge of the underwater seat. His knees brushed Caitlin's and they both jumped. Jack darted a look at Jeremy, as if expecting his friend to tell him to back off, but Jeremy just went back to kissing and licking Caitlin's neck, and toying with her nipples. Then he trailed one hand down her stomach, lightly circling her bellybutton, and cupped her mound, pressing one finger firmly against her slit.

Caitlin didn't realize she was moaning until both Jeremy and Jack shushed her. She opened her eyes—only then realizing she had closed them. Jack was looking apprehensively over her shoulder, clearly wondering if any of the others had heard her soft moan over the fortuitously loud music. Apparently the coast was clear. He went back to watching her avidly, devouring her with his eyes. He was still touching himself, his arm moving faster now. His hand under the frothy surface of the hot tub was just a wavery blur, undefined, but she could see his shoulder muscles tensing and shifting as he stroked.

Jeremy was close too—Caitlin could tell by how rock-hard his cock was, behind her, by the increased rhythm and pressure of his movements as he ground his crotch against her ass. Then Jeremy slipped his hand inside her bikini bottoms. With his index finger he circled her clit, lightly, teasingly. She clutched at his wrist, trying to create more pressure, and heard him chuckle in her ear. "Somebody wants it bad," he murmured. "You really like this, don't you? You like showing off for Jack?"

Caitlin's stomach flipped over—with excitement or fear, she couldn't tell. Was it wrong to feel this way? But she had to tell the truth. "Yes," Caitlin whispered. She looked straight at Jack, gratified to see his eyes widen at her admission. He licked his lips. "Yes," she said again. "I like it when Jack watches us. Watches me."

"Me too," Jeremy breathed raggedly in her ear, and she sighed with relief. He rewarded her admission with a firm grip on her clit, rubbing it rapidly. She was getting so close.

"Me three," Jack said shakily, sitting back a bit. His hands were still now, gripping his knees. "But I gotta stop, or I'm gonna shoot in my pants."

"Oh please," Caitlin heard herself beg. She hadn't meant to say anything, but she couldn't stop. "I would love to see that, Jack. Please?"

"Really?" Jack sounded taken aback, but also pleased. "You would?"

"Seems only fair," Jeremy added as Caitlin nodded, beyond words. "You've seen us come already, after all."

Jack cast another nervous glance toward the pool, but the others were apparently absorbed in a new game of volleyball, from the sounds of it. He hesitated a moment, then nodded. "Okay," he said.

He scooted forward again, his knees pressing firmly against Caitlin's once more. She watched through the churning water as he tucked his right hand inside his trunks. The rhythmic motion of his arm, the rippling of his strong chest and shoulder muscles, told her he was firmly stroking his cock.

Caitlin watched, her own pleasure mounting at the incredibly erotic sight. Jack was breathing raggedly, his hand pumping rapidly. His face was flushed, eyes locked on Caitlin's heaving breasts. It only took a minute. Then he froze, a strangled exclamation of ecstasy, half sigh and half groan, bursting involuntarily from his lips. His hips bucked beneath the water, and Caitlin knew he'd just come into his hand. She imagined the hot, slippery fluid spewing from the tip of his cock, wishing she could see it. Feel it. Taste it.

With that thought her own orgasm overtook her, and she clenched her thighs involuntarily, crushing Jeremy's hand against her pussy. And Jeremy was coming too. She could feel his cock pulsing against her ass, his hot breath on her neck. "Oh god," he whispered. "My god, so fucking hot."

Chapter Seven

ೞ

Jack leaned back in the hard plastic seat, taking in the incredible view. Rexall Place was packed, a significant majority of its almost seventeen thousand seats occupied—most by fans in white or dark-blue jerseys. The long, narrow LED billboard ringing the arena between the lower and upper decks was alternating commercial ads with information about tonight's game, sending bright colors racing around the enormous oval cavern. *YOU'RE IN OIL COUNTRY!* the billboard declared every few minutes.

Jack and his friends were sitting in the blues near the top of the upper deck—the nosebleed section—on the east side of the arena. If there had been windows behind them, they'd be overlooking part of the vast parking lot and, beyond it, Wayne Gretzky Drive.

Jack was excited about the hockey game—only the fourth home game of the regular season, the first one he'd had a chance to attend—and about finally being off work for a while. He and Jeremy had just finished their four-day night-shift rotation, and they now had four days off before rotating to swing shift.

He was also excited, he had to admit, about spending time with Caitlin again, for the first time in almost a week. He glanced down at the petite redhead beside him, who was looking around with obvious delight. Though she'd been an Oilers fan for years—a fact supported by her blue and bronze Oilers jersey, in a style and color scheme that told his knowing eye she'd purchased it at least five years before—this was the first time she'd attended a game at their home arena. And that, Jack knew, was a thrilling experience. Oilers fans were widely hailed as the most loyal and enthusiastic hockey supporters in the league—no matter how their team was ranked in current standings. Already, with a few minutes still to go before things got under way, and before the players were even out on the ice, the positive energy and anticipation radiating through the crowd were palpable.

Jeremy, on Caitlin's other side, was pointing out the enormous oil derrick, now folded up against the ceiling, which would be lowered to the ice just before game time. By longstanding tradition, the Oilers would enter the rink by skating through the metal legs of the thirty-foot-tall rig, accompanied by pyrotechnics, a laser light show and good old fashioned rock 'n' roll.

Mike, Kristy and Travis returned from the concession, inching back to their cramped seats along the crowded row, laden with beer in plastic glasses, cardboard containers of French fries and pierogi and foil-wrapped burgers.

Jack passed Jeremy and Caitlin their drinks and food, then accepted his own from Travis, who sat on his right. He turned back to Caitlin, watching as she unwrapped her hamburger. "Excited?"

"Yes," Caitlin said, her green eyes meeting his in a long look.

It felt like a ball of heat was uncoiling in Jack's stomach. Or maybe a bit lower than his stomach. He had a feeling Caitlin was talking about more than just the game. Maybe she had been looking forward to seeing him again too?

He glanced at Jeremy, beyond Caitlin. The big man—improbably crammed into a seat that looked far too small for him—had already downed half his beer. Jeremy caught Jack's eye, grinned, then put a hand on his girlfriend's knee, squeezing gently. "This is going to be great. Right, guys?" His tone too was invested with multiple layers of meaning.

Caitlin's smile took in the men on both sides of her. "Right," she agreed.

Jack shifted in his seat, his jeans suddenly feeling too tight. Though he hadn't seen Caitlin in several days, and neither he nor Jeremy had talked about anything personal at work, Jack had kept thinking about the new shift their friendship was taking. The night at Jeremy's place. The other night at his own apartment. The restaurant. And the hot tub.

He had a sudden memory of Caitlin's round white breasts, topped by delicate pink nipples hardened into tiny points, quivering as she came under Jeremy's skillful touch. The heat in his stomach expanded — and so did his cock.

Jack tugged his white jersey down over his crotch and shifted again, trying to ease the sudden constriction in his pants.

"Dude, careful!" Travis exclaimed, his beer sloshing as Jack's right knee hit his left elbow.

"Sorry, man," Jack said. He'd better get his mind on the game, or — considering the cramped quarters — he'd be spending the next three hours with the world's most uncomfortable tent in his pants.

Luckily, at that moment the lights in the arena dimmed, signaling the start of the pre-game show. The oil derrick was lowered, and the Oilers burst onto the ice, accompanied by fireworks, blue and orange lights and loud music drowned out by the even louder cheers of the crowd.

As they stood and *The Star-Spangled Banner* began, Jack couldn't help remembering Paul Lorieau, who had sung the anthems in Edmonton for thirty years before retiring in 2011. Jack would be the first to admit that Lorieau wasn't the world's greatest singer — and the French-Canadian's English pronunciation was still a bit off, even after all these years of singing the same words over and over. But Lorieau was an icon, a tradition. And like all Oilers fans, Jack would never forget the 2006 Stanley Cup run, during which Lorieau had started a new tradition.

After the Canadian national anthem was booed by Anaheim Ducks fans before games one and two of the Western Conference final, Edmonton fans, led by Lorieau, responded in true Canadian fashion before game three—the first game of that series on Edmonton ice. Far from returning the insult, the Edmonton crowd respectfully sang along with the American national anthem. Next, Lorieau sang only the first few lines of *O Canada*, then gestured to the crowd to take over.

And take over they did. Sixteen thousand, eight hundred and thirty-nine fans joyfully belting out their anthem in support of their team, their city and their country was a sight and sound that had moved many, those present in the arena and those watching the television broadcast—and later, YouTube videos—to awe and even tears.

Jack would always remember that as the moment he had realized just how much he loved his city.

As the American anthem ended, Caitlin leaned over to Jack. "I can't wait for *O Canada*," she said over the applause. "I've been waiting to be here for this ever since 2006."

Jack felt a sudden rush of affection for Caitlin, touched and delighted by their shared emotion in this moment. He found her hand, clasped it briefly, let go. She gave him a radiant smile. They both faced ahead as the Canadian anthem began.

Jack sang along with gusto. He wasn't a great singer—in fact, he was actually kind of terrible—but he had to do his part, in homage to Lorieau and the tradition begun in 2006. Around him he could hear the others, including Caitlin, joining in.

The Oilers' bench looked quite small from this distance, but he thought he could see Joey Moss there—the Oilers' dressing room attendant and another key part of the team's grand history—belting out the anthem with his usual unabashed enthusiasm. With that shining example to follow, Jack simply couldn't not sing.

* * * * *

The game was fantastic—the Buffalo Sabres scored the first two goals, but the Oilers came from behind as they so often did, to win with a score of 5–3. When it was all over, Jack and his friends joined the immense throng exiting the coliseum. Though they had cars, instead of driving to the arena they'd parked at Century Park and taken the Light Rail Transit, to avoid the high parking fees and, more importantly, the backed-up traffic that would take an hour or more to clear out of Rexall Place. So they joined the crowds heading to Coliseum Station.

The LRT was packed with hundreds of fans who had similarly chosen to take the train. Caitlin and Jeremy ended up squeezed into the back corner of the last car in the southbound train. Two young men, faces painted orange and blue, crammed in next, just in front of Jack. Mike, Kristy and Travis pushed in last, separated from the others by the men with face paint and two couples in their late twenties. Jack wiggled his way around the strangers to stand next to Jeremy and Caitlin. Their other friends remained close to the door, unable to move any farther through the packed crowd.

Caitlin smiled at Jack as he squeezed in next to Jeremy, and he winked at her before clapping Jeremy on the shoulder. "Some game, hey?" he said. "I got a bit worried after the first period, but Horcoff and Smyth came through eventually."

"Yeah, they usually do," Jeremy agreed. "But it was a real cliffhanger, for sure."

"I had fun," Caitlin declared.

"Me too," Jack said. "I've been having a lot of fun with you guys lately." Jack's voice deepened, and he took a half-step closer, letting his arm brush against Caitlin's. Someone bumped him from behind and he rocked forward another step. He could feel Caitlin's thigh pressing against his own—just as it had done for the past three hours. He had been conscious of her nearness for the whole game. He swayed closer again, and for a moment the swell of Caitlin's left breast brushed Jack's chest. The contact felt as though a low electric field was energizing him from head to toe.

Jeremy seemed to notice both the inadvertent touch and the effect it had on Jack, and looked intently at his partner. Jack took a step back, unsure if he'd gone too far. He couldn't deny he was attracted to Caitlin, that he was enjoying every moment of every voyeuristic opportunity she and Jeremy gave him—but he was acutely aware that Caitlin belonged to Jeremy, not to him. He had to let his friend call the shots.

Jeremy, however, just smiled. He turned slightly, and took a small step to his left. The movement nudged Jack even closer to Caitlin, and at the same time presented Jeremy's own back to the crowded train car beyond their cramped corner.

The train lurched as it pulled out of the station, filled to capacity at last, and Jack stumbled, caught off guard by the unexpected motion. He fell toward Caitlin, quickly catching himself by bracing his hands on either side of her, against the cream-colored wall. Caitlin smiled up at him. Her eyes glittered, and Jack knew she'd felt his half-hard cock press against her hip.

Jeremy glanced down, and grinned as he too noticed the bulge in Jack's pants. Jack shifted, trying to adjust himself within his suddenly too-tight jeans. He lowered his arms but didn't back up, and the swaying movement of the train bumped him periodically against Caitlin's hip.

Jack watched, aroused and envious, as Jeremy leaned down to kiss his girlfriend. He cupped her cheek in one hand, nuzzling her jaw, then spoke in her ear. "Baby," he whispered. Jack could just hear him over the noise of the crowd behind them. He waited, expecting and hoping for Jeremy to encourage Caitlin to let him touch her, to put on another show for Jack.

Instead, he heard Jeremy ask his girlfriend softly, "Would you like to touch Jack?"

Jack's breath caught in his throat, and Caitlin gasped too, flushed and wide-eyed. She glanced around. Jack looked around also. Behind him, the two "dye"-hard fans were oblivious to everything except their boisterous reenactment of the best moments of the game. Beyond them, he could see Travis, Kristy and Mike. Their friends were chatting easily, ignoring the noisy crowd around them. Travis glanced their way and grinned. Jack waved at him, as casually as he could, and Travis went back to his conversation with the others. No one on the train could see anything of Caitlin but the top of her head, Jack realized, except for Jeremy and himself. And he was facing away from the crowd, shielded by the wall on one side and his hulking best friend on the other. If Caitlin did touch him, no one would know it but them.

Jack turned back to Caitlin. She was looking from him to Jeremy, her gaze troubled. With nervousness? Reluctance? Jack couldn't tell. He wished, not for the first time, that he could read her mysterious eyes. "You don't have to do it," he said hoarsely. He wanted her to touch him—god, did he want her to touch him!—but only if she wanted it as well. "I mean, if it's too much, or you don't want to," he said, "I'll understand."

Caitlin hesitated, still looking at both men, unsure. "Would you like me to?" she asked.

"Yes," Jeremy and Jack said at the same time.

The tension broke, and they laughed. "Jinx—you owe me a beer," Jeremy said to Jack. He looked back at Caitlin. "No security cameras on the LRT yet," he added conversationally. "They have them in the stations, but not in the trains themselves."

Jack turned back to Caitlin. "Yes," he said softly. "I want you to touch me. If you want to."

Still she didn't move, and for one heart-stopping moment, Jack thought Caitlin was going to say no. But with a final glance up at Jeremy—who nodded firmly to indicate his approval—she turned to Jack, reaching toward him with her left hand.

Jack stood stock still, waiting with almost unbearable anticipation. He'd been fantasizing about Caitlin for days, hoping she and Jeremy would put on another show for him soon. But he never thought he'd be the one Caitlin was touching, with Jeremy as their enraptured audience.

Caitlin put her hand on Jack's chest, palm flattened against his sternum. Even through his jersey and t-shirt, he could feel the heat of her hand. Slowly, then, her eyes boring into Jack's own, she began inching it downward. Jack held his breath as she reached his waist, then reached lower. His cock was fully hard now, straining in the tight confines of his pants.

With agonizing slowness Caitlin's hand continued to slide down. Finally, she reached the bulge at his crotch and curled her hand around it, gripping his shaft firmly through his clothes. Jack drew his breath in sharply at her touch, and Caitlin smiled, pleased by his reaction.

She slid her hand up under his jersey and over his crotch once more, squeezing and pressing, stroking her hand up and down over the soft denim. The friction on his cock through several layers of clothing was simultaneously unbearably acute and not nearly enough. Jack swayed, steadying himself with a hand against the wall.

He glanced over at his best friend. Jeremy was looking down at Caitlin's hand, but then looked up, meeting Jack's eyes. His slight smile—and the large bulge Jack could see tenting Jeremy's own jeans—told him his friend was enjoying the show. Behind him, Jack could hear dozens of people talking and shouting, including their other friends, but none of them seemed to know what was going on in this back corner of the subway train.

Jack rocked forward and then back as the train lurched to a stop. Belatedly he realized this had happened once already, but here at Churchill Station, as with Stadium before it, few people had squeezed onto the train and even fewer had gotten off. The train probably wouldn't really start clearing out 'til they left downtown and got to the University of Alberta, across the North Saskatchewan River.

They pulled out of the station, continuing southward, and this time Jack was pushed away from Caitlin and then against her once more. As he was pressed forward she grasped him more firmly, and began to stroke him faster through his jeans.

Jack braced his arm firmly against the wall and let his eyes close, biting his lip to stifle a groan. He didn't know how this was going to end—probably with him going home with the world's most painful blue balls and one hell of a masturbation fantasy—but right now he didn't care. He just wanted to enjoy whatever he could get out of this while it lasted.

Caitlin's hand squeezed, relaxed and then released him. Jack froze, wondering if it was over already. Was she having second thoughts?

Then he felt her tugging at the button on his jeans. Jack's eyes flew open. The button popped open too, and next he felt Caitlin's fingers grasping the tab of his zipper. She pulled it down, easing some of the now almost unbearable pressure in his groin.

Jack held his breath, staring down at the curvy redhead. With a deep breath, and a final glance of inquiry at Jeremy — who smiled encouragingly, leaning down to give her a quick kiss—Caitlin slipped her hand inside Jack's jeans.

Her fingers brushed the shaft of his cock through his thin boxers, and Jack shivered. She slid her fingers up, located the waistband of Jack's shorts and slipped her hand beneath it, nails trailing lightly through the thin line of hair bisecting Jack's abdomen. Her fingers were deliciously cool on Jack's burning, sensitive skin. Caitlin pushed her hand in deeper, and at last—as Jack stood frozen, aching for her touch—her soft fingers found his cock, hot, hard and standing at full attention.

As she touched him Jack gasped, then looked around, feeling his face turn red. Jeremy nudged his shoulder, a warning to keep quiet.

Caitlin smiled and twisted her hand, cupping her fingers around the thick shaft of his cock. She slid her hand down, then up again, until the side of her hand pressed up against the underside of the flaring head. She ran her thumb lightly over the head, catching the pre-come beading at the small slit, rubbing it in as she drew her hand down once more.

Never mind trying not to moan and groan, Jack was having serious trouble just staying on his feet. If not for his hand braced against the wall, Jeremy supporting his left side and the face-painted fans pressed against his back, Jack thought he might have swooned like a Victorian heroine. Not that Victorian heroines were likely to get—or give—a public handjob, he thought inanely.

Caitlin was smiling up at him again, clearly enjoying his pleasure. "Do you like that, Jack?" Her voice was soft and sultry.

"God yes," Jack said huskily. He leaned in, afraid someone behind them would hear, smelling the clean apple scent of Caitlin's hair. This close he could see the amber flecks in her green eyes. "That feels incredible. You're incredible."

"Grandin Station," the cool female recording announced, as the train slowed. This was the last stop before the university, Jack realized. The train would likely clear out significantly there. Probably enough for the rest of their friends to join them.

"Maybe...maybe we should stop," Jack said breathlessly. He didn't want Caitlin to stop touching him, but he didn't want to get caught with his pants open and his dick out either. Not by anybody, and most definitely not by their friends.

"Not yet," Caitlin said impishly. She began to pump his cock faster. With her other hand she tugged at his boxer shorts, pulling the fabric away from his crotch. Suddenly that hand was inside his pants too, cupping his balls.

"Oh god," Jack said. "Caitlin, don't—I'm...uhh..."

"Yes," Caitlin insisted. "I want to make you come, Jack. Please. Please come for me."

She gripped him firmly, stroking hard and fast, gently squeezing his balls, and he was right there, the delightful pressure building in his testicles, surging into the base of his cock.

Biting his lips to stifle a groan, helpless to prevent the pleasure from overtaking him, Jack came. The hot fluid spurted out, over his stomach and Caitlin's hand, and he sagged against the wall, powerless to control it.

"Ohh," Caitlin breathed, and Jack's cock twitched again at the lust he could hear in her voice.

"University Station," the disembodied voice pronounced, and Jack felt the pressure leave his back as the passengers behind him surged toward the doors. The more welcome pressure in front of him disappeared too, as Caitlin let go of him, pulling her hands out of his pants.

"Here," Jeremy said, and Jack looked around, dazed, to find his friend holding out a handful of napkins from the Rexall concession, which he'd apparently put in his pocket earlier. Caitlin took two and hurriedly wiped the glistening white fluid from her hand. Jack grabbed the other three and tried to clean himself up. He got most of the mess off his stomach, but his boxer shorts, his jeans and his t-shirt were all soiled. He was a disaster.

Still, he thought ruefully as he hastily did up his jeans and yanked his jersey down over the whole mess, it could have been worse. He'd come so hard he might have splattered Caitlin, or even Jeremy. They'd have had a hard time explaining that to their friends.

"Dudes, why so quiet?" Speaking of their friends, that was Travis, dodging around the exiting passengers as he headed their way. Jack took Caitlin's used napkins, wadded them up with his own and stuffed them quickly in his pocket.

"And dudette," Travis added, nodding at Caitlin. He clapped one hand on Jeremy's shoulder, the other on Jack's. "You guys should be happy — we won, for crying out loud."

"We are happy," Caitlin assured Travis. She winked at Jack, and he hastily faked a cough, covering his mouth to hide the silly grin threatening to burst onto his face. Happy! He didn't think he'd ever been quite so happy in his life.

"You sure?" Mike asked, as he and Kristy joined them too. "'Cause you were all just standing around looking like your cat died, or something."

"Nah," Jeremy said, backing up to include Kristy and Mike in their circle. "We're just tired."

Jeremy's face and neck were flushed, and Jack could see a vein pulsing in his temple. He had untucked his own t-shirt — Jack could see it sticking out under the hem of his jersey — and had his fists balled in his pockets. Jack felt a wave of sympathy for his friend. At least he'd gotten to come. If Jeremy had enjoyed watching Caitlin touch him half as much as Jack had enjoyed watching Jeremy touch Caitlin on previous occasions, then Jeremy was probably so hard he was in pain.

"Yeah," Jack agreed. "I'm still jetlagged from night shift."

"Pussy," Mike said amicably. Kristy pretended to punch him in the stomach.

By the time they reached Southgate Mall, Jack was starting to feel almost normal again. If the absolute exhilaration he felt was normal, that is. Jeremy looked a bit calmer too — he was less red in the face and had taken his hands out of his pockets.

It was hard to tell whether Caitlin was as aroused as the two men. There were of course no telltale bulges in her pants — women sure had it lucky there — and her jersey was too thick for him to see if her nipples were hard. She was uncharacteristically quiet, though, not participating much in the conversation. And were her cheeks a bit pinker than usual? Her breathing a bit more rapid?

Caitlin looked up, apparently feeling Jack's eyes on her. Maybe she read his thoughts in his face, or maybe she just wanted to give him another thrill. Either way, as she held his gaze, she brought her left hand to her face—the hand that Jack had come all over only minutes ago—and deliberately licked her fingers.

Jack stared, riveted. Jeremy was watching too. He shoved his hands back in his pockets.

"Hungry?" Kristy laughed, watching Caitlin lick the palm of her hand.

"No, no," Caitlin explained innocently. "I just got something sticky on my hand."

Jack looked down, unable to meet anyone's eyes.

"God, me too," Mike bitched. Jack choked, trying not to laugh. He heard Jeremy clearing his throat noisily.

"I swear," Mike continued, oblivious, "some idiot spilled beer on every railing of every flight of stairs from the nosebleeds down to the ground floor. I am sticky as hell."

"That must be what it is," Caitlin said, smiling broadly.

"Hey, look," Kristy said. Jack realized with mounting alarm that she was pointing at his crotch.

"You got covered in beer too, huh?" Mike was peering at the wet stain on Jack's jeans.

"Yeah," Jack said uncomfortably. He tugged his jersey down again and pressed back against the wall of the train. He was afraid that if Mike got any closer his nose would tell him what Jack was really doused in.

Travis was grinning at his discomfiture. "You look like you pissed your pants. That's a class act, bro."

"Shut up," Jack told him, pretending to be annoyed. He was actually relieved. The others could think what they wanted—just as long as they didn't figure out what had really happened.

They pulled into Century Park—formerly Heritage Mall, now a public transit hub, condo complex and strip mall—and got off the train, heading for the ETS Park 'n Ride lot.

Shouting goodbyes, Mike and Kristy headed for Jack's truck—they'd ridden there with him. Travis, who'd come with Jeremy and Caitlin, waved and headed for Jeremy's SUV in the next row.

Jack stopped, torn. He couldn't say anything within earshot of the others, couldn't let them see that anything strange was going on...but he also couldn't let Caitlin and Jeremy go without thanking them for the most incredible experience of his life.

Jeremy and Caitlin stopped too, holding hands. "Well," Caitlin said. She sounded a bit lost as well. "See you around, Jack."

"Yeah," he said lamely.

"Jack!" Mike shouted from beside the truck. "Hurry up—it's cold!"

"Hold your ginch!" he shouted back without turning, still trying to come up with something to say.

"'Hold your ginch?'" Caitlin giggled. "What does that even mean?"

"It's like 'hold your horses'," Jeremy explained. "You know, 'wait a minute'."

"Yeah, I get that," Caitlin said, smiling. Jack was relieved she'd found a way around the tension that had started building between the three of them after what had happened on the train. "But what the hell is a ginch?"

"It's not *a* ginch, it's just ginch," Jack said. "It means underwear. Panties, undies, shorts, ginch, gonch, whatever."

"'Gonch?'" Caitlin echoed, laughing harder. "You guys are just making shit up now."

"For your information," Jeremy said, hugging his girlfriend, "ginch and gonch are legitimate expressions of Western Canadian culture."

"Just Western?" Caitlin asked next.

"Yep," Jack said, grinning himself. "As you head east, you're more likely to hear 'gitch' or 'gotch' instead—they drop the 'n'."

"Guys?" That was Travis chiming in now. "Are we going, or what?"

"Look," Jack said hastily, taking a step toward Caitlin, forcing himself to stop there. "I just wanted to say…thanks. To both of you."

Caitlin brushed her long red hair out of her eyes—the wind was picking up. "You're very welcome," she said.

"Yeah," Jeremy said. "No problem. We had fun too."

"Good," Jack said. He took another step forward and gave his best friend a brief but powerful hug. Turning to Caitlin, he bent down, wrapping his arms quickly around her. Caitlin hugged him back, arms around his middle, cheek against his chest.

Jack bent his head, allowing his lips to brush Caitlin's glorious red hair for the briefest of moments. Then he forced himself to let go, turn around and walk away.

Chapter Eight
ಬ

"So?" Jeremy said expectantly. He closed his locker and sat down on the narrow bench to lace up his boots.

"Yeah, I guess," Jack said reluctantly. He threw down the towel he'd been drying his hair and upper body with and reached for his shirt.

"You guess?" Jeremy repeated, surprised. "You love hockey. And you're always nagging me to let you come watch on my flat-screen. What gives?" His bootlaces finished, he stood, tossed his own towel in the corner bin and began doing up his pants, looking at his partner curiously.

Jack wasn't sure why he was reluctant to go hang out at Jeremy's place the next day. They'd been talking about it all through their shift. He hadn't spent any time with Jeremy outside of work lately, and he hadn't seen Caitlin at all in a week. Not since they all went to the game together. And since what happened on the LRT afterward.

He did want to see the hockey game, Jack reflected. And Jeremy was right, his flat-screen and sound system were pretty sweet—better than what Jack and Mike had at their place.

"I don't know," he sighed. "I'm tired, I guess. I was up late talking to Scott last night." And up even later jerking off, he thought but didn't say, pretending it was Caitlin's small but square hand on his cock again, instead of his own.

"Oh yeah?" Jeremy said. "How are Scott and Liz?"

"Good," Jack said noncommittally. Truthfully, they hadn't talked much about Scott, and hadn't talked about Liz at all. Scott had spent the whole time analyzing Jack's commitment issues and trying once again to persuade his former partner to join him in Toronto. Though he still had no intention of moving, the latter was almost a relief for Jack to hear, compared to the former.

"Guys!" Jack and Jeremy both looked up as John Radakovich, another member of their squad, came around the corner, wearing nothing but a towel slung low on his hips, and carrying a brown zippered toiletries bag. "Why are you still here? You're not usually this slow."

"We had a bet on," Jeremy grinned, winking broadly at Jack. "Wanted to see just how long you spend in front of the mirror, doing your hair."

Jack laughed involuntarily. They teased Rad often about his carefully slicked-back hair and meticulously groomed mustache. Rad and his beat partner, Cheryl Hamlett, could often be heard arguing good-naturedly about the image he projected. Rad insisted he came off as sexy and just a bit dangerous. Cheryl's frequently stated opinion was that he looked like a seventies porn star. The rest of the squad tended to side with Cheryl in this particular debate. Rad, who got a healthy dose of female attention in spite of—surely not because of?—his truly porntastic copstache, took it all with good humor.

"Hey, don't hate the player, hate the game," Rad said calmly, opening his locker.

Jeremy rolled his eyes expressively and Jack laughed again.

"You know, you think it's funny," Rad said to Jack, putting his bag of grooming products back in his locker and starting to get dressed, "but you play the field even more than I do. You just haven't got The Look."

"If that's The Look, I'll pass." Jack snickered, eyeing the tight polyester pants and pink shirt his friend was putting on. "And I can get plenty of girls without it. When I want to."

"Yeah, like that blonde at lunch?" Rad smirked. He and Cheryl had met Jack and Jeremy mid-shift for a quick lunch at Badass Jack's, a fast food chain serving subs and wraps.

They'd all noticed the busty blonde at the next table who had looked up from her meal several times to smile suggestively at Jack. "I can't believe you didn't get her number—you're really slipping, man."

"Hey, we had to run," Jack protested weakly. True, they'd gotten a call to assist before they'd finished eating, but Jack knew he could have taken a moment to ask the girl for her number. If he'd really wanted to.

Now it was Rad's turn to roll his eyes. "Whatever. You choked."

"Well, it won't happen again," Jack said. He had to do something to get Caitlin off his mind, that was for sure. Maybe this blonde would turn out to be just what he needed. "I'll go back there one of these days—I bet she eats there regularly."

"She probably will now," Jeremy said, smiling as he pulled on his shirt. "Hoping to see you again."

"Good luck with that," Rad said. He was dressed already. However much time he spent fussing with his hair, he always managed to make it up by dressing quickly and efficiently. "See you guys next shift." He tossed his towel in the corner bin and strode out of the locker room, whistling cheerfully.

"You really going to go back?" Jeremy asked, reaching for his coat. "Try your luck with that blonde?"

"Yeah, probably," Jack said, though he wasn't entirely sure himself. "It's been a really long time—I need to get laid." As he said this, it suddenly struck him that it had been well over a month since he'd had sex. God, no wonder he was thinking about Caitlin all the time—he hadn't had such a long dry spell in ages. He obviously needed to let off some pressure. He was relieved—that was clearly all that was going on.

"I bet," Jeremy agreed. "But are you sure this blonde is the answer?"

"Why not?" Jack asked, confused. "Who else is there? You know Leanne is long gone, and I don't see any other girls lining up to jump in bed with me."

"Well, maybe I can help you with that," Jeremy said, zipping up his jacket. "Lemme get back to you."

Jack rolled his eyes. "Whatev, pimp."

Jeremy laughed. "So, tomorrow, right? The game?"

"Yeah," Jack said. What the hell, it would be fun. Sure, he might be a bit uncomfortable—meaning horny as hell—sitting in the same room with Caitlin for three hours, but he could deal. Now that he'd realized it was just his hormones going nuts—a situation he expected to alleviate soon, with the blonde from this afternoon, or the next willing, attractive girl to cross his path. "I'll be there."

"Excellent," Jeremy said, tapping Jack's fist with his own. "See you tomorrow then."

* * * * *

Jeremy put the key in the ignition and started his SUV. He turned the heater up, cranked it to defrost, punched the rear defrost button as well and sat back, giving the car a few minutes to warm up. The warm weather had finally broken, the daytime high only reaching single digits, and by late evening—like now—it was already starting to get frosty. It would snow any day now.

He glanced at his watch, then at the clock on the dash for good measure. Though Caitlin was sometimes able to work from home, her job was basically a nine to five, Monday to Friday gig. They wouldn't have much time to hang out together before she'd have to go to bed, but she'd invited Jeremy to sleep over that night if he wanted to.

Which he did. He loved sleeping with Caitlin. In both senses—she had a real sense of adventure in bed and didn't mind talking dirty to him once in a while, which was a huge turn-on for Jeremy. But he also liked just being asleep with her.

When they lay on their sides, spooning, with Caitlin's wonderfully curvy backside snugged up against Jeremy's crotch, the top of her head only came up to his chin. He would press his mouth into her hair, feeling the silky strands glide over his lips, and fall asleep smelling the fresh apple scent of her conditioner.

The car had warmed up, and Jeremy pulled out, heading for Caitlin's apartment. He drove quickly, wanting to make sure they had time to talk before bed. He wondered what Caitlin's reaction would be to what he had in mind.

Maybe Jack couldn't think of a girl he already knew who'd want to have some no-strings sex with him, but Jeremy thought maybe he could.

Caitlin had clearly been enjoying herself the past few weeks with Jack, as they'd played their illicit little games. Jeremy knew as well, from past experience, that the more orgasms Caitlin had, the more sensitive and turned-on she got. There were occasions when he'd made her come as many as two or three times, with his hands and his mouth, before finally allowing himself to plunge his cock into her hot, tight wetness. And even after all that she would usually come at least one more time before Jeremy, unable to hold back any longer, would give in to his own release.

Caitlin had never said so, had never expressed anything but pleasure and satisfaction when they made love, but lately — since the first night they'd inadvertently put on a show for Jack — Jeremy had wondered if Caitlin ever secretly wanted to have sex with more than one man at a time. He had a feeling she'd be able to handle it. In fact, he had a hunch that if there was another man there to take over right after Jeremy had to pull out, spent, that Caitlin might end up getting the most intense and incredible fuck of her life.

If he was honest with himself, Jeremy also had to admit that it turned him on immensely to know just how excited Caitlin got Jack. Jeremy remembered the night at Jack's place when Caitlin had taken off her black lace panties and given them to the dark-haired man as a souvenir. Jeremy had been surprised, then amused and then gratified by the shock and arousal he'd seen on his best friend's face when Caitlin had held out her little surprise.

Jack hadn't given the panties back to Caitlin. Jeremy hadn't asked, but several times he'd caught himself wondering what Jack might have done with them in the weeks since that night. Did he take them out periodically and hold them to his nose, wanting to smell Caitlin's unique musk? Did he hold them in one hand while masturbating with the other, imagining that Caitlin was there with him? Had he even wrapped them around his cock while he touched himself, and spurted his own cum where Caitlin's pussy had so recently been?

Jeremy wasn't sure why, but thinking about these things excited him beyond belief. As did the other things they'd done—him touching Caitlin while Jack watched, and letting Caitlin touch Jack while he watched them.

He wasn't gay—though he had no problem with homosexuality, Jeremy had no urge to touch Jack himself, and didn't want his partner to touch him either. But something about the idea of sharing Caitlin with another man, letting someone else experience firsthand how incredibly sexy Caitlin was and watching, gratified, as Caitlin drove Jack wild the same way she did Jeremy, was indescribably exciting.

And it had to be Jack. Jack was his best friend, and Jeremy trusted him like he trusted no one else. And Jack was safe. Though he clearly lusted after Caitlin—that was obvious to Jeremy and had been for a while—Jeremy knew Jack wasn't a threat to their relationship. Jack seemed to be totally allergic to commitment—not that Jeremy could blame him for that, after the number Angela had done on him—but it did mean he never stuck with one girl for very long. Jack had said he was going to try to hook up with the blonde girl from that afternoon, so chances were he would soon be involved with her. And if that didn't end up happening, or didn't last very long, Jack would simply move on to someone else. The way he always did.

Though Jeremy knew Jack didn't like talking about Angela, they'd talked about girls and relationships in general enough for Jeremy to know that Jack wasn't looking for anything serious or long-term. He didn't want to fall in love, didn't want to tie himself down to one girl. So, while Jeremy knew that Jack wanted to be with Caitlin, he was confident that it wouldn't last. They could have their fun—the climax that their exhibitionist games had been building toward for the past several weeks—and then it would be over. Jack would move on to someone else, and Caitlin and Jeremy would still have each other.

So, if Jeremy's plan worked out, tomorrow would be a chance for Jack to finally get laid, and to scratch the temporary itch he'd developed for Caitlin. Jeremy hoped it might also be a chance to satisfy Caitlin in a way she hadn't had the opportunity to experience before. And last, but certainly not least, it was a chance for Jeremy to indulge his own newly discovered fantasy. He wanted to watch his best friend fuck his girlfriend. He wanted to witness as another man explored and marveled at Caitlin's exquisite surrender in bed. And he wanted to give his best friend a very meaningful gift…a chance to experience the best sex he had ever had.

Now he just had to see if Caitlin wanted this as much as he did.

* * * * *

Jack pressed the button marked 324. After a few seconds, a loud buzzing noise sounded, and he pulled open the security door, awkwardly—he was carrying a two-four of Kokanee, two bags of chips and some dill pickle dip. Old Dutch BBQ for Caitlin, of course, Old Dutch Rip-L and dip for him. And everybody else could help themselves to either.

He took the stairs, arriving at the door slightly out of breath from carrying the heavy beer case. He braced the beer against the wall with one hand and rang the doorbell with the other. The feeling of breathlessness intensified when the door opened and he saw Caitlin standing before him.

"Hi, Jack," she said, smiling warmly. Her gaze was as intense as always, and her cheeks flushed a delicate pink as their eyes met.

"Hey," Jack said, stepping forward as she backed up to let him in. He tried not to stare at her as she took the chips and dip from him, but it was hard. He hadn't seen her in over a week.

She was wearing a pink tank top with thin straps and one of those built-in stretchy layers around the boobs—whatever that was called. Jack didn't think she was wearing a bra—he didn't see any other straps or lines. He followed Caitlin into the kitchen. She wore soft flannel pajama bottoms in a light- and dark-pink pattern. Walking behind her, he couldn't help but notice how low they rode on her hips, how they clung to her sexy ass. Through the flannel he could see the lines of her panties, low and straight across. What did you call those ones—boy shorts? He couldn't remember. She definitely did not look like a boy.

"Jack! Finally made it, eh?" Startled, Jack tore his gaze from Caitlin's rear end and guiltily met his best friend's eyes. Jeremy was leaning against the counter, a bottle of Molson in his hand and a knowing smile on his face.

"Hey," Jack said again, blushing. This didn't seem to be his night for scintillating conversation. Good thing they'd be watching the hockey game, not talking.

"Kokanee?" Jeremy watched in mock disbelief as Jack slid the two-four onto the counter, beside the chips and dip that Caitlin had set down. "You actually expect us to drink that moose piss?" He wasn't a fan of Jack's favorite brand, and they often teased each other about who had better taste in beer.

"*I'm* going to drink it," Jack said, smiling in spite of himself. His friend always managed to cheer him up. "*You* can go fuck yourself."

Caitlin laughed. "It's all moose piss, in my humble opinion," she said. "I'm going to drink this." She got a supercan of Strongbow out of the fridge and popped the tab.

Jack helped himself to one of his beers and loaded several more into the fridge to stay cold. He popped the top and took a long swallow. Jeremy and Caitlin were both leaning against the counter now, side by side. Other than the low hum of the refrigerator, and the periodic swallows as they all sipped their drinks, the apartment was quiet.

"Mike and Kristy not here yet?" Jack asked. "And where's Travis?"

Jeremy and Caitlin exchanged a glance. "Actually," Jeremy said slowly, "there's been a change of plans. They're all watching the game at Brandon and Danika's."

"What?" Jack was startled. "Aren't we invited too?"

"Yeah, we were invited," Jeremy reassured him. He glanced at Caitlin again. "But we told them we wanted to hang out with you here. We haven't spent much quality time with you lately."

"Oh," Jack said. "Uh, okay." Not that he wasn't flattered, but the Kowalchuks' home theater made even Jeremy's flat-screen look like an iPhone. And the thought of spending the evening alone with Caitlin and Jeremy made him distinctly nervous. How was he supposed to forget about their little games and get his mind off Caitlin and on to some other — safer — girl under these circumstances?

They were both just standing there, looking at him. It made Jack even more uncomfortable. He looked at his watch. The game would be starting. "Well?" he said nervously. "Should we go watch it then?"

"Sure," Caitlin said. This time she threw a meaningful glance at Jeremy. Jack wasn't sure what all these secret looks meant, but they were starting to freak him out.

They headed into the living room. Caitlin settled on the couch, curling up like a cat. Jeremy stood next to the coffee table, punching buttons on several remotes to bring up the television, stereo and cable box.

Jack glanced longingly at the couch, but chose the recliner instead. He hated the rickety, ugly old thing—ironically, it was Travis' prize possession—but he felt the need to put some distance between himself and Caitlin. He hadn't touched her once but he could feel the curvy redhead's presence like an electric field, even from several feet away.

Finally satisfied with the volume and aspect ratio, Jeremy sat down on the couch beside Caitlin. He smiled over at Jack, and put one large hand on his girlfriend's thigh.

Jack smiled back but then quickly turned his attention to the TV.

He made it through the first period somehow. It helped a bit that the Oilers were playing the Calgary Flames tonight— the stakes were always a bit higher when these two rival teams met.

Still, he couldn't help but see, out of the corner of his eye, that Jeremy was nuzzling Caitlin's neck and ear. And that she was loving it—eyes closed, head thrown back. Nipples hard. Jack crossed his legs and propped his chin on one fist.

As the buzzer sounded to end the first period, Jeremy hit another button on one of the remotes, muting the sound.

"What?" Jack asked, looking around.

"You tell him, babe," Jeremy said, looking at Caitlin.

"Are you sure?" Caitlin asked. She bit her lip, staring intently at her boyfriend. "You're really, completely sure?"

"About what?" Jack said, not certain he wanted to know. There was definitely something big going on here.

"Yes," Jeremy said firmly, squeezing Caitlin's hand. "I'm sure."

"Okay," Caitlin said. She turned toward Jack, then got up and perched on the arm of the couch right next to his chair. Her knee brushed his elbow and he sat back, crossing his arms apprehensively.

"We wanted to ask you something," Caitlin said. She was gripping the knees of her pajama bottoms tightly enough to twist the fabric taut, and Jack realized with some surprise that she was at least as nervous as he was.

"I've enjoyed all the things we've done together over the past few weeks," she said. "Jeremy has too, and I think you have as well." Jack almost laughed—that was the understatement of the year.

"So," she continued, "we were wondering if…if…" She trailed off there, hands still clenched nervously, for once having trouble meeting his eyes.

Jeremy stepped up beside Caitlin, putting an arm around her shoulders encouragingly. "We were wondering," he said, "if you wanted to have sex with us."

Jack blinked. "With both of you? What do you mean?" God, was Jeremy attracted to him? Was that why he got off on this stuff they'd been doing?

Jeremy laughed, no doubt seeing the confusion and panic on his partner's face. "Well, I didn't actually mean with me," he clarified. "I love you, pal, but not like that. No offense."

"Ditto," Jack said, relieved.

"I meant," Jeremy continued, "we could both have sex with Caitlin. If you want to."

Jack looked at Caitlin, stunned. He could tell they'd had something planned, but he'd never suspected this. Finally she raised her head and met his eyes once more. "Is that what you want?" he asked the petite redhead. She nodded, slowly but firmly.

"Really?" Jack persisted. "You're not just going along with Jeremy on this?" This must have been what Jeremy meant about finding a girl who'd have sex with Jack. Another thought struck him. By now he had a feeling both Jeremy and Caitlin knew how much he wanted her. Maybe this was just a pity fuck, an attempt to acknowledge and ease those unreciprocated feelings? "You don't feel sorry for me?"

"Sorry for you? For what?" Caitlin's surprise sounded genuine.

"Nothing," Jack said, somewhat relieved. "Forget it. I just, I'm kind of in shock here. I came here expecting to watch the game, not...do this."

Caitlin grinned at him. "Well, if you'd rather watch hockey, we can go have sex without you. It *is* the Battle of Alberta, after all — that's pretty important."

"Nah, that's okay," Jack said, smiling back. "If there's one thing that's more important than hockey, it's sex."

"Well said, bro." Jeremy chuckled. "So, is that a yes?"

Jack couldn't believe he was seriously considering this. It was crazy. How was he supposed to go back to his normal life after this? And how would this affect their relationship in the future? Would he and Caitlin — and even more importantly, he and Jeremy — be able to remain good friends after sharing something like this?

Jack looked at Caitlin again, letting his eyes rove over her hungrily, as he'd wanted to do for so long. Maybe, if he gave in and finally scratched this itch, he'd be able to get her out of his head. Stop thinking about her and go on with his life. Find some other girl who would meet his physical needs without threatening to get under his skin. Or into his heart.

Jack took a deep breath. "Okay," he said finally. "Yes."

"Good," Caitlin said. She stood up and reached for Jack's hand. He let her take it, feeling her small but surprisingly strong fingers close around his, and stood up obediently when she tugged. "Let's go," she said, and pulled Jack toward the hallway, and the bedrooms beyond. With a glance at Jeremy, who fell into step behind them, Jack let himself be swept away.

Chapter Nine

As Caitlin led Jack down the hallway, she was outwardly calm, but inside, her thoughts were racing. Was this actually happening? Was she about to have a threesome with not only her sexy boyfriend but his sexy best friend as well?

She could appreciate the shock and confusion Jack was feeling, if the expression on his face was any indication. She'd felt much the same way when Jeremy had brought up the idea last night. The shock had come from Jeremy's suggestion to share her with another man—she had never expected that. She knew he loved her, and was incredibly protective of her and would never have expected him to be okay with—never mind actually eager for—something like this. But he had assured her that he was, over and over 'til she had no choice but to believe him.

The confusion had more to do with her own feelings. It had surprised and alarmed Caitlin how much the idea appealed to her. Some of the appeal came from the thought of having sex with two men—any two men—at the same time. Her sex life with Jeremy was fantastic—he was both a thoughtful and a playful lover. And considerate—he always made sure she came at least twice before he finally came himself. She couldn't ask for a better lover than Jeremy. But she had to admit she sometimes wished he could last even longer, or make love to her several times in a row. Each orgasm he gave her made her crave another, and another still. What would it be like to have another man there, ready and eager to fill her up and ride her hard after the first man was spent? She couldn't wait to find out.

But another large part of the appeal, Caitlin was forced to admit, was Jack himself. That was the part that was confusing.

She loved Jeremy and would never betray him with another man...but she couldn't deny her powerful attraction to Jack. She had always thought him handsome, with his crinkly, electric blue eyes, wavy black hair and long, lean muscles. Likewise he had always been fun, with his quick wit and generous nature.

But in the past few months, Caitlin had gotten to know him even better, and her feelings of friendship and mild physical attraction had deepened into something else. Something more. And in the past few weeks, their exhibitionist games had sharpened her attraction to acute desire. Letting Jack watch, seeing his own desire radiating from those impossibly blue eyes, filled Caitlin with a longing so powerful it frightened her.

Caitlin was afraid to give in to that longing, afraid of where it might take her. But Jeremy insisted he wanted to do this, that it would turn him on to see her with Jack. That he would still love her after, and nothing would change. If Jeremy wanted it too, why not give in to this craving?

There was still a small voice deep inside Caitlin that warned against it. It whispered that once she took this irrevocable step, it would awaken something in her that would never go away again. Caitlin was afraid to try to name this wakening feeling, even to herself. Just thinking about it felt like a betrayal of Jeremy.

Instead, she told herself resolutely that it was all irrelevant anyway. Jeremy had told her about the blonde girl who'd caught Jack's eye the other day, so it was pretty clear that soon Jack would be involved with her, or someone else. If he was seeing another girl, however casually, that wouldn't leave any room for games with Caitlin and Jeremy, no matter how Caitlin's subconscious felt about it. She would probably never have a chance like this again. Jeremy was offering it sincerely...she should just take it. And not look back.

"Shit," Jack exclaimed as they entered Jeremy's bedroom, startling Caitlin out of her thoughts.

"What?" she asked, letting go of his hand. Was he going to change his mind? For all the apprehensions racing through her head, Caitlin felt not relief but disappointment at the thought.

"I, uh, I don't have any condoms," Jack said. "Do you guys?" He sounded doubtful. From that, Caitlin assumed he knew she and Jeremy didn't use them. She didn't have any STDs, and had been on the Pill for years. After his routine, department-mandated blood test several months ago showed that Jeremy remained clean as well, they'd stopped using them.

"No worries," Jeremy said. He flicked the bedroom light on, closed the door and then crossed to his dresser. Pulling a box of Trojans out of the top drawer, he tossed it to Jack. "I picked these up on the way home."

"Oh," Jack said, sounding relieved. Then he shot his best friend a mock glare. "Had this all planned out, did you?"

"Yeah, pretty much," Jeremy grinned unrepentantly. "Is that a problem?"

"Guess not," Jack said. He looked over at Caitlin, who was standing in the center of the room, arms folded over her breasts. She must have looked at least half as nervous as she felt, because he took a step toward her, concern etched on his face. "Caitlin? Are you okay?" He hesitated, tossed the condoms on the bed. "If you want to change your mind..."

"No," she said, looking from him to Jeremy. "I'm just...a bit nervous."

"Me too," Jack admitted.

"Me three," Jeremy said.

"Really?" Jack was surprised. "Wasn't this all your idea?"

"Yeah," Jeremy said. He shrugged. "Doesn't mean it isn't a big deal." Then he laughed. "I mean, what if your dick is twice the size of mine?" he joked. "Then I'll have to kill myself."

Caitlin laughed too. "If Jack's dick is twice the size of yours, it'll kill *me*," she said. "Honestly, you guys, bigger is only better up to a certain point."

"Well, that's a relief," Jack said. He knew Jeremy didn't really have anything to worry about. He took another step toward Caitlin.

The joking had eased everyone's nervousness, but the sexual tension hadn't left the room. Caitlin could feel it building around her. Or was it all inside her? She wasn't sure.

Jeremy turned and sat down on the edge of the king-size bed. "Okay," he said softly. "Why don't you guys go ahead and do...whatever you want to do. I'll just watch, for now."

"You're sure?" Jack said. "You really want to do this?"

"Yes," Jeremy said. He looked at Jack and at Caitlin, holding their gaze, giving them both permission. "I really do."

Jack turned back to Caitlin and took one more step, closing the distance between them at last. They weren't touching yet, but he was so close she could smell him, the scents of spicy aftershave and clean laundry a pleasing complement.

She looked up at him. He was several inches shorter than Jeremy; still quite a bit taller than Caitlin, but not so tall it cricked her neck to meet his eyes. She took a deep breath. This was it. "Kiss me, Jack," she said softly. "Please."

Jack raised one hand to Caitlin's face, lightly tracing her generous mouth with a fingertip. Then he bent down and pressed his lips gently to hers. He explored slowly at first, nipping and then licking. She tasted sweet from the cider. Her tongue met his, flicked along his lower lip, met his again. Then Jack leaned in hungrily, tasting her mouth, drawing Caitlin close against him. He plunged both hands into her silky red hair, then slid them down her back, cupping her ass cheeks, using his grip to pull her even more tightly against him.

Caitlin gasped, her mouth leaving his for a moment. Then she kissed him again, rising eagerly to her tiptoes. Her hands traveled from his waist to his shoulders, then rose up into his hair.

Jack shifted slightly, trying to ease the increasing pressure on his cock, which was crushed against Caitlin's stomach, bent uncomfortably in his pants and growing harder by the second. It didn't work and he finally had to let go of Caitlin, reaching down to adjust himself. She watched, her gaze lingering on his crotch before returning to his face.

"That was hot," Jeremy said, and Jack turned, surprised. He'd been so wrapped up in kissing Caitlin that for a moment he'd forgotten they weren't alone.

"Sorry," Jeremy said, realizing he'd disrupted the mood somewhat. "Carry on."

Caitlin moved toward Jack once more. She grasped the hem of his v-neck sweater and pushed it up. Jack grabbed it too, pulled it up and over his head. He tossed it on the floor in front of the closet.

He stood still, trying not to move, enjoying the sensations as Caitlin explored his naked chest. She ran her palms over his stomach, up to his shoulders and down his arms. She traced her fingertips along the slight protrusions of his ribs, and through the wisps of dark hair dusting his pecs and trailing down his stomach.

She took a step closer, dropping her hands to his waist, and drew her tongue slowly up his chest and over one nipple. Jack twitched at that, and she smiled. She ran her tongue across his chest to the other nipple, then sucked it into her mouth, biting gently. "Oh," Jack breathed.

"You like that?" Caitlin said, looking up at him.

"Yes," he admitted. Then added, "But I'd like doing it to you even more."

Caitlin glanced at Jeremy, who still seemed content to sit back and enjoy the show. He definitely was enjoying the show,

Jack saw—he was sporting a tent in his pants to rival the one in Jack's own.

"I'd like that too," Caitlin said. She reached down to her waist, about to pull her tank top off, but Jack stopped her. "Please," he said. "Can I do it?"

When Caitlin nodded he led her over to the bed. Jack sat down next to Jeremy, and tugged Caitlin toward him, hands on her waist, 'til she stood between his spread thighs, her breasts level with his chin. Jack slowly slid his hands upward, over the soft fabric of her shirt, 'til his thumbs encountered the bottom swells of her breasts. As he reached higher he gazed intently into Caitlin's face, wanting to see how his touch made her feel.

He held her breasts firmly, cupping and squeezing, feeling her nipples hardening under the palms of his hands. As the peaks tightened he pinched one between his fingers, watching, gratified, as Caitlin gasped, her eyes widening.

He pulled her closer and buried his face in her soft, white cleavage. He could hear her heart beating rapidly. She swayed slightly, and steadied herself by bracing her hands on his shoulders. "Please, Jack," she said breathlessly.

Jack sat back and pushed the fabric up, slipping the elasticized band up and over the swells of her breasts, lifting the tank top off over her head. It joined his shirt on the floor.

Her breasts were even lovelier than he remembered, large and full, creamy white with high pink nipples circled by small areolas. There was a small brown birthmark under her right breast. He touched his tongue to it and then moved higher, kissing and nipping. He closed his mouth over her right nipple and sucked firmly, simultaneously pinching her other nipple with the fingers of his right hand.

"Oh god," Caitlin moaned. Her hands crept into Jack's hair and cupped the back of his head, urging him wordlessly to continue.

The rasp of a zipper made them both look up. Jeremy had undone his jeans and was fidgeting on the bed, spreading his legs farther apart. "You guys are driving me nuts," he said. "Do you have any idea how hard it is to just sit here and watch without joining in?" He pretended to be annoyed. "Especially when you're going so damn slow?"

Jack chuckled. "Again," he said, "this was all your idea. Don't blame us."

"He does have a point, Jack," Caitlin said. "You *are* going really slow. It's driving me crazy too."

"Oh really?" Jack said. Her admission delighted him. "Well, in that case..." He pulled Caitlin toward him again and suckled her breasts with increased fervor. With one hand he held her waist steady. He slipped the other hand between her thighs, cupping her mound through her flannel pajama pants, and squeezed.

"Is this what you want, Caitlin?" Jack murmured around the nipple in his mouth. He probed her crotch with one finger, finding her cleft through the rapidly dampening fabric.

"Yes," Caitlin cried. She reached for her pajama pants, trying to push them down. "Please, Jack, more."

He grasped her waistband and pulled her bottoms down himself, taking her underwear with them. He could check out her panties later. Right now he desperately wanted to see what was beneath them.

It was a beautiful sight. As he slid her pants off, Caitlin's sturdy, creamy white thighs were revealed. And at their center, a small triangle of closely trimmed golden-red hair, above her clean-shaven, rosy pink lips.

Jack had wanted to wait, to draw this out, to make every moment of this once-in-a-lifetime opportunity last. But when he finally saw Caitlin completely naked, when he smelled her feminine musk, he knew he had to taste her as soon as possible.

He guided Caitlin back a few steps so he could drop to his knees on the carpet in front of her. His already aching cock strained more as he kneeled and spread his legs. Bending forward, gripping Caitlin's ass to pull her against him, he darted his tongue between her folds.

Caitlin spread her legs apart too, to give him more room. Her fingers were clenched in his hair, pulling him against her. Jack let go of her waist with one hand and reached between her legs, parting her lips with his fingers to allow himself greater access. He pressed in farther, and found her hard little knob with the tip of his tongue.

"Oh my god, Jack," Caitlin cried, arching her hips toward him. She swayed suddenly, losing her balance, and Jack looked up, alarmed, trying to steady her. Jeremy leaped up from the bed and caught his girlfriend in his strong arms. Caitlin clutched at him unsteadily, pressing her face into his chest. "I think you guys better do this on the bed," Jeremy said.

"Yeah," Jack agreed, gripping the mattress to lever himself up off his knees. "Probably a good idea."

Jeremy guided Caitlin over to sit on the bed, then sat down beside her. She smiled ruefully at him, then turned to Jack as well. "Sorry, guys," she said. "Guess I was getting a bit carried away."

"That's good," Jeremy said, smiling. He leaned down to kiss her, and she responded eagerly, her hands sliding under his t-shirt and over his chest.

Jack watched, not sure what would happen next. His turn wasn't over, was it? There were so many things he still wanted to do. And if he didn't take his pants off soon, he felt like his cock would explode.

As if reading his mind, Jeremy ended the kiss and sat back, gesturing for Caitlin and Jack to continue. This time Caitlin pulled Jack over 'til he stood before her at the side of the bed. Caitlin smiled up at him, and then began undoing his pants.

Jack watched as Caitlin undid the button and pulled down the zipper. She pushed his jeans down and he stepped out of them, kicking them aside, now wearing only his gray boxer briefs.

Caitlin reached for him, lightly tracing the outline of his erect cock through the thin, soft fabric. It twitched and she grasped it for a moment, squeezing gently. Jack gasped. "Please," he said. It was his turn to beg.

With a smile, Caitlin gripped the waistband, stretching it out slightly, and then pulled his boxer briefs down. She slid them down his thighs and then let go, letting them drop to the floor. Her eyes went to his cock, red and throbbing, standing at full attention before her.

"Guess I have to go kill myself now," Jeremy sighed, and Jack blinked at him, confused. "Your dick is bigger," Jeremy explained.

"Seriously?" Jack said. He hadn't gotten a really good look at Jeremy's cock, the time he accidentally watched Caitlin giving Jeremy a blowjob, but they'd seemed about the same size to him.

"No, not really," Caitlin said, still staring. She wrapped her hand carefully around the shaft, and Jack let out a breath that was almost a moan. "You're a little bit longer," she said. "But Jeremy is a little bit thicker."

"Oh," Jack said. He didn't care. All he cared about was the feel of Caitlin's hand on his cock, stroking him with agonizing slowness. She let go after only a few moments, but before Jack could protest, her fingers were replaced by her tongue. She licked him slowly, deliberately, from the base of his shaft to the head, then traced the tiny slit at the end with the tip of her tongue.

"Jesus," Jack said. He felt cool softness slipping over his hands, realized he'd brought his hands up to tangle in Caitlin's hair. She licked him again, then drew the head of his cock into her mouth, sucking with firm pressure. Jack fought to keep his hands relaxed. He wanted to clutch her to him, to feel her hot wet mouth along the whole length of his aching cock.

As if sensing his need, Caitlin drew him in farther, sucking and licking. She curled her hand around the base of his shaft, stroking up as she sucked, feeding his length into her sweet mouth. He gloried in the sensation, watching his cock sliding between her plump lips.

Caitlin glanced up at him, her eyes flashing green, her lips curving into a sensual smile around his turgid flesh. It was just like his fantasy, just what he'd been picturing every time he touched himself, ever since he saw her going down on Jeremy a month—god, was it only a month?—before.

The fulfillment of his erotic fantasy was almost more than Jack could take. A familiar tingling in his balls warned him he was very close to coming—too close. Jack didn't want this to be over yet.

He took his hands out of Caitlin's hair and gently disengaged his cock from her mouth. "My turn," he said when she looked up at him questioningly. "I didn't get a chance to finish earlier."

Caitlin nodded obediently, allowing Jack to guide her backward, easing her down on the bed. She slid toward the far side so there would be room for Jack.

Jeremy stood, grabbed a pillow and handed it to Caitlin. "Thanks," she said, slipping the pillow under her head, smiling at her boyfriend. "My pleasure," Jeremy replied. He pushed his jeans down, yanked his t-shirt over his head and added his clothes to the growing pile on the floor. Then, clad only in his impressively tented plaid cotton boxers, he climbed back on the bed, sitting against the wall next to Caitlin. She reached for him, smiling, and he took her hand, cradling it in his.

Jack felt a wave of loneliness momentarily overwhelm his lust. This was a fantasy come true, and he was going to remember it—and jerk off over it—for the rest of his life. But it would be over all too soon. Jeremy and Caitlin would still have each other, and he'd have...what? Whatever he'd had with Leanne, with the other girls before her—even with Angela—it didn't even begin to touch this.

"Jack?" Caitlin was gazing up at him, her expression troubled. "You okay?"

"I'm great," Jack said, forcing himself to smile at her. He wasn't going to let anything ruin this—especially if it would never happen again.

He kneeled on the bed, between Caitlin's legs, and leaned down, kissing her bellybutton. She jumped, apparently ticklish there. "Sorry," Jack murmured. He kissed his way lower 'til he felt the short, reddish hairs brush his lips. Then he stretched out on his stomach, gently lifting Caitlin's legs over his shoulders.

He glanced up briefly. Caitlin was staring down at him, cheeks flushed, eyes wide with longing. Jeremy was watching too, his face also reddened, a vein pulsing in his temple like the night on the train. They were still holding hands.

Then Jack spread Caitlin's folds gently apart and lowered himself for a long, loving taste. She tensed beneath him, quivering. Jack licked all around her swollen pink opening, savoring her unique flavor. He darted his tongue inside her—relishing her gasp—and then licked his way higher, finding her clit. He circled it a few times with his tongue, then dove in deeper. He drew the little bud into his mouth and sucked firmly, while still flicking it gently with the tip of his tongue.

Caitlin's gasps turned into sharper cries. She must have let go of Jeremy—both of her hands were now fisted in Jack's hair. "Oh please, Jack, please!" she begged.

Jack shifted slightly left, freeing his right hand, still using his left to hold her open for him. He sucked Caitlin's clit harder, probing with his fingers until he found her opening. He pressed two fingers inside the slick cleft and she cried out wordlessly, her pussy squeezing tightly around him.

"Don't stop," Caitlin cried breathlessly, her hips bucking helplessly against him. "Like that, just like that, I'm so—ohh…"

Jack kept sucking and licking, his cheek muscles starting to burn, and kept pumping his fingers rapidly. Caitlin was coming, coming hard. Her voice had dissolved into wordless moans. Her thighs were squeezing his shoulders, her hips thrusting up at him. Her pussy clamped impossibly tight on his fingers, throbbing and pulsing around him.

When the spasms finally eased, Jack pulled back, relaxing his aching mouth and sliding his fingers out of Caitlin's pussy. As horny as he still was, desperately craving his own orgasm, he felt immensely gratified to have brought Caitlin pleasure.

"How was that?" he asked her. He sat up and wiped his mouth.

"Incredible," Caitlin said breathlessly. Her eyes were wide, bottomless, as mysterious as ever. "Now," she said, reaching for Jack, trying to pull him to her. "I need you, Jack, please."

A tearing noise interrupted Jack's wonderment at Caitlin's sensual pleas, and he looked around. Jeremy, ripping open the box of condoms, met his gaze. "I forgot to mention, she's totally insatiable," he teased. "Better get this on quick." He held out a plastic-wrapped square to Jack.

Jack stared, momentarily stunned. He knew what they'd planned, and he knew what he wanted. But somehow, deep down, he hadn't believed this moment would actually come. That he would actually get to make love to Caitlin. To his best friend's girlfriend.

"Here," Caitlin said. She snatched the package out of Jeremy's hand, tore it open and reached for Jack. The feel of her urgent hands on his cock, rolling the condom over the head and down the shaft, brought him crashing back to reality.

"Whoa, babe," Jeremy said, eyes twinkling. "Impatient much?"

"I need it," Caitlin said to both of them. Her tone suggested she was teasing, but her eyes were snapping green fire and she was tugging Jack toward her desperately. "I need a cock inside me right now." Her hot green gaze zeroed in on Jack alone. "Please, Jack."

He smiled shakily back. "If you insist," he said. Then he grasped his cock, lined it up with her moist opening and slid himself inside.

Somebody moaned. Jack wasn't sure if it was Caitlin or himself. She was hot, wet and impossibly tight. "Is that okay?" Jack gasped. He didn't want to hurt her.

"No, it's not okay," Caitlin moaned, and Jack froze, ready to withdraw. "It's amazing," she corrected. She lifted her legs, wrapping them around Jack's waist, drawing him to her. "Now please fuck me. Hard." She arched her hips in emphasis, clutching at Jack's chest with desperate fingers.

Jack was stunned, incredibly aroused by Caitlin's blunt words, her wanton lust. Obediently he lowered himself on top of her, bracing his weight with his elbows, and began pumping his hips, driving his cock into her in hard, sharp thrusts.

Caitlin's head was thrown back, eyes closed, her breath escaping in soft, mewling gasps. Never mind how incredible it felt to have his cock buried inside her at last; it was unbelievably exciting for Jack to see her like this, to know he was the cause of her pleasure.

"My god," Jeremy said beside them. "That is so hot." He had one hand on his crotch, not stroking his cock, but squeezing steadily through his boxers at the base of his shaft. Trying not to come, Jack knew. "I'm not sure I can hold on much longer," Jeremy added.

Caitlin's eyes flew open. "Jeremy, please," she said, alarmed. "I need you to fuck me too."

"I will, babe," Jeremy assured her. "Believe me, I will." He stretched out on his side and kissed Caitlin, then worked his way lower to suckle her breasts, which were bouncing with every thrust of Jack's pelvis. At first Jack was annoyed, wanting Caitlin all to himself in this moment. But her moans increased under Jeremy's attentions, and he had to admit it was exciting for him as well, to see her getting even more worked up.

"Do that thing," Jeremy said around the nipple in his mouth. "Jack will love it."

"What thing?" Jack panted. Then he groaned as Caitlin's already tight pussy suddenly got even tighter. She clenched her muscles around him, drawing him in, gripping his cock so hard he could barely move it anymore.

"Holy shit," Jack gasped, fighting for control. He was already close, and this heightened sensation threatened to drive him right over the edge.

Jeremy chuckled at his words and at the expression on Jack's face. "I know, right?" he said. "She's incredible."

"Yeah," Jack panted, polysyllabic words utterly beyond him now. "God yes."

Jeremy backed up slightly, and Jack lowered himself again, kissing Caitlin hungrily. She kissed back, and reached down to grab his ass, using her grip to pull him even more tightly against her. "I'm so close, Jack," she panted. "Please."

"What do you want me to do?" he asked. "You name it, it's yours."

"Harder," Caitlin said immediately. "Just fuck me, as hard as you can."

So Jack did. He raised himself up slightly and gripped the backs of Caitlin's thighs just above her knees. She pulled them apart and back willingly, until her knees were on either side of her chest. Bracing himself by his grip on her thighs, Jack pistoned his cock in and out of Caitlin's pussy with all the force he could muster.

Beside him he saw Jeremy tense, reaching out a cautioning hand, alarmed that it would be too much for the petite woman. But as Caitlin's cries rose, clearly indicating her pleasure, he relaxed once more.

Jack never wanted this to end, but he wasn't sure how much longer he could hold out. He was both relieved and saddened when Caitlin's cries turned to breathless gasps, and her pussy began to pulse in waves around his cock, signaling her orgasm at last.

The additional sensations on his already hypersensitive cock pushed him irretrievably over the edge. He felt his balls tightening, his cock swelling. He realized he was groaning aloud. "Caitlin, oh my god," he cried as he came. He felt the thick jets of fluid spurting out of his cock, his muscles spasming, helpless. "Caitlin," he said one more time. Then his muscles gave out and he sprawled on top of her, utterly spent.

Jeremy watched as Jack went down on Caitlin, fighting the almost unbearable urge to stroke his own cock. He knew if he started touching himself, he was done. He felt like a total deviant even thinking this, but watching his girlfriend having sex with his best friend was the most exciting thing he had ever seen.

He had a condom ready for Jack, knowing from past experience that as soon as Caitlin had one orgasm, she'd be desperate for another. Jeremy had expected to be at least slightly apprehensive when they made love, when the moment actually came that his girlfriend had another man's cock inside her. But he wasn't jealous or angry at all—just more turned-on than he'd ever been in his life.

He tried to hold himself back, to let Jack and Caitlin have this moment together, but he couldn't help kissing Caitlin, suckling and fondling her breasts. He was pleased by Jack's reaction when Caitlin did her special trick, squeezing him tightly with her internal muscles. The first time Caitlin had done that to him, he'd come immediately, overwhelmed. He was more used to it now, but it always brought him to the brink.

The only bad moment for him came when Jack, taking Caitlin's lust-filled pleas to heart, began pounding her more forcefully than the larger man had ever dared to do. Jeremy was alarmed, certain that Jack's powerful thrusts would hurt the tiny redhead. But to his surprise, she gave every impression of loving it, if her blissful cries and rapturous expression were any indication.

He watched intently as Caitlin orgasmed again, followed closely by Jack himself. Again he watched with some trepidation as the smaller man did something Jeremy would never allow himself to do—he collapsed, spent, on top of Caitlin. She didn't struggle to push him off though, and Jeremy forced himself to relax. His dick was throbbing desperately, and all he could think about was being inside Caitlin, but he made himself wait, giving Jack a moment to recover. Anyway, he had a hunch that Caitlin would make the next move herself at any moment.

Jack stirred at last, kissing Caitlin tenderly before lifting himself off her. He grasped his deflating cock with one hand, holding the condom in place as he withdrew from Caitlin's pussy, then collapsed on his side next to Caitlin. "My god," he said. "That was incredible." Slowly, reverently, as if he couldn't believe she was real, Jack put out his hand and laid it on Caitlin's breast.

"It sure was," Caitlin said, sounding reverent herself. She smiled at Jack, but when Jeremy moved, getting to his knees, she turned immediately to him.

Jeremy smiled at her as he pushed his boxers down, freeing one knee at a time and then kicking the plaid shorts off the bed. "Ready for more?" he asked suggestively.

"Yes please," Caitlin said immediately. She reached for him with both arms and legs, drawing him down toward her.

Jeremy knelt between Caitlin's thighs. He lined up his cock with her pussy, flushed red and dripping wet, and then pushed himself inside.

"Oh my god," he said, freezing with his dick halfway in. For a moment he was afraid he might come right then. Caitlin was still wonderfully tight, but after fucking Jack she was hotter and wetter than Jeremy had ever felt her before. He wondered fleetingly how much wetter still she would be if Jack hadn't used a condom, if he had come inside her. Jeremy thought the idea—of fucking a woman filled with another man's cum—should disgust him, but it didn't. It sounded really hot, actually. He fought for control—he had to hold on 'til Caitlin came at least one more time.

Jeremy took a deep breath and then locked his elbows, holding himself above Caitlin as he began to pump his cock into her slick tunnel. Caitlin moaned wordlessly. She wrapped her legs around his waist, as she had done with Jack, and put her hands on his torso, running her fingertips through the sparse brown hair on his chest.

Beside him, Jack pulled the condom off, tossed it in the garbage can beside the bed and cleaned himself with a handful of tissues from the bedside table. They went in the garbage too. Then he stretched out beside Caitlin and Jeremy once more, watching them avidly.

"Harder, Jeremy, please," Caitlin begged. She unwound her legs from his waist and snaked them up under his arms and onto his shoulders.

"Wow," Jack said admiringly. "Flexible."

"Mmm," Caitlin responded incoherently.

Jeremy sat up a bit, reaching down to lift Caitlin's hips. Jack, catching on, grabbed another pillow and slid it under her rear end, raising her up a bit higher. "Thanks, partner," Jeremy said. Then he bent forward again, bracing his hands on the bed on either side of Caitlin, and began to thrust harder.

"Yes," Caitlin said breathlessly. "Oh Jeremy, that's so good."

Jack slid closer to Caitlin, reaching out to cup her breast with one hand. She turned to him immediately, and he leaned down to kiss her. Caitlin responded hungrily, putting her arms around Jack's shoulders, pulling him closer.

"You like that, babe?" Jeremy said. He was loving it himself. Every time Jack pinched Caitlin's nipples, she unconsciously clenched her pussy muscles around Jeremy's cock. It felt amazing.

He leaned back a bit to give Jack more room, grasping Caitlin's hips to pull her against him with each thrust. Jack kissed his way down Caitlin's throat to her chest, exploring her breasts with his hands and his tongue. "You like fucking two guys at once?" Jeremy panted.

"Yes," Caitlin moaned. "Yes, oh god yes..." Then she arched her hips sharply, crying out, and Jeremy felt her muscles spasming gloriously all around his cock as she came for the third time.

He tried hard to hold on, but he just couldn't help it—he'd waited so long already. With a wordless cry, Jeremy came too, sending spurt after spurt of warm fluid into Caitlin's still-pulsing cunt.

Jeremy managed three more strokes, his whole body trembling with the pleasure shooting through his nerve endings. He had never come so hard in his life.

He pulled out slowly, tugged the pillow out from beneath Caitlin's hips and gently lowered her legs to the bed again. Then he collapsed beside her, breathing heavily.

"God," Caitlin said shakily after a moment. "That was incredible. Thank you both."

Jeremy said, "No problem," at the same moment Jack said, "Our pleasure." They both laughed. Jeremy turned on his side, meeting his best friend's eyes over Caitlin's heaving breasts. Jack had his head propped on one hand. He placed the other hand tentatively on Caitlin's stomach.

"Thank *you* both," Jack said quietly. "That was the most amazing experience I've ever had in my life. I'll never forget this."

Jeremy smiled. "I don't think we will either," he said.

"Definitely not," Caitlin agreed. She gave Jeremy a long, lingering kiss, then rolled on her other side, facing Jack. She kissed him too, pulling him against her, then stopped.

"What's this?" she teased, reaching down to stroke Jack's hardening cock, which was pressing against her hip. "You want more?"

Jack did want more. He didn't ever want this to end. But Caitlin wasn't his—he was acutely aware of that—and he wasn't the one calling the shots here. "Yeah, if you guys do," he admitted, trying to keep his tone light and playful. "I've had a bit of a dry spell here, don't forget."

"That's true," Jeremy said, laughing. He sat up, grabbed the box of tissues and cleaned himself up. "Guess we're lucky you didn't blow the end right off the condom."

"Speaking of which, could you get another one ready?" Caitlin asked her boyfriend, rolling to her knees.

"Are you sure?" Jack asked. She had taken quite a pounding already, from both of them.

Caitlin bent forward, her silky hair swirling around Jack's hips. He felt warm, wet pressure as she took the head of his cock into her mouth. She sucked it deep into her mouth once, slowly and deliberately, and then withdrew. "Yes," she said.

"Unh," Jack said as she went down on him again. His cock throbbed, fully hard once more, as Caitlin licked and sucked. Then she bent lower, lapping at his balls with the flat of her tongue while wrapping her hand around his shaft, stroking firmly.

Jack felt something poke his hand and he opened his eyes. He didn't remember closing them.

"Here," Jeremy said, pressing the condom into Jack's hand. He lay back down next to Caitlin.

"Thanks," Jack said hoarsely. Caitlin sat up, pushing thick waves of tousled hair back from her face. Jack tore open the package, took out the condom and rolled it onto his throbbing dick.

He held himself steady as Caitlin straddled him, impaling herself on his cock.

"Oh my god," Jack gasped, as Caitlin started rocking her hips. "You're so wet—that's fucking amazing."

Caitlin chuckled breathlessly. "You can thank Jeremy for that," she said.

"Oh right," Jack said. "Sloppy seconds." He didn't sound disgusted.

Jeremy laughed. "Technically, you're on thirds now," he pointed out, shaking his head. "Guy can't even count."

Caitlin smiled, shaking her head too. Trust Jeremy and Jack to keep teasing each other, even at a moment like this. She had been worried that their friendship would become awkward, or even end, if they went through with Jeremy's crazy plan. That was the one objection she'd felt comfortable discussing with Jeremy—her own feelings for Jack were a lot harder to articulate, and to share with her boyfriend. But Jeremy had assured her that nothing they did would change his relationship with his best friend. It looked like he'd been right about that.

Jack thrust his pelvis upward and gripped Caitlin's hips firmly, helping her move against him. Her breath quickened at the deliciously heightened pressure inside her. She rocked faster, and looked over at her boyfriend. Jeremy lay on his back watching them, a small smile on his face. He had his right hand wrapped around his rapidly growing cock, stroking it slowly but firmly.

Unconsciously, as she watched, Caitlin licked her lips.

"Go ahead," Jack invited, following Caitlin's gaze.

Jeremy got to his knees, and Caitlin bent forward and to the side, trying to suck his cock. The angle was awkward, though, and it was hard to keep bobbing her head and thrusting her hips at the same time. She sat back, smiling at her own ineptitude. "I'm not coordinated enough for this," she laughed.

Jack remembered the position Caitlin and Jeremy had been in the only other time he'd seen them in bed together — the moment, looking through the bedroom window, that had started this all. "I have an idea," he said. He patted Caitlin's thighs gently. "Hop off for a sec, okay?"

"Okay," she said. Jack held the condom in place as she pulled off him and backed up, waiting expectantly. Jack rolled awkwardly off the bed and stood up. "Why don't you kneel on the bed in front of Jeremy?" he suggested. "Then I can go behind you." Jeremy sat down and Caitlin moved obediently into position, getting to her hands and knees between Jeremy's spread legs. "That way," Jack continued, climbing up on the bed behind Caitlin, "Jeremy can have your mouth," he slipped a hand between Caitlin's legs, running it up and down her dripping slit. Caitlin whimpered and thrust back toward him, "and I can have this end," Jack finished. He leaned in and slid his cock back into Caitlin's quivering pussy.

The new position made Jack's cock rub against new places inside her, and Caitlin loved it. She spread her legs wide, arching her hips up. Jack gripped her ass and thrust into her firmly, setting a steady pace.

She looked at Jeremy. He was reclining against the wall, a couple of pillows stuffed behind his back, legs spread on either side of her. He was still slowly fisting his cock with one hand. With the other, he gently touched Caitlin's cheek. "Having fun, babe?" he asked huskily. His eyes, normally a deep brown, were now bottomless black pools of desire.

"Yes," Caitlin said fervently.

"Good," Jeremy smiled. He touched her lips gently, lowered his hand. Caitlin bent her head, stuck out her tongue and touched it lightly to the tip of his cock.

Jeremy tensed, his right hand slowing its movement. He let go of his cock, and Caitlin replaced his hand with hers. She stroked slowly, once, twice, then licked his cock, swirling her tongue around his hot shaft.

Jeremy's hands rose involuntarily to Caitlin's head, fingers sliding into her hair. He forced himself to relax, let go, drop his hands to his sides. But when Caitlin licked him lightly again, it was almost more than he could bear. "Please," he begged.

Caitlin drew back and looked up at him. Her breath was coming rapidly, her breasts heaving as Jack continued to thrust into her from behind. "Please what?" she asked.

"Please suck my dick," Jeremy said hoarsely. "Please, babe, I want it so bad."

Caitlin smiled. "Okay," she said. Then she bent forward once more. Gripping the base of his shaft firmly with her left hand, she drew Jeremy's cock deep into her mouth, sucking hard.

"Oh god!" Jeremy exclaimed. His hands clenched into fists at his sides. It took everything he had not to thrust up into Caitlin's mouth.

"Whoa," Jack said over Caitlin's shoulder. "That's really hot." Jack was incredibly turned-on, even more so than he had been earlier. To see his friends like this, exactly as they had been that night four weeks before—the night that he hadn't been able to get out of his head since—but to be part of the scene this time, fucking Caitlin himself as she sucked Jeremy's cock—was almost more than he could bear.

He pumped his hips harder, gripping Caitlin's waist to pull her firmly back against him with each thrust. "Yes," Caitlin moaned around Jeremy's cock. "God, Jack, that feels so good…"

"Good," he panted, thrusting even harder. Caitlin was whimpering steadily now, gobbling Jeremy's cock hungrily.

"Oh fuck," Jeremy said. His hands were in Caitlin's hair again, fingers twisted in the silky strands. His head fell back against the wall, eyes closed, face flushed red. "Fuck her hard, Jack, she loves it," he said raggedly. It was equally obvious that Jeremy loved the way Caitlin sucked cock when she was getting pounded hard.

"Mmm," Caitlin said around Jeremy's cock, obviously agreeing.

"You got it," Jack answered both of them. He began to pump even harder, slamming his cock into Caitlin's dripping wet cunt. Her cries of pleasure became even more frenzied around her mouthful of cock.

Jeremy came first. "Oh fuck," he gasped again. His hips bucked once, twice, and the cords stood out in his neck as every muscle in his body tensed in orgasm. The hot, salty liquid hit the back of Caitlin's tongue and she swallowed rapidly, still bobbing her mouth up and down on Jeremy's pulsing cock. Faintly she heard a high-pitched keening. She understood the sound was coming from her own throat, but she was powerless to control it. She thought she and Jack came at the same time—or at least, as her own orgasm washed over her, waves of ecstasy starting in her throbbing core and spreading into every part of her body, she was dimly aware of Jack's low-pitched groans behind her. His steady pace dissolved into frantic bucking. One last hard thrust, two, three, and the three of them collapsed together, utterly spent, in a jumbled heap on the bed.

Chapter Ten
∞

"Jesus," Jeremy gasped. He slid lower on the bed, putting his arm around Caitlin. "That was the most amazing sex I have ever had in my life."

"Ditto," Caitlin said shakily. She flopped over on her back, took Jeremy's hand on one side and reached out her other hand for Jack.

Jack peeled off the second condom, tossed it in the garbage can and lay back down. He took Caitlin's hand and kissed it. "Ditto," he repeated sincerely. "Thank you both again."

"You're very welcome," Caitlin said. She leaned over and planted a kiss, soft and sweet, on his lips.

"No problem," Jeremy said, then grinned. "We just had to try that once, you know?"

"Right," Jack said dully. "Yeah."

Once, he thought. *I never get to do this again.*

As that realization crashed down on him, Jack suddenly felt more alone than he had in years. Maybe ever. It didn't make any sense. He knew going in that this would be a one-time thing, and all he'd wanted was to finally get to have sex with Caitlin. Well, he had. And it was amazing. But now, he felt confused and bereft.

Jack sighed, sat up and began rooting around in the mess on the floor for his clothes.

He had his boxer briefs on and was just stepping into his jeans when they heard the front door of the apartment open and shut. He froze, staring at Jeremy and Caitlin, still cuddling naked on the bed.

"Shit!" Jeremy exclaimed, leaping up and grabbing his shorts. "It's Travis!"

They could hear Travis in the living room, calling out. "Guys? You home?"

Jack finished doing his jeans up and yanked his sweater over his head. "Go head him off, please," Jeremy said urgently, stepping into his own pants. Caitlin was putting on her undies. They were indeed boyshorts, Jack saw, in a bright bubblegum pink.

"Jack!" Jeremy repeated urgently, and Jack tore his gaze from Caitlin. "We can't let him walk in on this!"

"Okay," Jack said. He took a deep breath, and sneaked one more look—what he knew would be his last look, ever—at Caitlin's naked breasts. Then he opened the door and stepped out.

He found Travis in the kitchen, helping himself to a can of Kokanee. Travis didn't share his roommate's aversion to the brand. "Oh hey, Jack," Travis said. He held up the can. "This okay?"

"Yeah, help yourself," Jack said. He grabbed one for himself, popped the top and drained a third of it in a long swallow. He almost wished it was something harder. Getting totally oblivious seemed like a good idea all of a sudden.

"Talk about drowning our sorrows, eh?" Travis said, and Jack stared. Did Travis know what was going on?

"Man, that was brutal," Travis continued, shaking his head. "I really thought we were gonna come back in the third period, but that game misconduct was the last nail in the coffin."

"Right," Jack said, realizing at last that Travis was talking about the hockey game. The Oilers must have lost. "Yeah, that sucked."

Travis glanced around. "Where are Jeremy and Caitlin?"

Jack took another long swig of beer before replying. He wasn't sure what to say. "They're, uh…they were just…"

Thankfully, at that moment Jeremy's bedroom door opened, and Jeremy emerged, fully clothed.

"Hey, Travis," he said, walking into the kitchen. He grabbed a bottle of Molson from the fridge.

"Where's Caitlin?" Travis asked. He was looking curiously from Jack to Jeremy, and Jack wondered if he had any idea what they'd been up to.

"She went to bed early," Jeremy said. "Headache."

"Well, I can't blame her," Travis said, shaking his head mournfully. "That third period gave me a headache too."

"What?" Jeremy started to say, then caught himself. He met Jack's eyes, looked away. "Oh right," he said instead. "Um, yeah...that sucked."

Jack finished his beer, tossed the empty can in the box Travis and Jeremy used for returnables, and pushed off from the counter. If Caitlin was in bed with a "headache" he wouldn't get a chance to say goodbye to her, and he had no urge to sit around with Travis and Jeremy pretending to rehash a game he hadn't seen. He just wanted to go home.

"Well, I'm gonna head'er," he said. He picked up his case of beer, still more than half full, and turned to head for the door. "Thanks," he said to Jeremy. He couldn't meet his friend's eyes.

"Thanks for the beer," Travis said before Jeremy could say anything.

"No problem," Jack replied. Both Travis and Jeremy followed as he headed through the living room to the entryway.

"Here," Jeremy said, hands extended. Jack gave him the beer to hold while he put on his coat and shoes. He realized he'd left his socks on the floor in Jeremy's room. Well, there was no way to get them now. He slid his bare feet into his runners and stood up, holding his hands out for the beer.

"Well, have a good night," Travis said, oblivious to Jack's swiftly darkening mood. He clapped Jack on the shoulder, and then sat down on his ugly recliner.

"Thanks," Jack said quietly, as Jeremy gave him back the beer. "For everything."

"Thank *you*," Jeremy returned, equally quietly. He half-turned, glancing at Travis over his shoulder. Travis had un-muted the TV and was surfing channels, not looking their way.

Jeremy turned back to Jack. "Are we cool?" he asked.

Jack forced himself to raise his head and meet his best friend's eyes. He didn't think he flinched. "Yeah," he said. "We're cool."

"Okay, good," Jeremy smiled. He reached past Jack and opened the door for his friend. "Give me a call in a day or so — we can go get something to eat or whatever."

"Yeah," Jack said flatly. "Sounds good. Bye." Then he left, and didn't look back.

* * * * *

Jack winced, the flickering light from the television slicing through his brain like a scalpel. He hadn't been this hung over in years. Going home and drinking the rest of his case of beer had probably been a very bad idea, he reflected, sipping gingerly from a glass of water.

But he hadn't known how else to deal with the jumble of feelings that had threatened to overtake him as he drove home, alone. He had drunk himself into oblivion last night, and now, as soon as he felt well enough to shower and leave the house, he planned to go looking for the blonde from lunch the other day, or some other girl — any other girl — to take his mind off things again. Soon, he hoped, he could just lock all these crazy new thoughts in the back of his mind and get back to his life, the way it had been. Which was the way it was supposed to be...wasn't it?

The phone shrilled suddenly, and Jack winced again. On second thought, he probably wouldn't be up to going anywhere anytime soon. He squinted at the display to see who it was, then thumbed the "talk" button. "Hey, Scott."

Scott laughed at Jack's low, ragged voice. "Jack, what happened? You sound like shit."

Jack chuckled wryly. "Thanks, man," he said. "I watched the game with Jeremy and Caitlin last night, and I had too much to drink." That was all true, as far as it went...he had just left a few things out.

"Oh yeah? How was that?"

"We lost," Jack said. He hoped Scott wouldn't want to know more than that.

"Too bad," Scott said. "How are Jeremy and Caitlin?"

Nope, no such luck. "Fine," Jack said heavily.

There was a pause. Jack didn't know what Scott was thinking. He himself was trying to force all thought of Caitlin—heaving breasts, wide eyes, breathless gasps—out of his mind. It was hard.

Scott's next question didn't help at all.

"What does she look like again?" Scott asked slowly. "I forget."

Not sure where this was going, and still trying to resist the memories playing insistently through his head, Jack tried to describe Caitlin as succinctly as he could. "Five foot three or so, pale skin with a few freckles, long wavy red hair, bright green eyes, full lips, amazing boobs, incredible ass." He thought for a moment, wondering if he'd left out anything important. Anything important he could share with Scott, that is. "Strong hands, crooked smile."

"Aha," his former partner said, tone laced with significance.

"What's that supposed to mean?" Jack was confused.

"Did you just hear yourself?" Scott said. "Eye color, height and strong hands, for pete's sake?"

"What? She does have strong hands," Jack said defensively. "For a girl."

He could almost hear Scott rolling his eyes. "Jack, when you told me about Leanne a few weeks ago, you couldn't even remember if she was a blonde or a brunette. And the one before that—Robin? Renee?"

"Rebecca," Jack said. Or had it been Rachel? He couldn't remember.

"You never described her in such detail either," Scott insisted. "You know what this means?"

"No," Jack said tersely. He wasn't sure he wanted to know what Scott thought.

"You need a girl like this Caitlin," Scott said. "That's what you're really looking for."

Jack would have rolled his own eyes, but the mere thought of doing so made his head pound sickeningly. "If you say so, Dr. Phil," he muttered.

"I'm serious," Scott said. "Look, I know you have trust issues. Anybody would, after what Angela did to you. But you can't let her ruin the rest of your life, bro. You need to try."

"Try what, exactly?" Jack asked. Dammit, he'd *tried* with Angela, and it had gotten him nowhere. Worse than nowhere.

"Try letting a girl in. Find a girl you really like and then lower that playboy facade enough so she can meet the real you. So you guys can connect. About something you have in common, something real."

Christ, Scott really did sound like Dr. Phil, or some touchy-feely emotional counselor, anyway. Jack wanted to throw back some clever—and safe—retort. Maybe ask Scott exactly when he'd gotten in touch with his feminine side, and what kind of dresses she wore.

But as he pondered his friend's words despite himself, Jack found himself remembering the hockey game, with Caitlin at his side. When he'd learned how much it meant to her to hear *O, Canada* sung at Rexall Place. The same way it meant so much to him.

"It's worth it, pal, trust me," Scott was saying earnestly. "Once you find a girl like that, that you connect with on every level—mind, body and soul—you'll never want to let her go. Believe me."

Jack squeezed his eyes shut against the moisture that suddenly welled up. Damn, his hangover was relentless.

"So quit picking up all these bimbos in bars and give yourself a chance. A chance to meet *her*. The girl of your dreams. She's out there, pal, I just know it."

Now Jack's throat, already dry from his hangover, drew painfully tight. He wasn't sure he could speak. What was he supposed to say? *Yeah, I know it too, buddy*, he thought despairingly. *She's out there, all right. And yeah, she's the girl of my dreams. But here's the catch—she's already in love with my best friend.*

"Look," Scott continued when Jack didn't speak. "That's another reason for you to come out here, you know. First, it would probably be good for you to get away from there, away from your painful memories. Of Angela."

Jack still said nothing, but Scott's comment really hit home. Not about Angela—somewhere in the last month or so, he seemed to have finally gotten over what she'd done to him. He could remember her betrayal now with a sense of detachment, or at least a sense of distance. But now he had new painful memories to get away from. In fact, after spending one night with Caitlin, and knowing he could never have that again, Jack wasn't sure he could stand to be around her again. Maybe he *should* just leave.

"Second," Scott went on, "Toronto's a lot bigger than Edmonton. There are a lot more women to choose from. Maybe your girl is out here, just waiting for you. There's a cute redhead in dispatch, for example, if that's what floats your boat now. I'm pretty sure she's single. And if not, like I say, there are plenty of other fish in the sea."

"Yeah," Jack said finally, when Scott fell silent, waiting for a response. It seemed like too much work to explain to Scott that he wasn't just looking for a girl—any girl—with red hair. "Maybe."

"Really?" Scott sounded excited. "That's the first time you've said anything other than 'no'…am I finally wearing you down?" He laughed.

"I don't know," Jack said. His instinctive reaction was to say no, like he always did—he didn't want to leave Edmonton. He liked the city, he liked his job and he liked his friends. How could he move away from Mike, or Travis or Brandon? Or Jeremy. And Caitlin.

At that thought his mind recoiled. He didn't want to leave…but could he stand to be around Caitlin and Jeremy, watching them together, remembering what he'd had a single taste of, but knowing he could never truly have what they shared? He'd thought last night that he could take this, that he could just have some fun and then go on with his life. But now he realized he'd been completely wrong. Jack couldn't stand to even think about what they'd done, about what he would never have again. And yet he couldn't stop thinking about it either. All he knew was that he couldn't go on if this kept hurting as much as it hurt now. If he did what Scott wanted, made a fresh start in a new city far away, would he feel better? Could he just forget about Jeremy? And Caitlin?

"Maybe," he said again. "I'll think about it, okay?"

"Okay," Scott said cheerfully. "In the meantime, maybe you should go back to bed. You don't sound so good."

"I don't feel so good," Jack admitted. And it was true—though his hangover was only one of his problems.

"Well, call me later then," Scott said. "When you've had time to think about it."

"Will do," Jack said heavily. "Bye."

He put the phone on the nightstand and lay back carefully, putting one arm across his stinging eyes as if to shut out the world.

* * * * *

Caitlin forced herself not to start asking questions until Jeremy had kicked his shoes off, grabbed a drink from the fridge and stretched out on her couch. Then she couldn't hold back any longer.

"Well?" she said, curling up on the red leather Ikea Klippan sofa next to her boyfriend. "How is he?"

Jeremy sighed. "I don't know, Cait. I really don't. He says he's fine but...I don't know."

Caitlin stared at him, upset and confused. "But...did you talk to him? I mean, you guys just spent twelve hours together—you must have talked, right?"

"I tried," Jeremy said wistfully. "He wouldn't open up. He says everything's cool, everything's fine. He said to say hi to you."

"But?" Caitlin added in response to Jeremy's worried tone.

"But," Jeremy continued doubtfully, "he's shutting me out. He won't look me in the eye. We don't joke around like we used to. Something's bugging him." He clenched his fists in frustration. "I just don't know what it is."

Caitlin leaned against his shoulder. Jeremy put an arm around her, and she leaned in even more, wrapping her arms around his wide torso. "Jeremy," Caitlin said in a small voice. "Did we make a mistake?"

She pressed her face into Jeremy's chest, afraid she was going to start crying. She'd been having a hard enough time struggling with her own feelings since she'd had sex with Jeremy and Jack the week before. She thought Jeremy was working through some issues too. She caught him looking at her sometimes since that night, with a thoughtful, almost worried expression on his face. And the one time they'd made love since then, it had felt great, but they'd both been unusually subdued. As if there was a ghost in the room, watching them, coming between them. Caitlin was afraid to ask Jeremy what he'd been thinking, afraid to find out if his feelings toward her had changed since that night.

And now it seemed that their friendship with Jack was in danger too. Would nothing the three of them had had survive the terrible, wonderful night they'd spent together?

"I don't know," Jeremy finally answered the question Caitlin had almost forgotten she'd asked. "But I'm going to find out."

"How?" Caitlin asked.

"Well," Jeremy said, "For starters, Brandon got us all tickets to Captain Tractor on Saturday night. Jack too."

"Hey, that's great," Caitlin said. Captain Tractor was an Edmonton-based indie folk-rock band with a heavy Celtic influence, and a favorite among their circle of friends. Jeremy had all their albums, so she'd heard most of their music before. But she hadn't had the opportunity to see them play live yet.

"You think he'll come?" she asked. Jack loved Captain Tractor, but he also seemed determined to avoid both her and Jeremy these days.

"Brandon said he's not going to take no for an answer," Jeremy assured her.

"Good," Caitlin said. "So, if Jack still won't talk to you the rest of the week, at least we'll get a chance to see him at the concert. So maybe we'll get an idea what's going on."

"That's the plan," Jeremy confirmed. He stood up, scooping Caitlin up in his arms, and then set her gently down on the floor. "In the meantime," he continued, "we have a lot of work to do."

"Work?" Caitlin asked. "What kind of work?"

Jeremy smiled, pulling a handful of CDs out of the backpack he'd brought with him. "We need to make sure you know all the words to *Last Saskatchewan Pirate*, *Up the Hill* and other very important songs."

"Oh," Caitlin laughed. "Okay, then."

As Jeremy loaded *East of Edson* into the living room CD player, Caitlin deliberately pushed her worries out of her mind. Surely everything would be okay. And if it wasn't, well, they'd deal with it on Saturday.

* * * * *

Jack sipped his beer and fiddled with his French fries. He wasn't really hungry, but eating—or pretending to eat—gave him something to do with his hands. He was starting to think that coming to the concert was a big mistake.

He looked around the crowded pub, pretending to admire the scenery while avoiding his friends' concerned or confused gazes. They were in Dewey's, the largest bar on the University of Alberta campus. Jack wasn't sure when they'd changed the name. The last time he'd been there, it had been called the Power Plant—so named because the large brick structure was originally built to house the university's main power generator. At some point—Jack wasn't sure when, at least twenty years before—a new power station had been built, and the old power plant was converted to a popular bar and restaurant, serving cheap but tasty lunches and dinners during the week, and various forms of live entertainment on the weekends.

He checked his watch surreptitiously. Ten minutes until the band was supposed to start playing, and probably at least two hours until he could go home.

Jack sighed. Normally he'd have been excited to see Captain Tractor. They were one of his favorite bands and they always put on an amazing show. They had a kind of raw energy that few performers could match, and they were incredibly talented, with most band members playing multiple instruments as well as taking turns singing lead. But being so close to Caitlin — she was directly across the table from him — was almost more than he could bear.

Jack felt horribly confused. He'd thought the past week hadn't been so bad. Things at work were a bit awkward at first between him and Jeremy, but by the third day of their shift they'd been talking and laughing together — just like old times, he thought. He'd finally managed to stop thinking about that night in Jeremy's apartment. With Caitlin. He'd thought he was handling things fine.

He hadn't even hooked up with that blonde from Badass Jack's, or any other girl for that matter. Jack had decided Scott was right about one thing at least — it was time to stop picking up hot but one-dimensional girls for short-term fun, and start looking for someone he could have a real relationship with. And he'd about decided to tell Scott he was sorry, but he didn't want to move to Toronto. He didn't want to disappoint his former partner, but he didn't think he wanted to leave his job, his friends and his home behind. And he should be able to find a girl he wanted to be with in Edmonton if he put his mind to it, right?

Then he'd walked into Dewey's, and had seen Caitlin standing there with Jeremy and their other friends, and suddenly the world fell out from beneath his feet.

Images and sensations had washed over Jack, drowning him in memories of that one glorious night. His face had burned red as he remembered how Caitlin had tasted, the silky feel of her skin, the sounds she made when she came. His face was burning and he could only hope he looked and sounded normal as he said hello to his friends. After greeting everyone else first, he'd given Jeremy a quick hug but couldn't bring himself to touch Caitlin. She'd looked up at him, hurt and puzzled, as he'd backed away before hugging her, but Jack couldn't trust himself to embrace her at all. He was afraid if he did, he'd never let go.

Jack dragged his mind away from his painful thoughts, trying to focus on the conversation around him. From the sounds of things, Danika was describing some expensive new clothing line to Caitlin and Kristy.

"Do they come in petite?" Caitlin was asking.

"I don't think so," Danika said. "It's too bad, really—they're losing half their potential market that way."

"I always have a hard time finding clothes that fit," Caitlin said. "It's not just that I'm short—I'm not skinny either."

"Well, I envy you there," the tall, lanky Kristy said wistfully. "Wish I had your curves."

"She sure *is* curvy," Jeremy interjected admiringly, leaning down to give his girlfriend an affectionate squeeze. "I love that."

Caitlin smiled at Jeremy, giving him a quick but loving kiss. "Good," she said contentedly.

Jack didn't say so, but he loved it too. Most of his previous girlfriends, like Leanne and Angela, had been tall and rail thin. He didn't mind that look. They were classy, elegant and sophisticated, like models. But Caitlin looked amazing too—she was voluptuous and sexy, soft and beautiful and fun.

And belonged to his best friend.

Jack went back to staring morosely at his plate.

To his relief, the lights dimmed only moments later, and Captain Tractor mounted the stage to raucous applause. They opened with *Someday*, one of their most popular live tunes.

"Come on!" Kristy urged, bouncing up out of her seat. "Let's go dance!"

The others stood eagerly, and Jack rose as well. He joined his friends on the crowded dance floor—which was just an open space in front of the stage—glad to not have to talk, and glad for the chance to burn off some of his stress in physical activity.

The band played several of his favorites, including *Another Drinking Song* and *Frozen Puck to the Head*. When *The Bastard of Strathcona County*, another of their most popular live songs, began, the dancing changed. Complete strangers were clasping elbows, whirling each other about in a half-circle, letting go and then reaching out to grab the next person's arm with their opposite elbow. Jack had no idea what this kind of dancing was called—something Irish, maybe?—but it happened at every Captain Tractor concert, whenever they played a song with an appropriate beat.

He found himself swinging around a girl with a blonde pixie haircut, and then a tall skinny guy with brown hair and brown skin. Danika came next, laughing, then Brandon. Then Caitlin. As they hooked their bent arms together, Jack felt his elbow press against Caitlin's breast through her fitted t-shirt. Her eyes met his and for a moment he was looking into the same green fire that had blazed when she'd begged Jack to put his cock inside her for the first time.

Then the next person whirled Caitlin away in a sweep of red hair. Jack found himself swinging Jeremy around next. His best friend met his eyes steadily too, with concern and also, Jack thought, some kind of warning or censure. Jack followed Jeremy's gaze as he swung around again. First Jeremy looked at Brandon and Danika, dancing beside them, then his eyes flicked to Kristy and Mike. Then Jeremy grabbed Caitlin as she spun back from the opposite side of the dance floor. Grinning, he swung her up in the air. Caitlin laughed delightedly, threw her arms around his neck and kissed him.

Jack forced himself to keep dancing, but all he wanted to do was run away. The unspoken warning he thought he'd seen in Jeremy's eyes was all too bitterly clear—don't let anyone see there's anything strange going on! He remembered Jeremy's panicked exclamation when Travis had come home the other night. *We can't let him walk in on this*, Jeremy had insisted.

And with that, the inarticulate hope—that had begun to form when Caitlin looked at him in apparent longing—died, leaving nothing but a bleak emptiness in Jack's chest. He shouldn't kid himself—there was no hope for any real future between him and Caitlin. She belonged to Jeremy, and she always would. Even if Jack didn't start dating someone else, what he could possibly hope for from Jeremy and Caitlin? At best they'd throw him a pity fuck once in a while. And then he would have to sneak out, hiding his feelings from everyone. Never letting anything show, in front of anyone. And having to mutely endure Caitlin and Jeremy's real and open love for each other.

Jack knew he couldn't handle that. It would kill him to see that, all the time, inescapably, and know it was forever beyond his reach.

It was killing him now.

He whirled around, eyes burning, throat constricting, and bolted for the exit.

* * * * *

"Jack!" Caitlin burst out of the double doors and down the stairs, not caring that she was shouting, aware of Jeremy two paces behind her. She didn't know where Jack was going, but something was terribly wrong—that was obvious. She had to know what.

"Jack!" Behind her, Jeremy echoed Caitlin's shout. Jack was walking fast toward the parking lot, not turning back. Jeremy lengthened his stride, his longer legs catching him up to his partner. He put a hand on Jack's shoulder and spun him around. "Jack, for god's sake! What is it?"

"Nothing!" Jack said. He faced them at last but wouldn't look either of them in the face. "I just...had to get out of there," he said lamely.

"Jack, please," Caitlin said. She stepped closer to Jack but hesitated, afraid to touch him. "What's going on? Tell us, please," she begged.

Jack let his breath out in an explosive sigh, ran a hand through his black curls, but said nothing.

"Look," Jeremy began uncertainly. "If you're upset about what happened the other night—"

"And what exactly happened?" Jack interrupted viciously. "What would you call it?"

Jeremy took a step backward, alarmed by the venom in his best friend's voice. "You know what happened," he said. He glanced around. There were a few people in sight, but none of them appeared to be listening to their heated conversation. "When we had sex with Caitlin," he said quietly. "It's obvious you're upset about it. Just tell us what you want. If you want to pretend it never happened—"

"Right," Jack interrupted bitterly. "That's the solution."

"Well then," Jeremy scrubbed a hand across his face. He looked helplessly at Caitlin, who looked back with equal helplessness. "What do you think—"

"Honestly, it doesn't matter," Jack said. He took a deep breath. "I'm moving to Toronto. Scott's been asking me, and I'm going to do it. I'm going."

Caitlin and Jeremy stared at him, stunned. They both opened their mouths to speak, but another voice spoke first.

"What's up, guys?" Mike was coming down the steps toward them, Kristy a few steps behind, both with concerned looks on their faces.

"Did you know about this?" Jeremy demanded.

"About what?" Mike was clearly puzzled, looking from Jeremy to Jack.

"I didn't tell him yet," Jack said heavily. He hadn't meant to tell anybody anything—he thought he hadn't even made up his mind to go. But now he realized there was no other way out. He didn't want to leave, but he couldn't bear to stay either. He had no choice. "I'm moving to Toronto."

Mike looked as stunned as Caitlin felt. She watched helplessly as he stammered, asking Jack for more details. Caitlin's thoughts were racing too fast for her to follow what Mike and Jack were saying. *No!* she wanted to shout. In that moment the dangerous feeling that had been slowly building inside her, unnamed, unacknowledged, burst into full bloom, and she knew it for what it was. *Don't go,* Caitlin wanted to beg. *Don't leave, Jack – I love you!*

But she held her tongue, afraid. Not afraid of what Jack would say, or even of what Mike or Kristy would think. She was afraid of how Jeremy – the other man she loved equally – would react.

Caitlin knew Jeremy had enjoyed letting her play with Jack, that he had gotten off on watching his best friend fuck her. But she knew also that Jeremy had felt firmly in control of the situation – that he only meant for it to happen once. That had been a key point in his argument, the night he'd first proposed a threesome – that Jack would only be available, or interested, for one night, and that nothing would ever happen between them again.

How would he feel if he knew Caitlin not only wanted to have sex with Jack again but that she loved him? Truly loved him, the way she loved Jeremy himself?

Caitlin desperately wanted to say something, wanted to stop Jack from leaving them – from leaving her. But what would be the consequences if she did? Caitlin knew, as they all did, that love and long-term commitment were simply not things that Jack did. So, if she confessed her feelings for Jack, would she lose both of the men she loved?

Caitlin forced her attention back to the conversation going on before her. Mike was shaking his head slowly, and Jack seemed to be explaining – but heavily, hopelessly. Nothing was changing. He meant what he said.

Jack scrubbed a hand across his face and took a step back, away from all of them. He looked at Mike and Kristy, and glanced at Jeremy, but wouldn't – or couldn't – look at Caitlin.

"Bye, guys," he said quietly. He turned and started walking away, slowly, but with determination. Not toward the bar, but in the opposite direction, toward the parking lot.

Jeremy lurched forward, as if wanting to go after Jack, but stopped, powerless, after two steps. Caitlin watched too, torn and helpless, as Jack walked away.

Chapter Eleven

ஐ

Jeremy sat in his car, his thoughts as chaotic and relentless as the snow swirling down outside. He hadn't felt this helpless, bewildered and blindsided since he'd accidentally pricked himself on that damn druggie's needle three years before, and spent two weeks in numb disbelief, waiting to find out if that single moment would forever change—or end—his life.

At least he could pinpoint the cause of that moment. Whether you called it bad luck, malicious intent by the addict or carelessness on his own part, he could follow the chain of events, make sense of what had happened.

There was no sense here. What had gone wrong? They'd been having a wonderful time over the past few weeks—or at least he and Caitlin had, and he thought Jack had too. He'd certainly been enjoying himself physically, through their gradually escalating exhibitionist games—no guy could fake that. Granted, Jack had been surprised and maybe, now that Jeremy really thought about it, a little hesitant when they'd invited him to have a threesome...but he'd said yes. And, again, had given every indication of enjoying himself immensely. It should have been fun—just some harmless, momentary fun—and dammit, that was what Jack was always looking for, wasn't it?

But then, somehow, for some reason Jeremy couldn't puzzle out, everything had gone horribly wrong. And the act that he'd meant to be a special gift to his best friend, an acknowledgment of how much Jack meant to him and to Caitlin, had instead somehow driven Jack away.

He wished desperately that Jack would just talk to him, explain what was on his mind, tell Jeremy what he needed to do to make everything okay again. Whatever it was, Jeremy would do it.

But ever since the night at Dewey's, Jack had traded shifts and swapped patrol cars around, all to avoid Jeremy. And he wouldn't talk to him outside of work either, didn't answer or return his calls. He hid in his room, claiming to be too busy packing for Toronto, when Jeremy, frustrated, showed up at his apartment.

Jeremy just didn't know what to do. Again he remembered the only other time he'd felt this lost, this afraid. Jack had been by his side then—he'd only gotten through that terrible experience because of his best friend. He couldn't lose Jack now. And he didn't think Jack really wanted to go to Toronto anyway. He remembered the look on Jack's face when he'd told them that he was going, the tone of his words when he broke the news. The slow, heavy way he had walked away. It wasn't the demeanor of a man following his dreams—it was the despair of a doomed man accepting his sentence.

Jeremy resolved to find out what was upsetting Jack. He would do whatever it took to get his best friend to stay.

Jeremy's cell phone rang, interrupting his troubled thoughts. He checked the display. It was Caitlin.

"Babe, you okay?" he said. He knew Caitlin was upset about the situation too. They'd talked about it constantly since Jack had dropped his bombshell about Toronto four days before. He'd thought once or twice that Caitlin was holding something back, watching her words carefully as they endlessly rehashed what had happened and where they might have irretrievably offended Jack. But he knew she was just as confused and unsure as he was.

"I'm fine," Caitlin said. "Any news?"

He knew she meant about Jack. "No," he sighed. "I think I'm going to try going over there again."

She knew he meant to Jack's apartment. "You think that'll work?" she asked. "He wouldn't talk to you last time."

"Well, he's going to talk to me this time," Jeremy said resolutely. "Mike's home. He's already unlocked the front door for me. And I'll break Jack's bedroom door down if I have to."

"Okay," Caitlin said. "I'll meet you there."

"Are you sure?" Jeremy asked. The half-assed plan he'd been formulating involved him sitting Jack down for a no-nonsense, man-to-man talk. Of course, he'd been trying to do just that for four days so far, and none of his attempts had worked.

"Yes, I'm sure," Caitlin said firmly. "Whatever the problem is, it started after we...after we were all together. I'm part of this too."

"Okay," Jeremy said. Caitlin was right. "Meet you there in twenty minutes."

* * * * *

Jack sat on his bed, staring listlessly at the boxes and piles of clothes scattered around his bedroom. He'd phoned Scott back the day after the concert. Scott was delighted that Jack was finally coming to Toronto, and he and Liz had eagerly offered to let him stay with them until he got settled.

Jack was genuinely looking forward to seeing Scott. And Liz. And he didn't want to disappoint his friend and former partner by changing his mind again, after finally getting Scott's hopes up after all this time. But Jack was starting to have second thoughts about moving.

He was just as confused as ever, and he still didn't think he could stand to be around Caitlin if he couldn't have her for himself. But the more time he spent packing, the more he realized that moving to Toronto wasn't the answer to his problems.

Scott didn't know the whole story, but he was right about one thing—the fact that Jack could describe Caitlin in more detail than any woman he'd ever dated meant something. Ever since Angela had left him for another man, Jack had deliberately closed himself off, not letting himself care about any woman, trying to deny them the power to hurt him. But in doing so he'd also denied himself any chance for true companionship, true friendship, true love.

He'd been completely blindsided by his feelings for Caitlin. When had their relationship moved from friendship and physical attraction to something more? Looking back, Jack realized this was something that had been building for a long time. Maybe he hadn't recognized his feelings until the past few weeks—since Caitlin and Jeremy had started letting him watch—but those feelings had been there, under the surface. Now Caitlin definitely had the power to hurt him...but she had the power to complete him as well.

If only they could find some way to make that happen. And without hurting Jeremy.

Jack wouldn't do that to his best friend, and he knew Caitlin wouldn't leave Jeremy for him anyway. But he was finally realizing that she meant enough to him—and that he was so miserable without her—that he had to try something, say something to both of them. He didn't know what to say, but he knew he had to try.

There was a loud knock on the door. Startled, Jack jumped.

"Open the door!" It was Jeremy.

"Please, Jack." Caitlin was there too.

"Jack!" Jeremy shouted again. He pounded on the door 'til it actually shook in its frame. "We're not leaving until you let us in!"

Jack got up, strode over to the door and opened it, ending up face-to-face with Jeremy, whose fist was upraised to hammer the door again. Caitlin was at his elbow, looking worried but determined.

"It's open," Jack said mildly.

"Oh," Jeremy said lamely. He dropped his hand. "Well...you wouldn't let me in last time, so..."

Jack couldn't help it—he laughed. Caitlin giggled too. After a moment even Jeremy chuckled, though his face was bright red.

"What's going on?" The other bedroom door opened, and Mike stuck his head out, looking at his three friends curiously.

"Uh, we need to talk to Jack," Jeremy said, his eyes flicking to Mike and back to his best friend.

"Okay," Jack said. He took a look around his bedroom. There were bags and boxes everywhere, and the bed was completely covered by a heap of clothes. He stepped out, closing the bedroom door firmly behind him, and led his friends down the hall.

"About time," Mike said, rolling his eyes as they passed his room. He had been wondering why his roommate wouldn't talk to his best friend all of a sudden. "You two finally get over your lovers' spat?"

"Shut up," Jack said, only half joking. That was just a little too close to the truth. He pulled Mike's door closed too.

He led his friends into the kitchen. Jeremy sat down on one of the tall chairs—the same one, Jack remembered, that he'd been sitting in the night he'd first fingered Caitlin while Jack watched. Caitlin hopped up to sit on the counter, crossing her ankles. Jack leaned on the counter as well, next to the fridge.

"So," he said, when the others remained silent. "I, uh, I'm sorry for shutting you guys out. It took me awhile, but I finally figured out ignoring you isn't going to make the situation go away."

"You're right, it's not," Caitlin smiled with relief.

Jeremy leaned forward over the breakfast bar. "What exactly is the situation, Jack?"

Jack hesitated, not sure how to start.

Jeremy, clearly agitated, got up and came around the tall kitchen island to stand next to Caitlin. "Jack," he said. "You're my best friend. I don't want you to leave. At the very least, I need to know why you're leaving. I know you miss Scott sometimes, but that's not why. And it's not because you really want to live in Toronto either. It's something else." He hesitated. "Did I do something? Is it my fault?"

"Our fault," Caitlin amended quietly, her green gaze boring into Jack's tense blue eyes. "Something changed after we...got together. Tell us what. And how to fix it."

"That's just it," Jack said at last. "I don't know how to fix it. I'm not sure it *can* be fixed."

"But what is it? *What* can't be fixed?" Jeremy said anxiously.

Jack sighed. He looked up, meeting his best friend's eyes. "I want more. What we did together...I don't want that to end."

Jeremy looked from Jack to Caitlin. She took her boyfriend's hand encouragingly. "That's fine," Jeremy said hurriedly. "We can have a threesome again — whenever you want. If that's what it takes to make you stay here, we'll do it. Right, Caitlin?"

"No," Jack said resolutely, before Caitlin could do more than nod. "That's not enough. That's not what I want."

"What then?" Jeremy asked desperately. "Just tell me — tell us. Please, Jack."

Jack pushed off from the counter, facing both of them. "I want what you have," he said quietly. "I know you think this is all about sex for me, and I deserve that. That's all I've been looking for, for the past year." He took a deep breath. "But that's not all I want anymore. I don't want to just have the occasional threesome when you guys are feeling kinky — and when no one's around to figure out what we're up to. I don't want to sneak around. I don't want to have to pretend there's nothing going on." He turned to Caitlin, silently willing her to understand—and share—his feelings. "And I don't want to be second best."

Jack took a step forward. "I love you, Caitlin." He forced himself to meet her eyes as he spoke, wishing for the millionth time he could plumb their depths and figure out what she was thinking. "I think I have for a long time. I just didn't want to admit it to myself. I want you to be my girlfriend. I want what Jeremy has."

Caitlin blinked, biting her lip. A faint pink stain tinged her cheeks. She glanced at Jeremy. Jack looked up at the bigger man as well. He didn't look angry—not yet, at least. But he did look confused.

"Let me get this straight," Jeremy said. He kept his tone light, almost teasing, and Jack thought he was trying to smile, but his mouth twisted painfully instead. "You've finally decided to stop playing the field and have a real relationship...but you want to do it with *my* girlfriend?"

Jack tried to smile too, but he wasn't sure he did it any better than Jeremy had. "Yeah. I guess that's about it."

"You're asking her to choose between us?" Jeremy said. "Or you'll leave?" He swallowed, scrubbing one hand briefly across his face. "So I'm either going to lose my girlfriend or my best friend?"

"No," Caitlin and Jack said at the same time. Jack, surprised, turned to Caitlin.

"I can't choose between you. I won't," she said desperately.

"I'm not asking you to," Jack said. He turned back to Jeremy, gripping his partner's shoulder. "I wouldn't do that to you, Jer."

"Well, what then?" Jeremy asked. Then it hit him—Jack could see the realization in his eyes. "Are you saying you want Caitlin to date both of us? At the same time?"

"Yes." Again Jack and Caitlin spoke at the same time, and again Jack turned to Caitlin, surprised. Fear and hope warred inside his chest.

"Could you do that?" Jack asked her. "Would you?"

Caitlin hesitated, looking from Jack to Jeremy. For once Jack could read her expression—fear and doubt.

Jeremy took a step closer to Caitlin. "What do you say, babe?" He suddenly remembered Caitlin's odd hesitations as they'd talked over the past few days, the sense that she was choosing her words carefully, tiptoeing around something she didn't want to acknowledge—or didn't want to let Jeremy see.

Maybe it was her feelings for Jack.

"How do you feel about Jack?" he asked her. "How do you really feel? Do you love him?"

Caitlin took a deep breath. "Yes," she said in a trembling voice. Jack's heart leapt crazily as she met his eyes and said it again. "I love you, Jack." She smiled faintly, echoing his words of a few moments before. "I think I have for a while. I just didn't want to admit it to myself."

Then she turned to Jeremy, reaching out with trembling hands to grasp his. "But I love you too, Jeremy," she said earnestly. "That hasn't changed, and it's not going to." She let out a shaky breath. "I was afraid to tell you. I thought if I told you how I feel about Jack, I'd lose you. And I couldn't handle that."

She turned back to Jack. "I want both of you. If that's okay with Jeremy." Jeremy didn't say anything right away, and both she and Jack peered up at him anxiously.

Jeremy cleared his throat. The bottom had dropped out of his stomach when Caitlin said she loved his best friend, but the panic had started to subside when he realized she hadn't stopped loving him too. Maybe there was a way out of this, a way for all three of them to be happy. "And you'll stay?" he said hoarsely, looking intently at Jack. "If we do this, you won't leave?"

"No," Jack said. "Or yes. I mean, I won't leave. I'll stay."

He looked from Jeremy to Caitlin uncertainly. Could it really be this easy? "I need to know we're all on the same page here," he said slowly. "I want us to all be together again sometimes, like that other night...but sometimes I want to have Caitlin to myself. Just like you do," he said to Jeremy. "I want to be able to tell people she's my girlfriend. And I want to be able to kiss her, and hold her hand and cuddle with her too. Even if we're in public."

"When we're all together?" Jeremy said doubtfully. He looked at Caitlin with concern. "I could handle it, but what will other people think?" He turned back to Jack, worried. "Think about it—if we're in a bar or something, and some Neanderthal goon sees Caitlin swapping tongue with two different guys, he'll think she's available to any asshole who wants some. We can't allow that."

"No," Jack said. He ran a hand through his hair. "Look, I don't know how this would work," he admitted.

"You guys could take turns," Caitlin suggested, half joking, half serious. "Like, on even days, Jeremy gets the PDAs, and on odd days, it would be Jack's turn."

Both men stared at her. "That's not..." Jack began to protest, then fell silent.

Jeremy was mulling it over too. "That could actually work," he mused.

"And what about our friends?" Jack persisted. He needed to get this all on the table, so there would be no misunderstandings or mistakes. "We all hang out with them, all the time. I don't want to have to put on some casual act in front of them."

"No, of course not," Caitlin said.

"So you guys are okay with that?" Jack asked, turning from Caitlin to Jeremy. "You don't mind if we tell Mike and Travis and everybody the truth?"

"Tell us what?" Mike stood in the wide doorway between the kitchen and the living room.

They all turned to face him, surprised.

"Sorry," Mike said. He crossed the kitchen, grabbed a can of Coke out of the fridge and popped it open. "I was thirsty." He looked curiously at his three friends, Caitlin still perched on the counter, Jack and Jeremy on either side of her. "Tell me what?" he repeated.

Jack looked at Caitlin and Jeremy. Would they be willing to tell Mike the truth? They both said they were willing to share, but were they truly willing to do so openly?

"This," Jeremy said, standing up straighter, looking Mike directly in the eye. "Caitlin's dating Jack now."

Mike frowned, his eyes darting to Caitlin. "You dumped Jeremy for Jack?" he said, surprised.

"No," Caitlin said. She took a deep breath. "I'm still dating Jeremy. But now I'm dating Jack too."

The stocky Asian man blinked, needing a moment to absorb the unusual and unexpected news. "And you're cool with that?" he asked Jeremy.

Jeremy smiled, turning to include Jack and Caitlin as well as Mike. "Yes," he said. "I am."

"Okay," Mike said, shrugging. There was an awkward pause while Mike sipped his pop and nobody spoke. "How's that going to work?" Mike sounded genuinely curious. He didn't, however, sound disgusted or upset.

Jack laughed, shaky with relief. "Well, we're still working on the logistics," he admitted. "But we'll figure it out."

Mike nodded, then looked up as another thought struck him. "So are you still moving to Toronto, or what?"

"Oh right," Jack said. "I guess I better phone Scott." He glanced at Jeremy and Caitlin. "I'll be back in a minute, okay? Don't go away."

As Jack slipped out of the room, Caitlin turned to Jeremy. "Are you okay with this, Jeremy?" she asked. "Really okay with it?"

Jeremy smiled. He leaned close, gripping her knees reassuringly. "Yeah," he said. "I really am." She seemed to need more reassurance, so he groped for words, trying to articulate the relief, certainty and contentment that had been radiating inside of him ever since the unexpected, but happy, resolution to their situation.

"Jack's my best friend. I'd do just about anything for him. And I know he'd do just about anything for me. And for you." His smile turned mischievous. "And this is going to be fun. You know I liked watching while you and Jack—um..." he trailed off, abruptly becoming aware of Mike, still standing near the fridge, now grinning broadly as he listened.

"Don't mind me," Mike said, waggling his eyebrows suggestively. "I would love to hear how this all got started."

"Sorry," Jeremy laughed, putting his arms around Caitlin. "I think maybe we'll keep that part to ourselves."

Epilogue

ಐ

"So, have Scott and Liz forgiven you for staying here yet?" Travis asked. His question didn't prevent him from shoveling Double Chocolate Swirl cheesecake into his mouth.

"Yeah, I think so," Jack said, chuckling. "Or, put it this way—Scott's still mad at me for getting his hopes up for nothing, but he's glad I've finally found a girl to settle down with."

"Even if you're sharing her with someone else?" Kristy asked. She and Mike were sharing a piece of carrot cake that was practically the size of a loaf of bread. The Cheesecake Café was known for its generous portions as well as its delicious food.

"Yep," Jack said. "I mean, he thought it was kind of weird at first. And he was surprised that Jeremy's okay with it. But he said it's a good thing I'm sharing Caitlin with Jeremy, and not trying to share Liz with him." They all laughed, Jack included. "Seriously, though," he said, "Scott's just glad I'm finally happy. And I *am* happy."

As he spoke he put his arm around Caitlin, who was sitting in the booth next to him. He smiled down at her, then looked past her to Jeremy, sitting on her other side. Both Caitlin and Jeremy smiled back.

"Good," Caitlin said. She tilted her head up to kiss Jack, her mouth sweet from the red velvet cheesecake she and her boyfriends were sharing.

Jack kissed her back affectionately.

"I take it it's Jack's turn today," Travis said.

"Yep," Jeremy replied. He kept working on the generous slice of cheesecake. It was the 11th of December—an odd day—so it was Jack's turn to enjoy any overt public displays of affection while the three of them were out together. Jeremy didn't mind. He got his turns on even days. Caitlin's tongue-in-cheek suggestion for sharing was actually working out very well for all of them.

"Hey!" Jack said, letting go of Caitlin. He reached past her, yanking the plate away from Jeremy. "I want some of that too, you selfish bastard."

"You snooze, you lose," Jeremy teased.

As they polished off their dessert, talk turned to the weather, with everyone wondering whether the temperature would rise back out of the minus twenties any time soon. Jack leaned back in his seat, utterly content.

As they headed home, sitting three abreast in his truck, Jack reflected on how well things had been going for the past month. Their friends had quickly adapted to the new state of affairs among Jack, Jeremy and their shared girlfriend. Only Cindy had reacted with shock and disgust. Travis, far from siding with his girlfriend, had used the situation as an excuse to break up with her at last.

Travis and Mike were roommates now, living in the apartment Jack and Mike had previously shared, and both Jack and Caitlin had moved into the third-floor walk-up Travis had formerly lived in with Jeremy. That situation was only temporary, however—they were looking into buying a house in the spring. The housing market was pretty expensive in Edmonton, but with their three combined incomes, they were optimistic.

It only took ten minutes to get to their west-end apartment from the restaurant, even taking the icy roads into consideration.

"You guys want to watch TV?" Jack asked casually as they let themselves in and began stripping off their heavy coats and boots.

"Not really," Jeremy said.

"Nah," Caitlin echoed.

They both looked at Jack expectantly.

"Fine—let's go to bed," he said, grinning. "All of us," he added, winking at Jeremy.

They were referring to another part of their carefully crafted girlfriend-sharing arrangement—the details of which they hadn't shared with their other friends. Caitlin always slept in the king-size bed in what used to be Jeremy's room. On even days, Jeremy slept there with her, and also got to choose whether to invite Jack to join them, or whether Jack would spend the night alone in the smaller bedroom instead. On odd days, Jack got to call the shots.

In practice, they'd been living together for a month and—while they didn't have sex every night—no one had yet spent the night in the second bedroom. But the two men were careful never to presume on each other's generosity, and they all agreed that fairness and choice were critical to the continuing success of their relationship.

"So," Jeremy said, stripping off his shirt as they entered the larger bedroom. "What'll it be?" Though this wasn't actually part of their formal agreement, as a courtesy Jeremy would defer to Jack's preferences in bed as well. On Jack's days, that was.

"You go first," Jack decided, removing his own clothes. He pulled Caitlin to him, kissing her firmly, letting his growing erection press against her hip. "I want you all warmed up and dripping wet for my turn," he murmured against her lips.

"Oh," Caitlin breathed. As the two men had quickly discovered, it drove Caitlin wild to hear them talk about what they would do to her, together.

"How does that sound, baby?" Jack bent down to nuzzle her neck.

"Wonderful," Caitlin said breathlessly. Jeremy, also naked now, stepped up behind her, tugging at her shirt, and she obediently raised her arms so he could pull it over her head.

"Good," Jeremy said. He unclasped Caitlin's bra next, sliding it down her shoulders.

Jack leaned forward to capture a nipple in his mouth, his hands working at the waist of Caitlin's jeans. He got them open, and slid her pants and her panties down. Jeremy held her steady while Jack tugged the clothes off her feet.

Standing, Jack bent to kiss Caitlin again. She moaned into his mouth. Jeremy was pinching and rolling her nipples from behind. Jack reached between Caitlin's legs, sliding his fingers into her slick cleft.

"Oh man," he breathed as Caitlin whimpered. "She's ready for you, Jer."

"Yes," Caitlin agreed urgently. "Now, Jeremy, please."

"Okay, babe," Jeremy said reassuringly. "You got it." He sat down on the edge of the bed, guiding Caitlin back with him. He pulled her down onto his engorged cock—Jack felt his own cock throb with anticipation as Caitlin cried out in pleasure at being so suddenly and completely filled. Then Jeremy lifted Caitlin's legs, spreading them wide across his own thighs. With one arm he encircled her waist, pulling her back firmly against him as he thrust his own hips up. With the other hand he reached between her legs, pinching and caressing her clit.

"Oh god," Caitlin cried, throwing her head back on Jeremy's shoulder.

"Wow," Jack said reverently. He stroked his cock slowly as he took in the view. "Caitlin, baby, you are so sexy."

Then he smiled, knowing just what to say to drive her over the edge. "I love watching Jeremy fuck you," he said huskily, stepping closer. He cupped Caitlin's jiggling breasts in his hands. "I love watching you ride his cock."

"Oh my god," Caitlin cried again. Her hips bucked frantically, and she clutched desperately at Jeremy's knees.

"That did it," Jeremy panted, burying his face in Caitlin's hair. "She's coming. Oh Caitlin, god, that feels so good…"

Three more thrusts and Jeremy was coming too, unable to resist the pleasurable sensations as Caitlin's pussy spasmed around him.

Jack was ready. As Jeremy, spent, slipped out of Caitlin's dripping cunt and eased her to the bed beside him, Jack quickly kneeled on the mattress between her spread legs and slid his own cock home.

Caitlin cried out in wordless pleasure, and Jack too moaned at the amazing sensation. The things he'd been saying to Caitlin were geared toward getting her as excited as possible, but privately Jack had to acknowledge that he really did love fucking her after Jeremy had had a turn. The extra lubrication of the other man's cum felt amazing—especially now that he'd gotten Caitlin and Jeremy's permission to stop using condoms—and Caitlin, after one orgasm, was only getting warmed up.

"Oh Jack," Caitlin whimpered. She grasped his hips, pulled him to her longingly.

"I know," Jack said. That felt wonderful too—to be completely in tune with the woman he loved, to have been together long enough, and to know her well enough, to realize now exactly what she needed. "You want it hard."

"Yes," Caitlin gasped. Jeremy, recovered from his own orgasm, leaned over and held Caitlin's knees, pulling them back toward her chest.

"Thanks," Jack panted. He braced his hands on the bed, pumping hard, willing himself to resist his own pleasure long enough for Caitlin to come again.

Luckily, it didn't take long. With an inarticulate cry she arched her back, her pussy clamping down on Jack's cock. One long, glorious moment later, he came too.

The three of them lay in a sweaty tangle, limbs entwined, totally sated.

"Holy shit," Caitlin said after a moment. "That was incredible."

"It sure was," Jeremy said.

Jack couldn't agree more. "I keep thinking I'll get used to this," he said. "But it just keeps getting better and better."

"That's the plan," Caitlin said. She reached out to either side, grasping her boyfriends' hands in hers. "I love you guys," she said.

Jeremy grinned at Jack across Caitlin's chest.

Jack smiled back. "We love you too," he said sincerely.

Also by Cristal Ryder
∽

eBooks:
Elemental Heat
Hot Fusion
Switch Me Up

About the Author
∽

An expressionist through words and art from a young age, Cristal read her first romance at age twelve. Taylor Caldwell introduced her to passion and romance that fuelled a craving to read anything she could get her hands on. Reading long into the night until her father shouted for her to turn off the light.

Cristal wrote her first story at fifteen and spent many hours escaping into worlds she created on the walk to and from high school. Now, ready to experience all life has to offer, Cristal tempts her readers and takes them on journeys of passion to vivid locations with squirm-in-your-seat plots. The combination of artistic talent with her gift for the written word helps Cristal bring to life the characters and stories she weaves.

Cristal lives in a small Canadian town, is a single mom of two college-aged sons and, yes, they do fly home after their initial excitement of leaving the nest! Along with her writing, Cristal works full time in the law enforcement field, loves horses, the outdoors and will jet off at any given opportunity to see the world. Cristal is multi-published and excited to be an Ellora's Cave author.

Also by Katheryn Wallis

ಬ

eBooks:
Letting Jack Watch

About the Author

ಬ

Katheryn Wallis has worked as a tour guide, submarine pilot, laser tag manager, commercial diver, and editor of both fiction and non-fiction. She has published award-winning poetry and short fiction, but it wasn't until she got her Ph.D. (in history and philosophy of science) and worked as an academic for several years that she finally decided she actually wanted to be a novelist. Now Katheryn writes erotic and sensual romance, while still editing for several publishers and teaching at her local university. Katheryn lives in Western Canada.

ಬ

The authors welcome comments from readers. You can find their websites and email addresses on their author bio pages at www.ellorascave.com.

Tell Us What You Think

We appreciate hearing reader opinions about our books. You can email us at Comments@EllorasCave.com.

Why an electronic book?

We live in the Information Age—an exciting time in the history of human civilization, in which technology rules supreme and continues to progress in leaps and bounds every minute of every day. For a multitude of reasons, more and more avid literary fans are opting to purchase e-books instead of paper books. The question from those not yet initiated into the world of electronic reading is simply: *Why?*

1. *Price.* An electronic title at Ellora's Cave Publishing runs anywhere from 40% to 75% less than the cover price of the exact same title in paperback format. Why? Basic mathematics and cost. It is less expensive to publish an e-book (no paper and printing, no warehousing and shipping) than it is to publish a paperback, so the savings are passed along to the consumer.

2. *Space.* Running out of room in your house for your books? That is one worry you will never have with electronic books. For a low one-time cost, you can purchase a handheld device specifically designed for e-reading. Many e-readers have large, convenient screens for viewing. Better yet, hundreds of titles can be stored within your new library—on a single microchip. There are a variety of e-readers from different manufacturers. You can also read e-books on your PC or laptop computer. (Please note that Ellora's Cave does not endorse any specific brands.

You can check our website at www.ellorascave.com for information we make available to new consumers.)
3. *Mobility.* Because your new e-library consists of only a microchip within a small, easily transportable e-reader, your entire cache of books can be taken with you wherever you go.
4. *Personal Viewing Preferences.* Are the words you are currently reading too small? Too large? Too… ANNOYING? Paperback books cannot be modified according to personal preferences, but e-books can.
5. *Instant Gratification.* Is it the middle of the night and all the bookstores near you are closed? Are you tired of waiting days, sometimes weeks, for bookstores to ship the novels you bought? Ellora's Cave Publishing sells instantaneous downloads twenty-four hours a day, seven days a week, every day of the year. Our webstore is never closed. Our e-book delivery system is 100% automated, meaning your order is filled as soon as you pay for it.

Those are a few of the top reasons why electronic books are replacing paperbacks for many avid readers.

As always, Ellora's Cave welcomes your questions and comments. We invite you to email us at Comments@ellorascave.com or write to us directly at Ellora's Cave Publishing Inc., 1056 Home Avenue, Akron, OH 44310-3502.

Discover for yourself why readers can't get enough of the multiple award-winning publisher Ellora's Cave.

Whether you prefer e-books or paperbacks, be sure to visit EC on the web at www.ellorascave.com for an erotic reading experience that will leave you breathless.